KISSES
of
DEATH

KISSES
of
DEATH

A Nathan Heller Casebook

MAX ALLAN COLLINS

Crippen & Landru, Publishers
Norfolk, Virginia
2002

ISBN: 1-885941-56-0

Third Printing, 2006

Printed in the United States of America

Crippen & Landru Publishers
P. O. Box 9315
Norfolk, VA 23505
USA

Email: CrippenLandru@earthlink.net
Web: www.crippenlandru.com

For Larry Coven
who saw Del Close in this

TABLE OF CONTENTS

INTRODUCTION

The historical mystery wasn't a trend back in 1981 when I began work on my first Nate Heller novel. I was simply looking for a way to write my favorite kind of mystery — the private eye story — in a manner that didn't seem anachronistic.

Plenty of writers have come along in the intervening years who've found interesting ways to tell private eye stories in modern dress; but I wanted to do the traditional P.I., the tender tough guy in the trenchcoat and fedora with a bottle of wry in his bottom desk drawer. I didn't want to update him, and I didn't want to plop him down in contemporary times like a drunk who fell off a time machine.

This classic character — as devised by Hammett, refined by Chandler and redefined by Spillane — is a prototypical American hero, a child of the Old West by way of the Great Depression and a world war (or two), and whose voice is as wonderfully, distinctively American as Huckleberry Finn's. Chandler's first-person poetry attracted my ear, and Spillane's war-traumatized knight indicated the direction my hero's characterization might go.

But it was Hammett who showed the way. Back in the mid-'70s, I was re-reading for the umpteenth time the greatest of all detective novels, *The Maltese Falcon,* when I noticed the copyright, causing me to muse, "1929 . . . year of the St. Valentine's Day massacre — Al Capone and Sam Spade were contemporaries." In the comics business (like Spillane and Hammett, I'm a veteran of that field), a light bulb would've gone on over my head as it occurred to me that the private eye had been around long enough to exist in an historical context. In other words, rather than have Phillip Marlowe meet an Al Capone type, Al Capone could meet a Phillip Marlowe type.

It took me several years before I felt I was ready to attempt this ambitious approach — in the meantime, the film *Chinatown,* a couple TV shows (*Banyon, City of Angels*) and a few novels by a handful of mystery writers (Bergman, Gores, Kaminsky) were demonstrating that the "period" private eye story was becoming a niche within the genre.

But I didn't want to do a period piece: I wanted to do an historical novel.   Next to mysteries, historical fiction was my favorite genre growing up, and in particular I loved the (now unfortunately forgotten) Samuel Shellabarger, who wrote such vividly told tales as *Captain from Castille* and *Prince of Foxes,* in which swashbuckling fictional heroes mingled with historical figures; the first novel I remember reading and loving — *The Three Musketeers* — was of a similar bent.   My idea was to create a private eye who could enter history in the same fashion, and "solve" famous unsolved cases.

As a midwesterner, I figured Chicago was the ideal choice for setting, and — gathering a team of Windy City research experts (literacy advocate George Hagenauer and comics editor Mike Gold) — I prepared the first novel as if I were writing the definitive nonfiction treatment of the assassination of Mayor Anton Cermak.   But, of course, I wrote a mystery novel instead: *True Detective* (1983), the longest private eye novel ever written, at least until my later *Stolen Away* (1993) came along.   (Both novels won the "Shamus" Best Novel award from the Private Eye Writers of America in their respective years.)

Nate Heller was given an elaborate background — father, mother, grandparents, unusual trappings for a P.I.   Like Mike Hammer, Heller is a battle-scarred veteran of World War Two; unlike Hammer, Nate took us to Guadalcanal with him (*The Million Dollar Wound,* 1986) to see how he got that way.

Heller has solved the Lindbergh kidnapping, Huey Long's assassination, Bugsy Siegel's gangland hit, Sir Harry Oakes' locked- room murder, the Roswell incident, the Black Dahlia case and more, over the course of eleven novels and one previous casebook (short story collection).   He has played Paul Drake to Clarence Darrow's Perry Mason in *Damned in Paradise* (1996) and "found" Amelia Earhart in *Flying Blind* (1998).   He does a lot more than just find Amelia, actually — Heller has a unique way of finding out for his client (Amelia's husband) whether or not said client's wife is staying faithful.   Unlike Chandler's Marlowe, Chicagoan Heller doesn't always play by the "private eye" code.

Heller's "bad boy" qualities seem to endear him to women readers, which to his creator is very gratifying (and a relief).   In the postwar novels, Nate is frequently at least as psychotic as Mike Hammer and has often served up a rough justice that goes beyond just about anything I can think of in private eye fiction — in the most recent Heller, *Angel in*

Black, he even . . . well, let's just say I find it interesting and even a little odd that readers accept Heller's homicidal tendencies as casually as they do. Sign of the times, perhaps, or maybe Nate is just such good company, we forgive him the occasional righteous slaying.

It's been my hope that Nate could enjoy the conventions — even the cliches — of the classic private eye and yet be a fully dimensional character, growing and changing over the years. That the mysteries themselves are real — history mysteries — makes for challenging research, and a rewarding experience for a writer . . . for readers, too, I hope. The most unusual accolade Heller and I have received is the inclusion of the novels in the bibliographies of a number of non-fiction works. Not bad for a mystery writer and a fictional P.I.

The stories in this casebook cover just about the complete span of Heller's career to date: "Kaddish for the Kid" is an early '30s job, and "Strike Zone" the first recorded case of Heller's in the 1960s. Like the previous collection, *Dying in the Post-War World* (1991), the lead story is a novella, and like the title piece of that previous casebook, it's a tale I consider to be a significant entry in the Heller canon. I would be surprised if this is the last time Heller encounters Marilyn Monroe.

After this lead novella — which takes place in the '50s — the stories are arranged not in order of publication, but in chronological order. One of the challenges of writing these novels and stories is that they jump around in Heller's life, which means I have to keep track of the arc of his characterization. And I hope you will note differences in him, as a man and as a detective, according to his age and the time period in which he's operating.

My thanks to the editors of the anthologies and magazines where these stories originally ran — "Kisses of Death" appears here for the first time — and to Doug and Sandi Greene of Crippen and Landru for making this book possible. I also thank the loyal readers — the sort of avid fans who would buy a book like this one — who have helped keep Heller alive all these years.

In fact, when Doug asked me to come up with something extra that could be included in the special, limited edition of this book, my first thought was a five spot. After all, that's what Heller would have slipped a Chicago cop.

Of course, Nate would expect change.

Although the historical incidents in these stories are portrayed more or less accurately (as much as the passage of time, and contradictory source material, will allow), fact, speculation and fiction are freely mixed here; historical personages exists side by side with composite characters and wholly fictional ones — all of whom act and speak at the author's whim.

KISSES OF DEATH

Y ou can almost see it on the cover of *Photoplay* or *Modern Screen*, can't you, circa 1954? "I Was Marilyn Monroe's Bodyguard!" with a subhead reading, "A Private Eye's Hollywood Dream Assignment!". . . but in the end, "A New York Nightmare of Depravity" was more like it, worthy of *Confidential* or *Whisper*.

Not that Miss Monroe was involved in any of that depravity — no such luck — though we did have a promising first meeting, and it was in neither Hollywood nor New York, but in my native Chicago, at the Palmer House, where the A-1 Detective Agency was providing security for the American Booksellers Association's annual convention.

I didn't do any of the security work at the booksellers shindig myself — that was for my staff, and a few add-on ops I rounded up. After all, I was Nathan Heller, president of the A-1, and such lowly babysitting was simply beneath my executive position.

Unless, of course, the baby I was sitting was Miss Marilyn Monroe, curled up opposite me on a couch, sweetly sitting in her suite's sitting room, afternoon sunlight coming in behind her, making a hazy halo of her carefully coifed platinum page boy.

"I hope this isn't a problem for you," she said, shyly, with only a hint of the mannered, sexy exaggeration I'd noted on the screen. "Such short notice, I mean."

Normally I didn't cancel a Friday night date with a Chez Paree chorus girl to take on a bodyguard job, but I only said, "I had nothing planned. My pleasure, Miss Monroe."

"Marilyn," she corrected gently. "Is it Nate, or Nathan?"

Her manner was surprisingly deferential, and disarmingly reserved. Like other movie stars I'd encountered over the years, from George Raft to Mae West, she was smaller than I expected, though her figure lived up to expectations, partly because her black short-sleeved cotton sweater and her dark gray Capri pants were strategically snug.

"Nate's fine," I said. "Or Nathan." I would gladly have answered to Clem or Philbert, if she were so inclined. I was forty-seven years of age, and she was, what? Twenty-five? Twenty-six? And I felt like a school boy, tongue thick, hands awkward, penis twitching, rearing its head threateningly as I crossed my legs.

Her barefoot casualness (her toenails, like her fingernails, were painted a platinum that matched her hair) was offset by the flawlessness of her surprisingly understated make-up, her complexion luminously, palely perfect, a glorious collaboration between God and Max Factor. The startling red of her lipsticked lips was ideal for her world-famous smile — sex-saturated, open-mouthed, accompanied by a tilt-back of the head and bedroom-lidded eyes — only I never saw that smile once, that afternoon.

Instead, only rare tentative fleeting smiles touched those bruised baby lips, and for all her sex appeal, the in-person Marilyn Monroe's undeniable charisma invoked in me unexpected stirrings, which is to say, Not Entirely Sexual. I wanted to protect this girl. And she did seem a girl to me, for all her womanly charms.

"I read about you in *Life*," she said, dark blue eyes twinkling.

She'd read about *me* in *Life*. Was she kidding?

Actually, she probably wasn't. Last year the magazine had done a spread on me, and my career, touching on the Lindbergh kidnapping, the Sir Harry Oakes murder and several other of my more headline-worthy cases of years past, but focusing more on the current success of my Hollywood branch of the A-1, which was developing into the movie stars' private detective agency of choice.

On the other hand, I'd read about her not only in *Life*, but *Look*, and the *Saturday Evening Post*, and *Esquire*, not to mention the *Police Gazette*, *Coronet* and *Modern Man*. She was also the reason why I hadn't, in June of 1953, gotten around to taking down a certain 1952 calendar as yet. My most vivid memory of Miss Monroe, prior to meeting her face to face, was a rear view of her walking slowly away from the camera in a movie called *Niagara* (which I walked away from after her character got prematurely bumped off).

"When Ben told me about the party tonight, at Riccardo's," she said, "I simply had to be there. I'm afraid I invited myself . . ."

As if there'd be an objection.

". . . and Ben suggested we ask you to accompany us. He thinks it's a necessary precaution."

"I agree with him," I said. "That joint'll be crawling with reporters."

She shivered. "Oh, and I've had my fill of the press today, already."

Marilyn Monroe was in town on a press swing to promote the imminent release of *Gentlemen Prefer Blondes*; when I'd arrived at her suite, she had just wrapped up an interview with Irv Kupcinet, of the *Sun-Times*.

"If they see me at your side," I said, "they may be more inclined to behave themselves."

"That's sort of what Ben said. He said people know you in Chicago. That you have quite a reputation."

"Reputations can deceiving."

"Oh yes," she said with a lift of her eyes and a flutter of lashes. "Nathan, can I get you something to drink?"

"A Coke would be nice."

She flashed just a hint of the famous smile, said, "I'll have one, too," rose and walked to a little bar in one corner, and in those painted-on Capri pants, she provided a rear view even more memorable than *Niagara*.

Soon she was behind the bar, pouring Coca Cola over ice, saying, "How did you meet Ben? I met him on monkey business."

"Met him how?"

She walked over to where I was sitting, a tumbler in either hand, a study in sexy symmetry as her breasts did a gentle braless dance under the sweater. "On the movie — *Monkey Business*. Ben wrote it. That was a good role for me. Nice and funny, and light. How did *you* meet him?"

I took my Coke from her. "You better let Ben tell it."

I figured that was wise, because I had no idea where or when I'd first met Ben Hecht, though according to Ben we'd known each other since I was a kid. I had no memory of encountering Hecht back in those waning days of the so-called Chicago literary Renaissance of the late teens and early twenties, though when he approached me to do a Hollywood job for him, a few years ago, he insisted we were old friends . . . and since he'd been the client, who was I to argue?

Hecht, after all, was a storyteller, and reinventing his own life, revising his own memories into better tales, was in his nature.

She sat up, now, and forward, hands folded in her lap around the glass of Coke, an attentive school girl. "Ben says your father had a radical bookshop."

"That's right," I said. "We were on the West Side, and most of the literary and political shenanigans were centered in Tower Town . . ."

"Tower Town?"

"That's the area that used to be Chicago's Greenwich Village; still is, sort of, but it's dying out. On the Near North Side. But most of the freethinkers and radicals and artsy types found their way into Heller's Books, from Clarence Darrow to Carl Sandburg."

Her eyes went wide as Betty Boop's. "You know Carl Sandburg?"

"Sure. He used to play his guitar and sing his God-awful folk songs in this little performance area we had."

Her sigh could only be described as wistful. "I love his poetry."

"Yeah, he's become a big deal, hasn't he? Nice guy."

Hope danced in the wide eyes. "Will he be there tonight?"

Imagine a homely wart like Charlie getting a dish like this warmed up over him.

"I kind of doubt it. He doesn't get back to Chicago all that much."

Her disappointment was obvious, but she perked herself up, saying, "Ben's arranged this party as a benefit for Maxwell Bodenheim, you know."

"Are you serious?"

Misinterpreting my displeasure as something positive, she nodded and said, "Oh, yes. Ben said Mr. Bodenheim and his wife flew in from New York last night. Do you know him?"

"Yeah. Yeah, I know Max. I'm surprised you've even heard of him, Marilyn."

"I read a lot of poetry," she said. "His *Selected Poems* is a delightful collection."

Who was I to rain on her parade? How could she know that Bodenheim, who I vividly remembered from childhood, had been a womanizing, sarcastic, self-important, drunken leech? The only writer my soft-hearted father had ever banished from his store, when he caught Bodenheim shoplifting copies of his own books.

"I haven't thought of that guy in probably thirty years," I said. "I didn't even know he was still alive."

Her brow furrowed with sympathy. "Ben says Mr. Bodenheim has fallen on hard times. It's difficult to make a living as a poet."

I sipped my Coke. "He used to write novels, too. He had some bestsellers in the '20s."

Sexy potboilers, with titles like *Replenishing Jessica, Georgie May* and *Naked on Roller Skates*, that had seemed pretty racy in their day; *Jessica* had even been busted as pornography. Of course, in the modern era of Erskine Caldwell and Mickey Spillane, the naughty doings of Bodenheim's promiscuous jazz age heroines would probably seem pretty mild.

Still, if Bodenheim was broke, it was only after squandering the fortune or two a bestselling writer would naturally accrue.

"I just think it's wonderful of Ben to help his old friend out like this," she said, her smile radiant, as madonna-like as she imaged Hecht's intentions to be saintly.

Bodenheim was indeed an "old friend" of Hecht's, but my understanding was that they'd had a major falling out, long ago; in fact, while I don't remember ever meeting Hecht in the old days, I do remember my father talking about how violently these two one-time literary collaborators had fallen out. Hecht had even written a novel, *Count Bruga*, lampooning his pretentious former crony, to which Bodenheim replied with his own novel, *Duke Herring*, about a self-centered sell-out clearly patterned on Hecht.

The gathering tonight at Riccardo's was a Renaissance reunion, organized by Hecht, who was one of that movement's stellar graduates, albeit not in the literary way of such figures as Sandburg, Vachel Lindsay, Sherwood Anderson, Edgar Lee Masters and Margaret Anderson. Hecht — whose archly literary novels and would-be avant garde pornography of the twenties had made him a king among local bohemians — had literally gone Hollywood.

After the success of his play *The Front Page*, a collaboration with Charlie MacArthur, another former Chicago newspaperman, Hecht began a wildly successful screenwriting career — *Scarface, Gunga Din, Spellbound, Notorious*, to name a few of his credits — that would be impressive by anybody's standards. Except, perhaps, those of the literary types among whom he'd once dwelled.

Like Bodenheim.

Of course, I didn't figure — other than Bodenheim — there would be many people at the party that Hecht would owe any apology to. The crowd that Ben and Bodenheim had hung out with, sharing the pages of literary magazines, and the stages of little theaters and the wild and wooly Dill Pickle Club, was pretty well thinned out by now. The most exotic demise was probably that of Harriet Monroe (presumably no relation to Marilyn); the editor of the prestigious magazine *Poetry*, Harriet had died in 1936, on some sort of mountain-climbing expedition in Peru (Sherwood Anderson also died in South America, but less exotically, succumbing to peritonitis on a goodwill tour). Vachel Lindsay had died a suicide, Edgar Lee Masters died broke in a convalescent home. This poetry was a rough racket.

The beautiful, enigmatic (i.e., lesbian) editor of the *Little Review*, Margaret Anderson, wasn't dead, but she might as well have been: she lived in Paris. I figured the party attendees would mostly be Renaissance refugees who had drifted back into the newspaper business, from whence most of the players had come in the first place, seasoned veterans of Schlogl's, the legendary Loop tavern where *Daily News* reporters gathered, even those without literary pretensions.

Of course, Riccardo's was a newspaper hangout in general, and the entertainment scribes Marilyn had already encountered, this trip — Kup, Herb Lyon, Anna Nangle, among others — might be there, as well. I knew all of them and could keep them at bay in a friendly way.

I sipped my Coke. "I gather you and Ben are embarking on some sort of project together."

"Well, we're seriously discussing —"

And a knock at the door interrupted her. I offered to answer it for her, and did, and as if he'd arrived specifically to answer my question, there was Ben.

"Madhouse down there," he said, gesturing with a thumb, as if pointing to Hell, but in reality only meaning the floor where the meetings and seminars of the ABA were being held.

Ben Hecht, a vigorous sixty years of age, brushed by me and went over to greet Marilyn, who rose from the couch to give him a Hollywood hug. His frame was square, large-boned, just under six foot, his attire rather casual for a business occasion, a brown sportjacket over a green sportshirt; a Russian jew, he looked more Russian than Jewish — a pleasant, even handsome-looking man with an oval head, salt-and-pepper curly hair, a high forehead that was obviously in the process of getting higher, trimmed mustache, deep-blue slightly sunken eyes, and strong jaw worthy of a leading man.

She sat back down, and he nestled next to her, and took her hands in his as if about to propose marriage.

"I talked to the Doubleday people," Ben said, "and they're very excited."

Her eyes Betty Booped again. "Really?"

"They did somersaults over the idea."

Now she winced. "I still think I'm a little young to be writing my life story . . ."

"You're the hottest thing in show business, kid. Strike while the iron is hot. You liked the sample chapters I wrote, didn't you?"

"I *loved* them." She turned to me, and I was relieved to see that one of them realized I was still there. "We spent an afternoon at the Beverly Hills Hotel, Ben and I, with me talking into a tape recorder, and then a few days later we met again. Ben had turned my ramblings into something marvelous. I laughed . . . I cried . . ."

"Well," he said, withdrawing a cigar from a silver case from inside his sportjacket, "you'll laugh and cry with joy when you hear the deal Doubleday's offering. Plus, I talked to some people from the *Ladies' Home Journal*, and they're going to make an offer to serialize."

For a guy famous for writing ping-pong back-and-forth dialogue, Ben nonetheless spoke in paragraphs, though the words did flow at a machine-gun clip.

"Oh, Ben . . . this is so wonderful . . ."

He bit off the end of his cigar. "Kid, they're going to pay you bushel baskets of money, and the end result is, publicity for you. Only in America."

"Ben, how can I ever repay you?"

It was a question millions of American men would have died to hear Marilyn Monroe ask.

Ben, patting his jacket pockets as if he were frisking himself, replied with, "You got a light?"

She nodded and pranced over to the bar and got some hotel matches and came bouncing back and fired up his Cuban. It had a strong, pleasant aroma, but the mixture of it and Marilyn's Chanel Number Five was making me a little queasy.

I asked, "What time's the party?"

"They got a buffet over there for us," Ben said, "at seven. I'm kind of the host, so I'll head over a little early. Marilyn, what time would you like to make your appearance?"

"Maybe around eight," she offered. Then she looked at me. "Could you meet me in the lobby, Nathan, and escort me over?"

"Be delighted."

She stood. "Then you boys better scoot. I have to get ready."

"You are ready," Ben said, but he was rising at her command just the same. He gestured with his cigar in hand. "These are writers and poets, kid. Come as you are."

"I'll wear something nice and casual," she promised. "But I'd like to relax with a nice long hot bubble bath . . ."

That was a pretty image to leave on, so we did. In the hall, as we waited for the elevator, I said, "*Boden*-heim?"

"Yeah," Hecht said, as if throwing a benefit for his arch literary enemy was a natural thing to do. "We flew him and his wife in. I got them over at the Bismarck, if he hasn't burned it down by now."

"What's he need a benefit for?"

Hecht snorted, spoke around his cigar. "Are you kidding? He's been living in Greenwich Village for the last, I don't know, twenty years. Poor bastard's turned into a bum. Complete alky. You know how he makes his living, such as it is? Hawking his poems on street corners, pinnin' 'em on a fence, sellin' 'em for quarters and dimes."

"Jesus. Even I wouldn't wish that on him. I mean, he was famous . . . respected . . ."

"There was a time," Hecht said, and the sunken eyes grew distant, "when he was near the peak of poetry in this nation. Ezra Pound wrote him goddamn fan letters. William Carlos Williams, Conrad Aiken, Marianne Moore, all expressed their public admiration. Now? Now the son of bitch is sleeping on park benches and, when he's lucky, in flophouses."

"What's this about a wife?"

Hecht got a funny smile going; he flicked ashes from the cigar in the wall ashtray by the elevator buttons. "Her name's Ruth. He looks like shit, but she's kind of foxy, in a low-rent kind of way." Hecht shook his head, laughed. "Son of a bitch always did have a way with the ladies. You know the stories, don't you, about the suicides?"

I did. There was a period in the twenties, shortly after Bodenheim traded Chicago for New York, that the national papers were filled with the stories of young women driven to suicide by the fickle attentions of the author of *Replenishing Jessica.*

"I know you fancy yourself a ladies' man, Nate," Hecht said with a sly grin. "But committing suicide over your favors never has become a national fad, now, has it?"

"Not yet," I granted, and the elevator finally arrived. We stepped on. Hecht pushed the button for his floor and I hit lobby. We had the elevator to ourselves, so our conversation remained frank.

"What's all this about you writing Marilyn's autobiography? Since when are you reduced to that kind of thing, or are you trying to get a piece of that sweet girl's personality?"

Hecht had his own reputation as a ladies' man, or at least, womanizer.

He shrugged. "Straight ghost job. Good payday. I don't always sign my work, kid. Hell, if I put my name on every script I doctored, I'd be the most famous asshole in Hollywood."

"Well, doesn't scriptwriting pay better than books?"

"Hell yes." His voice remained jaunty but his expression turned grave. "But, frankly, kid — I got my ass in a wringer with this big fat mouth of mine. I'm blacklisted in England, you know, and if a producer uses me on a script, he can't put my name on the British prints, and if the Brits find out my name was on the American version, they might pass on the thing, anyway." His sigh was massive. "If you ever hear me gettin' messed up in politics again, slap my face, okay?"

"What are friends for?"

Hecht, whose apolitical nature was probably the reason why my father's radical bookshop was an unlikely place for us to have met, had gotten uncharacteristically political, right after the war. Specifically, he got vocal about Israel, outspoken in his opinion that England was the enemy of that emerging state, publicly praising Irgun terrorists for blowing up British trains and robbing British banks and killing British "tommies."

"Maybe it's for the best," he said, as the bell rang and the door drew open at his floor. "It's putting me back in the world of books, where I belong. Hey, I talked to Simon and Schuster this afternoon, and they're makin' an offer on my autobiography . . . See you at Riccardo's, kid!"

And with that final machine-gun burst of verbiage, he was gone.

✗ ✗ ✗

Just to be safe, I returned to the Palmer House at seven-thirty, walking over from my suite of offices at the Monadnock Building, going in on the State Street side, through the business arcade and up the escalator to the vast high-ceilinged lobby, a cathedral-like affair with arched balconies, Roman travertine walls and an elaborately painted Italian classical ceiling depicting gods and goddesses, which was only fitting considering who I was escorting tonight.

And since Hollywood divinity occupies a time and space continuum all its own, I had plenty of opportunity, seated comfortably in one of the velvet-upholstered chairs, to study each and every shapely nude, and near-nude, cloud-perched goddess.

As my delight at this assignment gradually wore to irritation (shortly after nine), I began toying with calling up to Miss Monroe's suite to see if I'd misunderstood when I was to pick her up, or if she'd run into a problem, and just as irritation was bleeding into indignation (nine-thirty), she stepped out of an elevator, a vision of twentieth-century womanhood that put to shame the classical dames floating above me.

She wore a simple black linen dress, spaghetti straps and a fairly low, straight-across the bosom neckline — no sign of a bra, or any pantyline, either; her heels were black strappy sandals, her legs bare. No jewelry, a small black purse in hand. Doffing my coconut-palm narrow brim hat, I rose to approach her as she click-clacked toward me across the marble floor and by the time I'd slipped my arm in hers, and gazed into that radiant face with its blazingly red-lipsticked baby-doll pout, my annoyance disappeared, and delight had bloomed again.

She issued no apology for her tardiness, but what she said instead was much better: "Don't *you* look handsome."

And for the first time I witnessed, in-person, the practiced, patented open-mouthed smile, as she stroked the sleeve of my green Dacron sportjacket, then straightened and smoothed the lighter-green linen tie that matched my sportshirt, under which my heart went pitty pat.

"I thought bodyguards tried to blend into the woodwork," she said, eyeing my canary yellow lightweight slacks.

"This bodyguard wants to be noticed," I said, as we walked through a lobby whose patrons were wide-eyed with wonder at the presence among them of this goddess. "Not that anyone will..."

In back of the cab, on our way to Riccardo's, I ventured a question: "Do you mind if I ask something a little personal?"

"Ask and see."

"Is what I read about in the papers true, about you and Joe DiMaggio?"

She shrugged. "We've been dating, kind of off and on."

"Is it 'on' right now?"

"Off."

"Ah," I said. "I'm sorry."

"Are you really, Nathan?"

"No."

She smiled at that. Then, looking out the window at the Loop gliding by, she said rather absently, "I'd never heard of him."

"Never heard of Joltin' Joe?"

She looked back and me and a tiny laugh bubbled in her throat. "It was a blind date. My girl friend said he was a famous ballplayer who liked blondes. I didn't even know what kind of ballplayer she meant, football or baseball or what. Didn't want to look any dumber than I already did, but he was a real sweetheart on the date, and you should've seen people slapping him on the back, asking him for autographs. They were completely ignoring me."

"And you liked that?"

"I respected it . . . Are you married, Nathan?"

"Not right now."

Riccardo's was a converted warehouse at 437 North Rush; it began in '34 as a hole-in-the-wall gathering place for artists, writers and theatrical types, but had been revamped and expanded a decade ago to accommodate the wider clientele its arty atmosphere and exotic reputation attracted.

The evening was pleasantly warm, with just the right hint of lake breeze, and the tables that spilled out from under the awning onto the sidewalk were packed with patrons enjoying dinner and drinks and a magnificent view of the parking lot. Heads swivelled and eyes widened as I guided Marilyn through the tables and into the restaurant, which somehow managed an intimate ambience despite expansive, open seating and bright lighting designed to show off the framed paintings that were everywhere.

"Looks more like an art gallery than a restaurant," Marilyn said breathlessly, her gaze skimming above the heads of diners who were admiring the work of art walking among them.

"It's both," I said, moving her gently through the crowd. "This main dining room is an exhibit hall for young midwestern artists."

"What a lovely notion! So the paintings are constantly changing?"

I nodded. "One-man shows lasting a month."

This month's genius seemed adept at filling canvases with dull-gray backgrounds on which danced ameba-like blobs of garish purple, red and green.

"Ah," I said, "here's Ric . . ."

In a black suit and tie, tall, slender, a youthful fifty with his gray crewcut and black eyebrows and mustache, looking like a Mephistophelean maitre d', Ric Riccardo approached, eyes twinkling, hand outstretched.

"The Chicago Sherlock," he said, as we shook hands. "And no introduction is required of this lovely lady . . ."

He gently took her fingertips in his and kissed the back of her hand and she smiled and raised her eyebrows, appreciation murmuring behind her kiss of a pursed smile.

"Marilyn, this is Ric Riccardo."

`She frowned. "You don't look much like Desi Arnaz."

Ric looked mildly wounded. I wasn't sure whether she was kidding or not, but somehow with her it didn't matter.

"This is the original," I said, "and he's Italian, not Cuban."

Her bare shoulders lifted and sat themselves down, doing a fine job of it, too, I must say. "I just love the idea of your restaurant, Mr. Riccardo! You're a true patron of the arts."

Ric made a dismissive gesture. "I'm afraid I only did it to have a place to hang my own canvases."

"You're an artist, too?"

"I've never been able to decide whether I paint badly," Ric sighed, "or whether people just can't understand what I paint. But at least, here, I sell a canvas now and then."

"Don't let him kid you," I told her, "his artwork's even better than his veal scaloppine."

Ric's eyes narrowed. "Which brings us to a difficult subject — my friends, you've missed the buffet, and I'm afraid the party has moved from my private dining room into the bar."

He led us down into the lower level, where I spotted Ben chatting with a pair of *Trib* talents, obsessive Sherlock Holmes buff Vincent Starrett and literary section editor Fanny Butcher. Here and there were the likes of bookseller Stuart Brent, *Herald American* columnist Bob Casey, various other well-known local scribes, John Gunther, Bill Leonard, Bob Cromie, among the bigger names. Mostly, as I had predicted, the crowd consisted of second-stringers and tail-end members from the Renaissance movement, who had gone back to the newspaper world that spawned them.

"Ooo," Marilyn said, "look at that odd-shaped bar!"

"It's a big artist's palette," I said.

"Oh, it is!" And her laughter chimed.

"Our murals back behind there," Ric said proudly, as he led us to a corner table for two, plucking the "reserved" sign off, "are the work of our city's most well-known artists — the Albrights, Aaron Bohrod, Vincent D'Agostino . . ."

"And Desi Arnaz, here," I said.

And our host smiled, bowed, and — with us deposited at our cozy table — moved on. Like Ben Hecht, Ric was a pragmatic Renaissance survivor, an artist turned businessman. And like Ben, Ric liked to think he was still a bohemian at heart.

For all its premeditated hipness, however, Ric's restaurant bore the square stigmata of Italian restaurants immemorial: instead of the cool tinklings of jazz piano, the air resounded with the strains of "O Sole Mio," accompanied by violin, mandolin and concertina, courtesy of strolling singers and musicians in ruffled sleeves and satin trousers.

Wandering in from the dining room and sidewalk cafe, where they provided a welcome backdrop for couples romantically dining, came a trio of these singers with a violinist in tow, warbling "Come Back to Sorrento." This was a misguided sortie into enemy territory, as Ben and other self-styled intellectual and literary lights attending the reunion glanced at them irritably over cocktail-glass rims and cigarettes-in-hand.

A slender ponytail brunette, her olive complexion a stark contrast next to her short-sleeved cream-color dress, planted herself in front of the musicians, hands pressed around a tall glass, swaying to their serenade. At first glance she seemed attractive, even strikingly so, and I pegged her for her mid-twenties.

"She's having fun," Marilyn said, not at all judgmentally.

As the musicians moved through the bar, and closer to us, and the brunette danced sensuously along, I got a closer look at her. The dress was a frayed secondhand-store frock, and she had to be in her thirties. Her big brown eyes were cloudy and dark-circled, her wide mouth slack.

This girl wasn't tipsy: she was a lush.

About this time, the musicians noticed Marilyn — or at least noticed a beautiful blonde — and made their way to our table. I was digging for a half dollar to tip them, and make them go away, when the slender bombed brunette inserted herself between us and the strolling musicians and hip-swayed to their music in a manner that would suit Minksy's better than Riccardo's.

Marilyn's glance at me was more sad than disapproving.

The brunette clutched the arm of the nearest singer — a handsome if chubby kid in his twenties, the tenor — and her other hand began moving up and down the thigh of his satin pants.

"Gentlemen!" a male voice cried, above the syrupy strains. "Please cease."

And an absurd figure who might have walked in off a burlesque stage appeared at the fringe of this little tableau, positioning himself alongside the violinist, a foul-smelling corncob pipe in one hand, a double-shot glass of straight whiskey in the other. The four musicians trailed off into stunned silence, and their eyes travelled from the drunken dame to the latest character in this farce, stooped, obviously inebriated, a frail sack of bones swimming in a dark, shabby, slept-in suit set off ever so nattily by a dark frayed food-stained tie and shoes that had long since exploded in wear.

His face was misshapen from years of drink, the blobby careless first-draft of an indifferent sculptor, skull beneath the flesh asserting itself as his features threatened to fall off, his complexion a mottled albino, eyes dark rheumy haunted pools, nose a lumpy sweet potato, mouth a thin crumpled line. His hair, unkempt and shaggy as it was, his ears half-covered, sideburns bordering on mutton chop, was the garish reddish brown of a Mercurochrome dye job; it might have been a wig, had this pitiful creature been able to afford one.

"Could it be," he said, revealing a jack-o'-lantern smile, his near-toothlessness giving him a Karloff lisp, "that angelic choristers of heaven have invaded this bistro, wings tipped with music vibrating like a flock of wild swans skimming the surface of some enchanted sea?"

"Shut-up, Max," the brunette said; she had a husky voice that under the right circumstances might have been sexy.

"Who is that?" Marilyn whispered.

"The guest of honor," I said.

And this was indeed Maxwell Bodenheim, an astonishing husk of the tall, slim, golden-haired ladies man I remembered from my father's bookshop; back then, only his eyebrows had been a devilish red-brown.

He leaned against the shoulder of the violinist. "And are these the heart-warming, bell-like tones of a Heifetz? Or does the angel Gabriel lurk in your barrel-like form?"

"Max!" she said. "Can't a girl *dance?*"

He raised the whiskey glass sloshingly, a parody of a toast, underlined by the threat of flinging it in the nearest face (not much of one, because Bodenheim was unlikely to waste such precious fluid in so foolhardy a manner).

"Or," he proclaimed, "are you heathens tempting an innocent child into the ways of the nymph, stirring the wildness in her nature and fomenting the bestial longings in her blood?"

The brunette threw her hands up. "Jesus Christ, Max!"

The musicians were looking at each other like the Three Stooges wondering how to explain their latest botched wallpapering job to their boss. Wide eyes peered out of the drifting cigarette smoke around us as the Renaissance reunion got a good look at the man of the hour, who was dramatically draining the whiskey glass, handing the empty vessel to the nearest bewildered musician.

Then, moving with unexpected quickness, and force, Bodenheim grabbed the woman by the arm and she squealed with pain as he intoned, "Or is this 'innocent' the heathen? If we are to believe Schopenhauer, women are incapable of romantic love, yet infinitely capable of unfathomable treachery . . ."

"Excuse me," I told the horrified but spellbound Marilyn, and got up and put my hand on Bodenheim's shoulder.

"It is rather unfortunate," he was saying, still clutching her arm, his face inches from hers with its wide eyes and lips drawn back in a snarl, "that the legs of a girl cannot be nailed to the floor . . . It's hard to keep them in one place, except when they are locked up in closets."

I said, "Been a long time, Max."

The rheumy blue eyes tried to focus, and he suddenly noticed the hand on his shoulder, looking down at it as if it were an oversize, unpleasant moth that had landed there. "I don't know you, young man. Kindly remove your meat hook from my shoulder."

I did, then extended my hand. "Nate Heller. Mahlon's son."

A wrinkled smile formed under the lumpy nose and the eyes tightened in remembrance. "Heller's Books. Ah yes. The West Side. Wonderful days. Days of youth and passion."

Ric, just behind us, was rounding up his musicians and herding them out of the bar and back up into the dining room.

In the meantime, Bodenheim had unhanded the brunette and was gesturing to her rather grandly with his corncob pipe in hand. "Heller's Books, allow me to introduce Mrs. Maxwell Bodenheim."

The pretty, lanky lush smiled at me, looked me up and down with open appreciation, and said, "I'll have to get Max to bring me to Chicago more often."

"You'll have to forgive Ruth," Bodenheim said, his smile tightening. "She has the morals of an alley cat, but she can't help it. She, too, comes from a newspaper background . . ."

"You mean like *me*, Max?" Ben asked, stepping into our rarefied social circle. He had a cigar in the fingers of the hand that held his glass of Scotch. He had the uneasy smile of a host who suddenly realized he had invited a disaster area for a guest.

Bodenheim beamed at the sight of his old friend and adversary; his smile had more holes than teeth. "I was referring . . ." He gestured and sneered and stage-whispered: ". . . to these lesser lights. Literary section editors. Book reviewers. Columnists . . ."

Ben smirked. "Try not to alienate them too bad, Bodie, till I pass the hat for ya."

Ruth floated off and I returned to the small table where a stilted

Marilyn was talking to Herb Lyon of the *Trib*. He was trying to wrangle an impromptu follow-up interview for his "Tower Ticker" column; I gently let Herb know this was a social occasion and he drifted off. Soon Marilyn was sipping a glass of champagne; I had a Coke — I was working, after all — while Bodenheim (who had somehow acquired another drink) had Hecht up against a wall, the former getting worked up and Hecht's patient smile wearing thinner and thinner.

I only got bits and pieces of it, mostly Bodenheim, saying, "I have always liked your work, my cynical friend, I can honestly say I've never slammed it . . . *Count Bruga*, of course, excepted . . . Ben, you had great ability in fields of prose, where money alone lies. I am an indifferent prose writer and a very good poet. That explains the difference in our purses!"

"Such a sad, brilliant man," Marilyn said, working on her second glass of champagne.

"Sad, anyway."

"You don't think he's brilliant?"

"He's got an impressive line of bullshit," I said, "for a deadbeat."

"How can you say that? His language is beautiful!"

"But what he says is ugly."

"I don't care. I want to meet him."

I didn't argue with her. Mine was not to reason why. Mine was but to do and sigh.

As I approached Bodenheim, he continued filibustering his old friendly foe: "If we don't raise at least twenty dollars tonight, Ben, I shan't be able to get my typewriter out of hock when I return to that shallow, mean and uncouth frenzy known as New York."

"Then as you wend your way around this room, Bodie," Ben said, smiling the world's tightest smile, "I suggest you find some topic of discussion beside the 'stench of Capitalism.' Your old friends, the ones still alive anyway, aren't radicals anymore. They're democrats."

"I do need my typewriter," Bodenheim said, as if Ben had said nothing, "even though I have not sold one of my short stories or poems yet this year." He took a healthy swig from his latest glass of whiskey. "But hope is a warmly smiling, stubbornly tottering child — and without a typing machine I would feel like a writer with spinal meningitis."

I whispered to Ben: "Marilyn wants to meet the Great Man."

Ben rolled his eyes, and said, "All right, but let's both chaperon him, then."

Bodenheim was saying, "You might consider it a persecution complex, but I'm convinced these rejections stem from the days when I threw many a caustic jab at the intellectual dwarfs who pass as literary editors and critics . . ."

Taking his toothpick arm, I said, "Max, that lovely blonde would like to meet you. She's quite famous. That's Marilyn Monroe."

"Heller Books, it would be my immense pleasure!" he said, something flickering in the cloudy eyes, the ghost of a once-great womanizer, perhaps.

I ushered him over to the table, where Marilyn rose, smiling, almost blushing, saying, "Mr. Bodenheim, I've worn my copy of your *Selected Poems* simply to tatters."

He took her hand and, much as Ric had, kissed it; I hope she washed it, later. With antiseptic soap.

"My dear," Bodenheim said, bowing, "your taste is as impeccable as your skin is luminous. May I sit?"

She gestured eagerly. "Please."

Ben and I commandeered a couple extra chairs and the four of us crowded around the postage-stamp table as the Tattered King of Greenwich Village conferred with Hollywood's reigning Sex Queen.

"Miss Monroe, I have admired your contributions to the cinema," he said.

"I would think an artist of your stature wouldn't find much of value in what I do," she said, obviously as flattered as she was surprised.

Ben said, "I never knew you to go to a picture show, Bodie."

"I have slept in some of the finest grindhouses on Forty-Second Street," he said rather grandly. He was looking around, probably for his wife. She was nowhere in sight. He returned his gaze to the incandescent beauty who hung on his every word.

"I adore your contribution to the arts, my dear," he said, the sarcasm so faint I wasn't sure it was there. "You remind me of the Bali woman who walks naked down to her navel, and proudly displays her beautifully formed breasts; making love is as a natural to her as breathing, or singing. Sex is really the song of the spirit as well as the flesh, and my dear, you are a prima donna, a diva, of your art."

This slice of condescension-laced sexual innuendo made Ben wince, but Marilyn seemed not to mind, even to take it as a compliment.

"But what I do is so . . . ephemeral," Marilyn said. "Your poetry will live forever."

He leaned forward. "Do you know what poetry is, my dear?"

"I think I do . . . I don't know if I could put it into words . . ."

Now he sat back again. "It's the deep, unformed longing to escape from daily details . . . to enter delicately imaginative plateaus, unconnected with human beliefs, or fundamental human feelings . . ."

"Oh, but Mr. Bodenheim . . ."

He puffed the corncob. "Call me Max, child — or Bodie, as my friends do."

Ben rolled his eyes, as if to say, *What friends?*

Marilyn's expression was heartbreakingly sincere. "But, Max . . . your poems are *filled* with human feeling . . ."

He nodded, exhaling foul smoke; I had a feeling if you took the smoke away, he wouldn't smell much better.

"I am cursed with a malady of the soul," the poet said. "I am constantly tempted to desert the sleek jest of this physical existence."

Her eyes tightened. Her question was a whisper: "Suicide?"

"My life has been a dirty, cruel, involved, crucified mess — with the exception of my glittering words. And sometimes I even hate them, my pretty, glittering words. But where would I be without that golden braid of language that lifts me up out of my life?"

"Would you . . . would you ever do it? Take your own life?"

"I think not, child. We demonstrate the truth or falsity of our lives by the manner of our deaths."

"What do you mean?"

"Those who die in a tavern brawl like Christopher Marlowe or in a fit of desperation like Hart Crane leaping off a ship in mid-ocean reveal in their violent deaths the inadequate inner workings of their secret beings . . . Are you familiar with this one?

I shall walk down the road.
I shall turn and feel upon my feet
The kisses of Death, like scented rain."

"*For Death is a black slave with little silver birds,*" Marilyn said, "*perched in a sleeping wreath upon his head.*"

"You do me great honor," Bodenheim said, touching a hand to his chest, lowering his head, then chugging some whiskey.

"So many of your poems are about death . . . and love."

"I am a man, and man is human, all-too-human, placed by the theologians a little below the angels. Life is the struggle between the pull of the divine and the downward drag of the beast."

She was leaning forward, rapt in the wise man's words. "Is suicide divine, or beastly?"

"Neither. Both. Perhaps I'll answer your question in my next poem." Then he shrugged and began working on relighting his corncob. "But as long as Ruth lives, I'll not take my life."

"Ruth? Your wife?"

"My sweet better half, with whom I share park benches, flophouse suites and what remains of my tattered existence. We have an exquisite arrangement — she cheats on me, and I beat on her. An inventive girl. Burned down her parents' house, you know. There are those who say that she is mad, but who among us does not have eccentricities?"

"Is she a poet, too?"

He had the corncob going again. "She's a writer."

Marilyn swallowed, summoned bravery and said, "I write poetry."

His smile was benevolent. "You do, my child?"

"Would you like to hear one?" She smiled. "I think I've had enough champagne to get the nerve . . .

Life — I am of both your directions
Somehow remaining
Hanging downward the most
Strong as a cobweb in the wind . . ."

"You wrote that?"

"Yes."

Bodenheim shook his head. "Sentimental slush." He stood suddenly. "Stick to the silver screen, sweetie."

And he rose and stumbled off into the crowd.

Marilyn had turned a ghostly white, her mouth slack, her face without expression, her eyes wide and vacant and yet filled with pain.

Ben touched her arm and said, "Marilyn, I'm sorry . . . he's a drunken no-good bastard. Hell, he thinks *Ezra Pound* stinks . . ."

"Nathan . . . could you please take me back to the hotel?"

"Sure."

But Marilyn was already up and moving out, and I was working to keep up with her. She didn't begin crying until we were in back of the cab, and I held her in my arms and comforted her, telling how much I liked her poem.

At the door of her suite, I said, "He's a Skid Row bum, you're a goddess. They'll be watchin' your movies when this guy's poems turn to dust."

She smiled, just a little, and touched my face with the gentlest hand imaginable. Then she kissed me.

Sweetly. Sadly.

"Do you want me to come in?" I asked.

"Next time, Nathan," she said.

And sealed herself within.

✗ ✗ ✗

I met Ben for lunch at the Pump Room at the Ambassador East. It was an atmosphere perfect for Marilyn Monroe — deep-blue walls, crystal chandeliers, white-leather booths, waiters in English Regency attire serving food elegantly from serving carts and off flaming swords.

But the only celebrities in the room were local newspapermen — fewer than last night at Riccardo's, actually — and, of course, Ben Hecht and that celebrated "private eye to the stars," Nathan Heller.

"She flew out this morning," Ben said, his bloodshot eyes matching the Bloody Mary he was drinking. His second.

"When was she supposed to leave?"

"Not until late this afternoon. We were going to meet with the Doubleday people after lunch."

"Hope your book deal didn't get queered."

"Nah. I'll meet with Marilyn back in Hollywood, it'll be fine. How would you like to bodyguard her again?"

"Twist my arm."

"You two seemed to hit it off."

"I kept it business-like."

"You mean, that fucking Bodie blew it for you."

I grinned, sipped my rum and Coke. "Bingo."

"Well, Doubleday wants Marilyn to make an appearance at next year's ABA, kicking off a promotional tour for the book. If I can talk her into it, which I think I can, I'll toss the security job A-1's way."

"I appreciate that, Ben. Maybe I'll let you ghost my autobiography."

"Write your own damn book." He laughed hollowly; he looked terrible, dark bags, pallid complexion, second chin sagging over his crisp blue bow tie. "Guess how much we raised for Bodie last night?"

"Five bucks?"

"Oh, much more . . . twelve."

I chuckled at this pleasant bad news. "He must have got even cuter after I left, to get such an overwhelming acclamation."

Ben's smirk made the fuzzy caterpillar of his mustache wriggle. "He caught his wife coming onto a waiter and started screaming flowery obscenities at her and finally slapped her face. When Ric stepped between them, Ruth slapped him and started shouting, 'I'm Mrs. Maxwell Bodenheim! I'm Mrs. Maxwell Bodenheim!'" He sighed and shook his head and sipped his Bloody Mary. "I think Max may have made the record books on this one — the only guy in history ever to get thrown out of his own benefit party."

"He's a horse's ass. What possessed you to fly him and his harpy out here, anyway?"

He didn't answer the question; instead he said, "That was awful, how he crushed that poor kid, last night. Little Marilyn may be built like a brick shithouse, but she's delicate, you know, underneath that war paint."

"I know. I'd have knocked the bastard's teeth out, if he had any."

Ben snorted a second to that motion, finished his Bloody Mary, and waved a waiter over, telling him we'd have another round before we ordered lunch.

"Don't be too tough on Bodie," Ben said. "Language and a sense of superiority are all he has. He doesn't have money to eat or buy clothes, just words he can use to make other people feel like they're bums, too."

"He's just a mean old drunk."

Ben shook his head, smiling grimly. "Problem is, kid, there's a young man in that old skin. He lives in sort of a child's world filled with word toys. He's a poet who lives in a world of poetry . . ."

"He's a stumblebum who lives in the gutter."

The waiter brought Ben's third Bloody Mary. Ben stared into the drink, as if it were a crystal ball into his past. His voice was hushed as he said: "We made a sort of pact, Bodie and I, back when we were young turks, cynical sentimental souls devoted to Art." A sudden grin. "Ever hear about the time we spoke at this pompous literary society for a hundred bucks? Which was real cabbage in those days . . ."

"Can't say I have."

"We agreed to put on a full-scale literary debate on an important topic. The hall was full of these middle-class boobs, this was in Evanston or someplace, and I got up and said, 'Resolved: that people who attend literary debates are imbeciles. I shall take the affirmative. The affirmative rests.' Then Bodie got up and said, 'You win.' And we ran off with the hundred."

I waited till Ben's laughter at his own anecdote let up before saying, "So you grew up and made some real money, and Peter Pan flew to the gutter. So what?"

Ben sighed again. "I was hoping last night we'd raise some real money for the son of a bitch . . ."

"Why?"

"Because, goddamnit, I've been supporting him for fucking *years!* He'd send me sonnets and shit, in the mail, and I sent him two hundred bucks a month. Only, I can't afford it anymore! Not since my career hit the fan."

"You got no responsibility to underwrite that bum."

"Not any more, I don't. Fuck that toothless sot." He opened the menu. "Let's order. I'm on expense account with Doubleday . . ."

✗ ✗ ✗

I had every reason to expect I'd seen and heard the last of Maxwell Bodenheim, and his lovely souse of a spouse, and to take Ben Hecht at his word, that he was finished with subsidizing the bard of Skid Row.

But the first week of February, at the office, I got a call from Ben.

"You want to do another job for me, kid?"

"If it involves Marilyn Monroe."

"It doesn't, really. Unless you consider it an extension of what you did for me, before. Did you hear what happened to Bodenheim, after the party at Riccardo's?"

"You told me," I reminded him. "He and the missus got tossed out their deserving backsides."

"No, I mean after that. Remember how I told you we raised a grand total of twelve bucks for him?"

"Yeah."

"Well, he spent it on rubbing alcohol. He was found in the gutter the next morning, beaten to shit, with half a bottle of the stuff clutched in his paws."

"Mugged?"

"I doubt it. More like he'd been mouthing off and got worked over for it."

"This didn't make the papers or I'd know about it."

"See, you don't know everything that goes on in Chicago, kid. Even out in Hollywood, I know more about the town than you . . . I got a call from Van Allen Bradley."

Bradley was literary editor over at the *Daily News*.

He continued: "Seems the lovely Mrs. Bodenheim, Ruth, came around begging for a book review assignment for Max, so they could raise bus fare back to New York."

"Ben, don't tell me you flew 'em out *one-way,* for that benefit?"

"Hell, yes! I expected to raise a couple thousand for the no-good son of a bitch. How did I know he was going to disintegrate in public?"

"Yeah, who woulda guessed that?"

"Anyway, Bradley assigned some new collection of Edna Vincent Millay, and Ruth brought the review in a day or so later. Bradley says it was well written enough, but figures Ruth wrote it, not Bodie. She stood there at Bradley's desk till he coughed up the dough."

"They're a class act, the Bodenheims."

"Listen, Heller, do you want the job?"

"What is it?"

"In June, back at the ABA, I talked to an editor with a low-end paperback house, about reprinting some of Bodie's books — you know, that racy stuff about flappers fucking? Slap on cover paintings of sexy babes and Bodie's back in business. I got nearly two thousand in contracts lined up for him, which is big money for him."

"So what do you need me for? Just send him the damn contracts."

"Nate, I can't find the S.O.B. He's a goddamn street bum, floating somewhere around Greenwich Village, or the Bowery. I know for a while he was staying at this farm retreat on Staten Island, for down-and-outers, run by Dorothy Day, with the *Catholic Worker*? I had a letter from him from there, and I called Dorothy Day and she said Ruth and

Bodie showed up on her doorstep, with his arm and leg in a cast from that beating he took. He was there for several months, healing up, and I guess he even managed to sell a poem or two, to the *New York Times,* if you can believe it, for I guess ten bucks a piece . . . but Ruth started flirting with some of the male 'guests,' and once his leg healed, Bodie dragged his blushing bride back into the city."

"I'll line up a man in New York to handle it for you, Ben. It'll be cheaper."

"No, Nate — I want *you* to do this. Yourself. You got some history with Bodie; you might get through to him where somebody else wouldn't."

"This could end up costing you more than these contracts are worth."

"Hey, I had a little upturn. I can afford it. I want to get some money to Bodie without gettin' back in the routine of me supportin' him. Anyway, I think it would do him good to see his work back in print."

I laughed, once. "You really are that bastard's friend."

"He doesn't deserve it, does he?"

"No."

✗ ✗ ✗

The Waldorf Cafeteria, on Sixth Avenue near Eighth Street, was within a stone's throw of MacDougal Alley and its quaint studios and New York's only remaining gas street lamps, in the midst of one of Greenwich Village's several centers of nightlife. Here, where skycrapers were conspicuous in their absence, and brick buildings and renovated stables held sway, countless little bistros and basement *boites* had sprung up on the narrow, choatically-arranged streets like so many exotic mushrooms. Longhaired men and shorthaired women wandered in their dark, drab clothes and sunglasses, moving through a lightly falling snow like dreary ghosts.

Finding Maxwell Bodenheim took exactly one afternoon. I had begun at Washington Square, where I knew he had once pinned his poems to a picket fence for the dimes and quarters of tourists. A bearded creator of unframed modernistic landscapes working the same racket for slightly inflated fees informed me that "Mad Max" (as I soon found all who knew him in the Village referred to him) had given up selling art to the tourist trade.

"He got too weird for the room, man," the black-overcoat-clad artiste of perhaps twenty-five told me, between alternating puffs of cigarette smoke and cold-visible breath. "You know, too threatening — half-starved looking and drunk and smelly . . . the Elks won't do business with a crazy man."

"The Elks?"

"Out-of-towners, man — you know, Elks and Rotarians and Babbitts. Or cats from Flatbush or the Bronx who let their hair down when they hit Sheridan Square."

"So what's Max up to, now?"

"He's around. Moochin' drinks and peddlin' poems for pennies in bars. Been runnin' the blinkie scam, I heard, with some Bowery cats."

I didn't relish hitting that part of town.

"No idea where he lives?"

"Used to be over on Bleecker, but they got evicted. Him and Ruth got busted for sleepin' on the subway. Didn't have the twenty-five bucks fine and spent the night in the can."

"It's a little cold for doorways and park benches."

He shrugged. "They probably still got enough friends to flop for free, here and there. Just start hittin' the coffee houses and clubs and somebody'll lead you to him."

"Thanks," I said. "Here's a contribution to the arts." And slipped him a fin.

I started to walk away and the guy called out, "Hey man! Did you check with Bellevue? He's been in and out of there."

"As a nutcase or alcoholic?"

"Take your pick."

I called Bellevue, but Max wasn't currently a guest.

So I hit the streets, which were alive with native bohemians and wide-eyed tourists alike — it was Saturday and the dusting of snow wasn't stopping anybody. I covered a lot of ground in about three hours, entering smoky cellar joints where coffee and cake were served with a side of free verse, stepping around wildly illustrated apocalyptic Bible verses in chalk on the sidewalks outside the gin mills of West Eighth Street, checking out such tourist traps as the Nut Club and Cafe Society and the Village Barn, gandering briefly at the strippers at Jimmy Kelly's, stopping in at cubbyhole restaurants that advertised "health food" in conspicuously un-healthy surroundings, but eating instead at the Cafe

Royal, which advertised itself as "The Center of Second Avenue Bohemia" and served up a mean apple strudel. The name Maxwell Bodenheim was familiar to many, from the Cafe Reggio to the White Horse Pub, but at the Village Vanguard, a deadpan waif with her raven hair in a pixie cut told me to try the Minneta Tavern, where I learned that the San Remo Cafe on MacDougal Street was Mad Max's favorite haunt. But at the San Remo, I was sent on to the Waxworks, as the Waldorf Cafeteria was known to hip locals.

What could have possessed the owners of a respectable, pseudo-elegant chain of cafeterias to open a branch in the heart of Bohemia, a place Maxwell Bodenheim had once dubbed "the Coney Island of the soul"? Its wallpaper yellowed and peeling, its "No Smoking" signs defaced and ignored, its once-gleaming fixtures spotted and dull, its floors dirty and littered, its fluorescent lighting sputtered with electrical shorts even while casting a jaundiced glow on the already-sallow faces of a clientele who had taken this cafeteria hostage, turning it from eating place to meeting place. The clatter of dishes and the ring of the pay-as-you-go cash register provided a hard rhythm for the symphony of egos as poets and painters and actors announced their own genius and denounced the lack of talent in others, while occasionally sipping their dime's worth of coffee and nibbling at sandwiches brought from home, the cheap flats they called "studios."

Holding forth at a small side table was the man himself, decked out in a World War One-vintage topcoat over the same shabby suit and food-flecked tie he'd worn to the Renaissance reunion, months ago. On the table, as if a meal set out for him, was a worn bulging leather briefcase. Sitting beside him was Ruth, in the pale-yellow dress she'd worn to Riccardo's. Both were smoking — Bodie his corncob with that cheap awful tobacco, Ruth with her elbow resting in a cupped hand, cigarette poised near her lips in a royally elegant chainsmoker posture. To the cups of coffee before them Bodenheim was adding generous dollops from a pint of cheap whiskey.

Bodenheim, of course, was talking, and Ruth was nodding, listening, or maybe half-listening; she sat slumped, looking a little bored.

I bought myself a cup of coffee and walked over to them, and bobbed my head toward one of the two untaken chairs at their table. "Mind if I join you?"

As he slipped the pint back in his topcoat pocket, Bodie's rheumy eyes narrowed in their deep shadowy holes; his lumpy face was the color of tapioca, his cheeks sunken to further emphasize the skull beneath the decaying flesh. Sitting up, pretty Ruth, with her big bedroom eyes, one of which drooped drunkenly, again gave me the onceover, like I was another entree on the cafeteria serving line.

"My wife and I are having a private conversation," Bodie said acidly, then cocked his head. "Do I know you, sir?"

"Yes," I said, sitting down, "from a long time ago, on the West Side of Chicago. But we ran into each other at Riccardo's last June."

The thin line of a mouth erupted into a ghastly array of brownish teeth and sporadic gaps. "Heller's Books! You accompanied that lovely young actress."

Ruth smirked and snorted derisively, as if compared to her Marilyn Monroe was nothing. Smoke came from her nostrils like dragon's breath.

"Yes," I said, "the lovely young actress you humiliated and sent from the room in tears."

He waved that off with a mottled hand. "That was for that sweet child's benefit. Cruelty was the kindest gift I could give her."

"You think?"

"I know." He patted the bulging briefcase before him. *"This* is poetry, my poetry, not sentimental drivel, but the work of a serious artist, a distinguished outcast in American letters — hated and feared, an isolated wanderer in the realm of intellect. If I were to encourage the amateurs, the dilettantes, even ones like Miss Monroe, whose skin shimmers like pudding before the spoon goes in, I would lessen both myself and them."

Ruth cocked her head toward me, rolled her eyes, then winked. She was pretty cute, for a drunk; but I would have had to be pretty drunk, to want to get cute.

"What's your name?" Ruth asked. Her eyes added "Big Boy."

"Nate Heller."

"You're from Chicago? What brings you to the Village?"

"Ben Hecht asked me to look your husband up."

That got Bodenheim's attention and elicited a bitter smirk. "Does my ex-friend wish me to make another cross-country pilgrimage for a twelve-dollar stipend?"

"He's got a publisher interested in reprinting some of your sex books."

Ruth's eyes sobered up and her smile turned from randy to greedy. But the crooked thin line under Bodenheim's sweet-potato nose was curling into a sneer.

"My novels may indeed be inferior to my poetry — I am nothing if not brutally honest with myself where my literary prowess is concerned — but they are hardly 'sex books.' They are not gussied-up pornography, like Hecht's *Fantazius Mallare*. Despite certain flaws, those novels sparkle with social satire and a genuine —"

"Whatever they sparkle with," I said, "there's a publisher willing to pony up a couple grand for the privilege of putting naked women on the covers."

Ruth's eyes were dancing with dollar signs, but Bodenheim was scowling.

"The last time I allowed a cheap pulp publisher . . . when was it, five years, eight years ago? . . . they bowdlerlized the text, even while presenting my work with the sort of sensational gift-wrapping to which you refer. I won't have my work simultaneously exploited *and* censored!"

I leaned forward. "I don't know anything about that. I would guess the last thing this publisher would want to do is trim the dirty parts. So I wouldn't worry about your literary integrity."

Bodenheim froze, his sneering smile dissolving into a hurt, surprised near-pout. "Why, Heller's Books — you don't like me, do you?"

"I wasn't paid to like you. I was paid to find you, and deliver this message." I patted my chest. "I've got the contracts in my inside pocket, if you want me to leave 'em with you. The publisher's right here in New York, you can talk with them, direct. Ben doesn't want any finder's fee, he just wants to see you make a buck or two off your 'prowess.' "

"I don't understand who you are," Bodenheim said, bewildered, the murky eyes suddenly those of a hurt child.

"I'm a private detective."

"I thought you were a literary man . . . your father . . ."

"Ran a bookstore. Me, like the man says on TV, I'm a cop. In business for myself, but a cop."

"You deal in violence," Bodenheim said quietly.

"Sometimes."

Now a look of sadistic superiority gripped the ravaged face. He leaned forward, gesturing with the foul-smelling corncob. "Are you aware, Heller's Books, of the close connection between the art of murder and the murder of art?"

"I can't say as I am."

"Artists are not killed overnight. They are murdered by being kept alive, as poverty, the unseen assassin, exacts from them one last full measure of agony."

"Is that right."

"When the arts go down to destruction, the artist perishes with them. For some of us, who do not sell our souls to Mammon, the final resting place is Potter's Field. For others it is Hollywood."

"Ben's just trying to help you out, old man. Why in hell, I don't know."

"Why?" Fire exploded in those cloudy eyes. "Because I am the closest thing to a conscience that Ben *Hack*'t has or ever *will* have."

I snorted a laugh. "What do you use for a conscience, old man?"

He settled back into the chair and the eyes went rheumy again; he collapsed into himself and said, very quietly, "My own crushed life sits beside me, staring with sharp, accusing eyes, like a vengeful ghost seeking retribution for some foul murder committed at a time of delirium and terror."

"I don't mean to barge in," a male voice said.

He was a good-looking kid in well-worn jeans and a short-sleeve, slightly frayed white shirt; he had the open face, wide smile, dark-blond pompadour and boyish regular features of the young Buster Crabbe; same broad shoulders, too, only he wasn't as tall, perhaps five eight at most. He only seemed clean-cut at first glance: then I noticed the scars under his left eye and on his chin, and how that wide smile seemed somehow . . . wrong.

"Joe," Ruth said warmly, "sit down! Join us."

"This is something of a business discussion," Bodenheim said, tightly.

"Don't be silly, Bodie," she said. "Sit down, Joe."

Joe sat down, next to me, across from Ruth. He was eyeing me suspiciously. I would have sworn the kid was looking at me through the eyes of a jealous boyfriend, but that would be impossible. After all, Ruth was married . . .

"Joe Greenberg," he said, offering his hand, wearing that big smile, though the eyes remained wary.

"Nate Heller," I said. His handshake let me know just how strong he was.

Bodenheim said, "Mr. Greenberg is a dishwasher here at the Waxworks. It's a career he's pursued with uncommon distinction at numerous establishments around the Village."

"Nice to meet you, Joe," I said. "If you'll excuse me, I was just going . . ."

I began to rise but Ruth touched my arm. "Stay for just a little while. Joe, Mr. Heller has wonderful news. A publisher wants to bring some of Max's books back out."

Joe's grin managed to widen, and words streamed out: "Why, Max, that's wonderful! This is a dream come true, I couldn't be happier for —"

"It is not wonderful," Bodenheim said. "It is, like you, Joseph, possibly well-meaning but certainly insulting."

"Max, don't say that," Joe said. "You and Ruth are the best friends I have around here."

"Look," I said, "do you want me to leave the contracts or not?"

"My old friend Ben is not aware," Bodenheim said, with strained dignity, ignoring Joe, who was looking quickly from husband to wife to intruder (me), "that I am currently engaged in the writing of my memoirs for Samuel Roth, publisher of Bridgehead Books."

"That's swell," I said. "Sorry to have bothered you . . ."

Again, I began to rise and Ruth stopped me, her brown eyes gazing up, pitifully beseeching. "Mr. Heller, what my husband says is true, he's been going in and writing every day, but the pay is meager. We don't have enough to even put a roof over our heads . . . we've been sleeping in doorways, and it's a cold winter . . ."

Bodie seemed to be pulling down pay sufficient to afford whiskey.

Joe leaned forward, chiming in, "I told you, Ruth — you and Max are welcome to stay with me . . ."

Now it was Ruth leaning forward; she touched Joe's hand. "That's sweet, Joe, but you just have that one small room . . . it's an imposition on you . . ."

Joe squeezed her hand, then with his other hand stroked it, petted it. His mouth was moist; so were his eyes. "I'd love to have you stay with me . . ."

"Leave her alone," Bodenheim spat, "or I'll kill you!"

Joe removed his hand and his face fell into a putty-like expressionless mask. "You hate me, don't you?"

"Of course I do," Bodenheim said, and withdrew his pint and refilled his coffee cup.

"What if I let you two take my room," Joe said nobly, "and me move in with my friend, Allen."

And he nodded toward a skinny redheaded bus boy with glasses and pimples who was clearing a table across the room.

"I'll pay the rent," Joe said, "and when you get on your feet, and get your own place, I'll move back in."

"I once warned a girl named Magda," Bodenheim said as if latching onto a stray thought just floating by, "against the possibility of falling into the hands of some degenerate in whom the death of love and the love of death had combined into a homicidal mania. She was strangled in a hotel bed."

Joe was shaking his head. "What are you talkin' about? I'm tryin' to be *nice . . .* "

Ruth said, "Oh, Bodie, don't you see? Joe's our friend. Don't say such cruel things."

"Today," Bodie said, patronizingly, "when the world is falling apart like scattered beads from a pearl necklace that once graced the lovely throat of existence, the bestial side of man's nature is revealing itself . . . blatantly."

"Now *you're* insulting *me!"* Joe said. "I know when I'm being insulted."

"The indignation of fools," Bodenheim said grandly, "is my crown."

I'd had enough of this touching scene. I got up, saying, "I'm in town till Monday. At the Lexington. If you change your mind, Max, give me a call."

As I left, Joe moved around to where I was sitting, nearer to Ruth, and he was leaning forward, speaking quickly, flashing his most ingratiating smile and issuing the best words he could muster, about how his good intentions were being misinterpreted, while Bodenheim sat uncharacteristically silent, frozen with contempt, a sullen wax figure in the Waxworks cafeteria.

✗ ✗ ✗

By the time I got back to my hotel, a message from Max was waiting at the front desk. It had been written down faithfully by the hotel operator: "Mr. Heller — my lovely companion has convinced me to come to my financial senses. Please be so kind as to bring the book contracts tomorrow afternoon between 3 and 4 o'clock to the following address — 97 3rd Avenue, near 13th Street. Fifth floor, room 5D."

I showed the desk clerk the address. "Where is that?"

"Lower Fifth Avenue," said the clerk, a boy in his twenties wearing a mustache to look older. "Pretty rough neighborhood. On the fringe of the Bowery."

So I was going to make it to the Bowery, after all. What trip to New York would be complete without it?

I spent the rest of the evening in the Lexington bar making the acquaintance of a TWA stewardess, the outcome of which is neither germane to this story nor any of your business; we slept in the next morning, had a nice buffet lunch at the hotel and I took her to Radio City Music Hall, where *How to Marry a Millionaire* was playing, one of those new Cinemascope pictures trying to replace 3-D. My companion was lovely, as were the Rockettes, and Betty Grable and Lauren Bacall; but Marilyn made me ache in so many places. She always would.

My new friend caught a cab to the airport, and I grabbed one to the Bowery, where I asked the cabbie to wait for me with the meter running. He warily agreed, and I entered a shambling five-story tenement that looked to be the architectural equivalent of Maxwell Bodenheim himself.

I went up five flights of spongy, creaky stairs, glad I was wearing a topcoat; the building wasn't heated. A window on the fifth floor offered a sweeping city view, more worthy of a postcard than a dingy rooming house; the Third Avenue El was just below. 5D was at the end of the hall, on the right, the numbers hammered haphazardly into the wall next to the gray-painted door, which had no knob, simply a padlocked hasp.

There was no answer to my repeated knocks. I considered saying to hell with it — so Bodenheim wasn't here, so what? How reliable was a boozehound like Max, anyway?

Pretty reliable, if money was waiting — and I had the feeling his brown-eyed soul mate wouldn't have missed this appointment if even fifty cents were at stake, let alone several thousands. The tiny hairs on the back of my copper's neck were tingling . . . and was it my imagination, or was there a stench coming from that room that drowned out the disinfectant and cooking smells and mildew and generally stale air? An all too familiar stench, worse even than Bodie's corncob pipe . . .

On the first floor I found the pudgy, fiftyish, groundhog-pussed operator ("Not the super! I'm the lessee! The operator!") of this grand hotel. His name was Albert Luck, which was something his tenants were all down on.

"So you know this guy in 5D?" Luck demanded, just outside his door, squinting behind thick-lensed wireframes as if my face were tiny print he was trying to make out; he wore baggy pants and suspenders over his long johns. "This guy Harold Weinberg, you know him?"

"Sure," I lied.

"Son of a bitch Weinberg sneaks in and out like a goddamn ghost," Luck said. "I can't never catch him, and he padlocks the place behind him. If you're such a friend of his, maybe you wanna pay his goddamn rent for him. He's behind two weeks!"

"How much?"

"Ten bucks."

"Five a week?"

He nodded. "Five's the weekly rate; it's eighty-five cents a night."

"I'll pay the back rent," I said, "if you give me a look around in there."

"Can't. It ain't my padlock on the door."

I showed him a sawbuck. "Wouldn't take much to pop the hasp."

"Make it twenty," he said, groundhog eyes glittering, "to cover repairs."

Soon I was following him up the stairs; he wore a plaid hunter's jacket and was carrying a claw hammer and a heavy screwdriver. "Tenants like your friend I don't need . . . This ain't a flophouse, you know. These are furnished rooms."

It took him two tries to pop the latch off. I let him open the door, just in case it was a situation where I wouldn't want to be leaving any fingerprints.

It was.

The blood splashed around in the eight- by nine-foot cubicle was mostly on one wall, and the ceiling above, and on the nearby metal folding cot, and of course on the body of the woman sprawled there on her stomach, still clad in the frayed yellow dress, splotched brown now, the same-dried-blood brown that, with the smell of decay, indicated she had been dead some time; this happened at least this morning, maybe even last night.

She had been stabbed in the back, on the left, four times, over her heart and lungs, deep wounds, hunting-knife type wounds, and from the amount of blood that had soaked her dress and painted the wall and ceiling with an abstraction worthy of Washington Square's outdoor art displays, I figured an artery had been hit. Another slash, on her upper left arm, indicated an attempt to ward off a blow. Her face was battered, bloodied, and blue-gray with lividity.

"Sweet lord Jesus," Albert Luck said. "Who are they?"

"That's Ruth Bodenheim," I said, and then I pointed at the other body. "And that's her husband, Maxwell."

Max was on the floor, on his back, feet near his wife's head where it and its ponytail hung down from the side of the bed. The poet's eyes were wide, seeing nothing, his mouth open and, for once, silent, the flesh as slack on his dead face as if it were melting wax; he had been shot in the chest, a small crusty blossom of brown and black on his dingy white shirt, blood stain mingled with powder burns, near his tattered tie. His loose black suitcoat was on, unbuttoned, open, and his arms were spread as if he were trying to fly, a sleeve torn and bloody with an apparent knife gash. A book lay near him: *The Sea Around Us* by Rachel Carson; his reading had been interrupted by his killing.

"I better call the cops," Luck said, his eyes huge behind the magnified lenses.

"Keep your shirt on, pops," I said, taking a look around.

A small table near the bed, slightly splashed with blood, had the empty pint bottle of whiskey and a wine bottle with a label that said Blackberry; also, a pad and pencil and some scribbled lines of poetry obscured by blood spatter. A window nearby opened on an airshaft. On a small electric stove sat a three-gallon pot of beans, cold; resting nearby was Bodie's corncob pipe and a half-eaten bagel.

In one corner was Bodenheim's worn leather briefcase, the repository of his art; leaned up against it was a tool of a more recent trade: a crudely lettered beggar's sign saying, I AM BLIND.

No sign of a gun, or a knife.

"I'm callin' the cops," Luck said.

"What does this Harold Weinberg look like?"

Luck frowned. "He's *your* friend."

I gave him a hard look. "Refresh my memory."

The landlord shrugged, said, "Good-lookin' kid, pile of greasy hair, talks too much, smiles too much."

I touched under my left eye, then pointed to my chin. "Scars, here and here?"

"That's him."

I got my wallet out and handed him a C-note. "I wasn't here, understand? The rent was overdue and you got fed up and popped the latch, found them like this."

Luck was nodding as he slipped the hundred in his pants. "Okay by me, mister."

My cab was still waiting.

"What scenic part of the city do want to view next?" the cabbie asked.

"The Waldorf."

"Astoria?"

"Cafeteria. Near MacDougal Alley."

✗ ✗ ✗

Late Sunday afternoon at the Waxworks was pretty slow: a sprinkling of hipsters, a handful of civilians catching an early supper or a slice of pie before heading back to the real world after a few hours in Little Bohemia.

The skinny redheaded bus boy, whose horn-rimmed glasses were patched at the bridge with adhesive tape, his pimples mingling with freckles to create a Jackson Pollock canvas, was taking a break, slouched in a chair propped against a wall, smoking beneath a NO SMOKING sign decorated with cigarette burns. He had the gawky, geeky look of a teenager having a hard time with puberty; but on closer look he was probably in his mid-twenties, and he had a tattoo of a hula girl on his thin right forearm. His bus boy's tray was on the table before him like a grotesque meal.

I sat down beside him and he frowned, irritably, but said rather politely, "You want this table, mister?"

"No, Allen," I said, and smiled, "I want to talk to you."

His eyes, which were a sickly green, narrowed. "How do you know me?"

"Friend of a friend."

"What friend?"

"Joe Greenberg. Or do you know him as Harold Weinberg?"

He swallowed nervously, almost lost his balance in his propped-back chair; righting it, he sat forward. "Joe just works here is all. He's off right now."

"He's off, all right. You wouldn't happen to know where I could I find him?"

Another swallow. He started drumming his fingers on the table and he didn't look at me as he said, tremulously, "No. I ain't seen him today. You try his flop?"

"Matter of fact, yeah. He wasn't there."

"Oh, well . . ."

"Two friends of his were. Dead ones."

The eyes locked right onto me now; he was surprised, genuinely surprised — these murders were news to him.

"Oh, didn't he mention that, Allen? That he killed two people? Maybe you knew 'em — Max Bodenheim and his wife Ruth. Good customers."

The ruddy flesh around the pimples and freckles got pale. "Hell. Shit."

"If you're letting him hole up at your place, Allen, you're putting yourself in line for an accessory to murder rap."

His lips were quivering. "Jesus Christ. Jesus Christ . . . Are you a cop?"

"Private. I was hired to find Bodenheim on a business matter. I don't want to get involved anymore than you do."

His voice lowered to a whisper; what he said was like a profane prayer: "Shit . . . I gotta get him out of there!"

Sometimes it pays to play a hunch.

"Allen, let's help each other out on this . . ."

✗ ✗ ✗

In 1954, I was licensed in five states to carry firearms in the course of my business, and New York was one of them. I had learned long ago that while my need for a weapon was infrequent, travelling naked could be a chilly proposition; after all, even the most innocuous job had the potential to turn ugly.

So, after a detour back to the Lexington to pick up my nine millimeter and shoulder harness, I took a cab to the address Allen Spiegel had given me: 311 East 21st, near Second Avenue. Joe/Harold had come up in the world, all the way from the bleak Bowery to the godforsaken Gashouse district.

A wind was whipping the remnants of yesterday's snow around in a chilly duststorm. Stepping around a derelict huddling in the doorway, I entered the four-story frame roominghouse, a cold, dank breeding ground for cockroaches. Allen was waiting just inside, a frightened host in a shabby sweater and faded jeans.

"The pay phone's on the second floor," he whispered, nodding toward the stairway. "Should I go ahead and call 'em?"

"After you see me go in. It's down that way?"

He nodded and pointed.

"Don't let him see you," I advised.

"Don't worry," he said.

The bus boy's room was toward the back of the first floor, with (Allen had informed me) a window that looked out on a backyard that served as a courtyard for adjacent tenements. I glanced around to see if anyone was looking — nobody was but Allen, peeking from beside the stairwell — and I took out my nine millimeter and, with my free hand, knocked.

The voice behind the door was Joe's: "What?"

"Allen sent some food over from the Waxworks," I said. "He thought you might be hungry."

The silence that followed lasted forever. Or was it ten seconds?

Then the door cracked open and I got a sliver of Joe's pasty face before I shouldered my way in, slamming the door behind me, shoving the gun in Joe's face.

"You want to tell me about it, Joe?"

He backed away. He wore a blue workshirt and jeans and he wasn't smiling, anymore; his eyes bore raccoon circles. He didn't have to be told to put up his hands.

The room was no bigger than the one at the other rooming house — another of those "furnished rooms," which is to say a scarred-up table, a couple ancient kitchen chairs, a rusty food-spotted electric stove, unmade army cot and a flimsy nightstand, fixtures any respectable secondhand store would turn down. The wallpaper was floral and peeling, the floor bare, the window by the bed had no curtains, but a frayed shade was drawn.

On the nightstand was a hunting knife in a black sheath. No sign of a gun.

"You," he said, pointing at me, eyes narrowing, "you're that guy from the Waxworks . . ."

"That's right."

"What are you doing here? What are —"

"I had an appointment this afternoon with Max and Ruth. They couldn't keep it, so I'm keeping it with you."

He ventured a facial shrug. "Gee, I haven't seen them since last night at the Waxworks."

"Gee, then how'd they wind up dead in your flop?"

He didn't bother trying to take his lame story any farther. He just sat, damn near collapsed, on the edge of the cot. That hunting knife was nearby but he didn't seem to notice it. Anyway, that was what I was supposed to think.

I dragged over a kitchen chair and sat backwards on it, leaning forward, keeping the nine millimeter casually trained on him. "What went wrong with your little party, Joe?"

He exploded in a rush of words: "They were just a couple of low-life Communists! Mad Max, hell, he was a walking dead man, and his wife was a common slut! A couple of lousy Reds, through and through!"

"Not to mention inside and out," I said. "When you hit that artery, it must have sprayed like a garden hose."

His eyes widened with the memory I'd just triggered.

"You didn't mean for this to happen, did you, Joe? You just wanted to get laid, right?"

And that wide smile flashed, nervously. "Yeah. Just wanted to tear off a little piece from that gutter-trash quail, like half the fucking Village before me . . ." The smile turned sideways, and he shook his head. "Shit. She sure was *cute,* wasn't she?"

"How'd it happen, Joe?"

Slumping, staring at nothing, he spoke in the sing-songy whine of a child explaining itself: "I thought he fell asleep, reading, the old fart. When he ran out of whiskey, you know, I gave him some wine, and after he drained that, I thought the bastard was out for the night. Or I else wouldn'ta, you know, started fooling around with Ruth on the bed . . ."

"Only he woke up and caught you at it."

He shrugged, said, "Yeah, so I took my knife off the table and kind of threatened him with it, told him to get back away from me . . . then the old fucker took a *swing* at me . . . I think he cut his arm when he did . . . and the knife, it kind of went flying."

"What did you shoot him with?"

"I kept this old hunting rifle, .22, next to my bed. That's a rough neighborhood, you know. Bad element."

"No kidding. So you shot him point-blank with the rifle."

Another shrug. "It was self-defense."

"Why did you do the woman, Joe?"

His face tightened with indignation; he pointed to himself with a thumb. "That was self-defense, too! She started screaming and clawing at me, after I shot her old man, so I threw the bitch down the bed, and started just kind of slapping her, you know, just to shut her up, but she wouldn't put a lid on that screaming shit so I hit her a couple times, good ones, only she just yelled louder, and so what the hell else could I do, I grabbed that knife off the floor, and . . ."

He stopped, swallowed.

So I finished for him: "Stabbed her in the back four or five times. In self-defense."

That's when he lunged for me, launching himself from the bed and right at me, knocking me and the chair ass over tea kettle. Then he dove for the knife, but I was up and on him and slammed the nine-millimeter barrel into the back of his hand, crushing it against the nightstand. He yowled and pulled the hand back, shaking it like he'd been burned, and I laid the barrel along the back of his neck, hard, sending him to the floor, where he whimpered like a kicked dog.

I tucked the sheathed knife in my waistband. "Where's your damn rifle?"

"Down . . . down a gutter . . ."

I gave the place a quick toss, looking for the other weapon, or any other weapon, but he was apparently telling the truth. He sat on the floor with his legs curled around under him, like a pitiful little kid who'd just taken a fearsome beating; he was crying, but the eerie thing was, he had that big crazy smile going, too.

"You stay put, Liberace," I said. "I'm calling the cops."

I shut him in there, tucked my gun away and listened for the sound of the window opening and him clambering out into the courtyard.

It was muffled, but I heard it: "Hold it right there!"

Then a gun shot.

And Joe's voice, pleading: "Please don't kill me! I'll tell you everything!"

Seemed the cops had been waiting when Joe went out that window.

Seemed my friend Allen had spotted a suspicious character in the roominghouse hallway, trying various doors, then out back, trying windows, and Allen, being a good citizen, called it in. He thought it might be a fellow he knew from work, a dishwasher named Joe Greenberg with scars on his face and a greasy pompadour, and sure enough, that's who'd been caught, climbing out Allen's window, then trying to scramble over a fence when that cop fired a warning shot. Seemed the police were looking for an individual on a Bowery killing who answered Greenberg's description. Later, a sheathed hunting knife used in the Bowery slaying turned up on the grass by some garbage cans behind Allen's roominghouse.

Anyway, that's what the papers said.

How I should I know? I was just the Little Man Who Wasn't There, slipping out the back.

✗ ✗ ✗

Harold Weinberg (Joe Greenberg was an alias) had a history of mental illness, having been first institutionalized at age ten; in 1945, at seventeen, he'd been medically discharged from the Army, and had since racked up a long record of vagrancy and breaking-and-entering arrests. He confessed to the police several times, delivering several variants of what he told me, as well as a version that had Bodenheim killing Ruth and prompting Weinberg to retaliate with the .22, as well as my favorite, one in which a person hiding under the bed did it.

Weinberg sang "The Star Spangled Banner" at his arraignment, bragged about ridding the world of two communists, assured spectators he was "not crazy," and was promptly committed to Bellevue, where Maxwell Bodenheim and his wife Ruth were also registered, albeit in the morgue.

I claimed the bodies, at Ben Hecht's behest, who shared funeral expenses with Bodenheim's first wife, Minna, subject of Max's first book of poetry. Three hundred attended the poet's funeral, including such leading literary lights as Alfred Kreymborg and Louis Untermeyer, among a dozen other nationally known figures in the arts, who mingled with lowly Village poets, painters and thespians. Kreymborg gave a eulogy which included the prediction, "We need not worry about Maxwell Bodenheim's future — he will be read."

And Bodenheim's murder did receive enormous national coverage — probably no Bowery bum in history ever got such a send-off — and by dying violently in a sexually charged situation, the one-time bestselling author of *Replenishing Jessica* gained a second fifteen minutes of fame (to invoke a later oddball Village luminary).

But Kreymborg's prediction has otherwise proved less than prescient. Every one of Bodie's books was out of print at his death, and the same is true as I write this, forty-some years later. As far as I'm aware, the last time a Bodenheim book was in print was 1961, when a low-end paperback publisher put some sexy babes on the cover of the Greenwich Village memoirs he was writing at the time of his death.

The body of the former Ruth Fagan was claimed by her family in Detroit.

As I had intended, and done my best to arrange, my participation in the official investigation into the murder of Maxwell Bodenheim and his wife Ruth was minimal; I gave a statement about the argument I'd seen at the Waxworks on the evening of Saturday, February 7. I was not required to testify, and while I'm sure at some point Weinberg must have told the cops about the guy with the automatic who took a confession from him in Allen Spiegel's roominghouse room, it was likely written off as just another of the numerous ravings of a madman who was eventually committed to Matteawan State Hospital for the Criminally Insane; he was released in 1977, and was behind bars again within a year on an attempted murder charge.

Until his death in 1964, Ben Hecht continued to write (and doctor) movie scripts, if with far less distinction than the glory days of the '30s and '40s. His real comeback was as a writer of nostalgic, wry memoirs, including *A Child of the Century* in 1954, in which he waxed fondly of Max; he tended to write of Chicago, not Hollywood or New York, and glorified the Chicago Renaissance (and himself) whenever possible, never letting the truth stand in the way of a good yarn.

He also completed the Marilyn Monroe "autobiography," which was entitled *My Story,* but the project hit an unexpected snag.

"Looks like I won't be paying you to make goo-goo eyes at Marilyn Monroe at this year's ABA," Ben said to me on the phone, in April of '54.

"Hell you say. Why not? Isn't she making an appearance?"

"Yeah, but not at the ABA. In court. That bimbo's suing me!"

Ben's British agent had peddled the serialization rights to the book overseas, without Marilyn's permission. Her new husband, Mr. DiMaggio, convinced her she was being swindled and, besides, he didn't like the idea of the book, anyway. Ben's agent had violated the agreement with Marilyn, who hadn't signed a final book contract; the book was pulled, the lawsuit dropped. *My Story* wasn't published until 1974, when Marilyn's former business partner, Milton Greene, sold it to Stein and Day, without mentioning Hecht's role.

I did, however, encounter Marilyn again, and in fact had heard from her prior to Ben's news about the busted book project. About a week after Bodenheim's death, when I was back in Chicago, I received a phone call, at home, at three in the morning.

"I'm sorry to call so late," the breathy voice said.

"That's okay . . ." I said, sitting up in bed, blinking myself awake, pretty sure I recognized the voice, but thinking I was possibly still dreaming.

"This is Marilyn Monroe. You know — the actress?"

"I think I remember you. Very little gets past me. I'm a trained detective."

She laughed a little, but when the voice returned, it was sad. "I couldn't sleep. I was thinking about what I read in the papers."

"What did you read?"

"About that poor man. Mr. Bodenheim."

"He was cruel to you."

"I know. But life was cruel to him."

We talked for a good hour, about life and death and poetry and her new husband and how happy she was. It was a sweet, sad phone call. Delicate, gentle, poetic in a way that I don't think Maxwell Bodenheim ever was, frankly.

The best thing you can say about Max is that, unlike a lot of writers who hit the skids and the bottle, he never stopped writing. He never stopped filling paper with his poetry.

On the other hand, I think about the sign I found in that ten by ten hellhole where he died, the cardboard on which he'd scrawled the words: I AM BLIND.

Probably the truest poem he ever wrote.

KADDISH FOR THE KID

The first operative I ever took on, in the A-1 Detective Agency, was Stanley Gross. I hadn't been in business for even a year — it was summer of '33 — and was in no shape to be adding help. But the thing was — Stanley had a car.

Stanley had a '28 Ford coupe, to be exact, and a yen to be a detective. I had a paying assignment, requiring wheels, and a yen to make a living.

So it was that at three o'clock in the morning, on that unseasonably cool summer evening, I was sitting in the front seat of Stanley's Ford, in front of Goldblatt's department store on West Chicago Avenue, sipping coffee out of a paper cup, waiting to see if anybody came along with a brick or a gun.

I'd been hired two weeks before by the manager of the downtown Goldblatt's on State, just two blocks from my office at Van Buren and Plymouth. Goldblatt's was sort of a working-class Marshall Field's, with six department stores scattered around the Chicago area in various white ethnic neighborhoods.

The stores were good-size — two floors taking up as much as half a block — and the display windows were impressive enough; but once you got inside, it was like the push carts of Maxwell Street had been emptied and organized.

I bought my socks and underwear at the downtown Goldblatt's, but that wasn't how Nathan Heller — me — got hired. I knew Katie Mulhaney, the manager's secretary; I'd bumped into her, on one of my socks and underwear buying expeditions, and it blossomed into a friendship. A warm friendship.

Anyway, the manager — Herman Cohen — had summoned me to his office where he filled me in. His desk was cluttered, but he was neat — moon-faced, mustached, bow-(and fit-to-be)tied.

"Maybe you've seen the stories in the papers," he said, in a machine-gun burst of words, "about this reign of terror we've been suffering."

"Sure," I said.

Goldblatt's wasn't alone; every leading department store was getting hit — stench bombs set off, acid sprayed over merchandise, bricks tossed from cars to shatter plate glass windows.

He thumbed his mustache; frowned. "Have you heard of 'Boss' Rooney? John Rooney?"

"No."

"Well, he's secretary of the Circular Distributors Union. Over the past two years, Mr. Goldblatt has provided Rooney's union with over three-thousand dollars of business — primarily to discourage trouble at our stores."

"This union — these are guys that hand out ad fliers?"

"Yes. Yes, and now Rooney has demanded that Mr. Goldblatt order three hundred of our own sales and ad people to join his union — at a rate of twenty-five cents a day."

My late father had been a diehard union guy, so I knew a little bit about this sort of thing. "Mr. Cohen, none of the unions in town collect daily dues."

"This one does. They've even been outlawed by the AFL, Mr. Heller. Mr. Goldblatt feels Rooney is nothing short of a racketeer."

"It's an extortion scam, all right. What do you want me to do?"

"Our own security staff is stretched to the limit. We're getting *some* support from State's Attorney Courtney and his people. But they can only do so much. So we've taken on a small army of nightwatchman, and are fleshing out the team with private detectives. Miss Mulhaney recommended you."

Katie knew a good dick when she saw one.

"Swell. When do I start?"

"Immediately. Of course, you do have a car?"

Of course, I lied and said I did. I also said I'd like to put one of my "top" operatives on the assignment with me, and that was fine with Cohen, who was in a more-the-merrier mood, where beefing up security was concerned.

Stanley Gross was from Douglas Park, my old neighborhood. His parents were bakers two doors down from my father's bookstore on South Homan. Stanley was a good eight years younger than me, so I remembered him mostly as a pestering kid.

But he'd grown into a tall, good-looking young man — a

brown-haired, brown-eyed six-footer who'd been a star football and basketball player in high school. Like me, he went to Crane Junior College; unlike me, he finished.

I guess I'd always been sort of a hero to him. About six months before, he'd started dropping by my office to chew the fat. Business was so lousy, a little company — even from a fresh-faced college boy — was welcome.

We'd sit in the deli restaurant below my office and sip coffee and gnaw on bagels and he'd tell me this embarrassing shit about my being somebody he'd always looked up to.

"Gosh, Nate, when you made the police force, I thought that was just about the keenest thing."

He really did talk that way — gosh, keen. I told you I was desperate for company.

He brushed a thick comma of brown hair away and grinned in a goofy boyish way; it was endearing, and nauseating. "When I was a kid, coming into your pop's bookstore, you pointed me toward those Nick Carters, and Sherlock Holmes books. Gave me the bug. I *had* to be a detective!"

But the kid was too young to get on the force, and his family didn't have the kind of money or connections it took to get a slot on the PD.

"When you quit," he said, "I admired you so. Standing up to corruption — and in *this* town! Imagine."

Imagine. My leaving the force had little to do with my "standing up to corruption" — after all, graft was high on my list of reasons for joining in the first place — but I said nothing, not wanting to shatter the child's dreams.

"If you ever need an op, I'm your man!"

He said this thousands of times in those six months or so. And he actually did get some security work, through a couple of other, larger agencies. But his dream was to be my partner.

Owning that Ford made his dream come temporarily true.

For two weeks, we'd been living the exciting life of the private eye: sitting in the coupe in front of the Goldblatt's store at Ashland and Chicago, waiting for window smashers to show. Or not.

The massive graystone department store was like the courthouse of commerce on this endless street of storefronts; the other businesses were smaller — re-sale shops, hardware stores, pawn shops, your occasional Polish deli. During the day things were popping here. Now, there was just us — me draped across the front seat, Stanley draped across the back — and the glow of neons and a few pools of light on the sidewalks from streetlamps.

"You know," Stanley said, "this isn't as exciting as I pictured."

"Just a week ago you were all excited about 'packing a rod.' "

"You're making fun of me."

"That's right." I finished my coffee, crumpled the cup, tossed it on the floor.

"I guess a gun is nothing to feel good about."

"Right again."

I was stretched out with my shoulders against the rider's door; in back, he was stretched out just the opposite. This enabled us to maintain eye contact. Not that I wanted to, particularly.

"Nate . . . if you hear me snoring, wake me up."

"You tired, kid?"

"Yeah. Ate too much. Today . . . well, today was my birthday."

"No kidding! Well, happy birthday, kid."

"My pa made the keenest cake. Say, I . . . I'm sorry I didn't invite you or anything."

"That's okay."

"It was a surprise party. Just my family — a few friends I went to high school and college with."

"It's okay."

"But there's cake left. You want to stop by pa's store tomorrow and have a slice with me?"

"We'll see, kid."

"You remember my pa's pastries. Can't beat 'em."

I grinned. "Best on the West Side. You talked me into it. Go ahead and catch a few winks. Nothing's happening."

And nothing was. The street was an empty ribbon of concrete. But about five minutes later, a car came barreling down that concrete ribbon, right down the middle; I sat up.

"What is it, Nate?"

"A drunk, I think. He's weaving a little . . ."

It was a maroon Plymouth coupe; and it was headed right our way.

"Christ!" I said, and dug under my arm for the nine millimeter.

The driver was leaning out the window of the coupe, but whether man or woman I couldn't tell — the headlights of the car, still a good thirty feet away, were blinding.

The night exploded and so did our windshield.

Glass rained on me, as I hit the floor; I could hear the roar of the Plymouth's engine, and came back up, gun in hand, saw the maroon coupe bearing down on us, saw a silver swan on the radiator cap, and cream colored wheels, but people in the car going by were a blur, and as I tried to get a better look, orange fire burst from a gun and I ducked down, hitting the glass-littered floor, and another four shots riddled the car and the night, the side windows cracking, and behind us the plate glass of display windows was fragmenting, falling to the pavement like sheets of ice.

Then the Plymouth was gone.

So was Stanley.

The first bullet must have got him. He must have sat up to get a look at the oncoming car and took the slug head on; it threw him back, and now he still seemed to be lounging there, against the now-spiderwebbed window, precious "rod" tucked under his arm; his brown eyes were open, his mouth too, and his expression was almost — not quite — surprised.

I don't think he had time to be truly surprised, before he died.

There'd been only time enough for him to take the bullet in the head, the dime-size entry wound parting the comma of brown hair, streaking the birthday boy's boyish face with blood.

✗ ✗ ✗

Within an hour I was being questioned by Sgt. Charles Pribyl, who was attached to the State's Attorney's office. Pribyl was a decent enough guy, even if he did work under Captain Daniel "Tubbo" Gilbert, who was probably the crookedest cop in town. Which in this town was saying something.

Pribyl had a good reputation, however; and I'd encountered him, from time to time, back when I was working the pickpocket detail. He had soft, gentle features and dark alert eyes.

Normally, he was an almost dapper dresser, but his tie seemed hastily knotted, his suit and hat looked as if he'd thrown them on — which he probably had; he was responding to a call at four in the morning, after all.

He was looking in at Stanley, who hadn't been moved; we were waiting for a coroner's physician to show. Several other plainclothes officers and half a dozen uniformed cops were milling around, footsteps crunching on the glass-strewn sidewalk.

"Just a kid," Pribyl said, stepping away from the Ford. "Just a damn kid." He shook his head. He nodded to me and I followed him over by a shattered display window.

He cocked his head. "How'd you happen to have such a young operative working with you?"

I explained about the car being Stanley's.

He had an expression you only see on cops: sad and yet detached. His eyes tightened.

"How — and why — did stink bombs and window smashing escalate into bloody murder?"

"You expect me to answer that, Sergeant?"

"No. I expect you to tell me what happened. And, Heller — I don't go into this with any preconceived notions about you. Some people on the force — even some good ones, like John Stege — hold it against you, the Lang and Miller business."

They were two crooked cops I'd recently testified against.

"Not me," he said firmly. "Apples don't come rottener than those two bastards. I just want you to know what kind of footing we're on."

"I appreciate that."

I filled him in, including a description of the murder vehicle, but couldn't describe the people within at all. I wasn't even sure how many of them there were.

"You get the license number?"

"No, damnit."

"Why not? You saw the car well enough."

"Them shooting at me interfered."

He nodded. "Fair enough. Shit. Too bad you didn't get a look at 'em."

"Too bad. But you know who to go calling on."

"How's that?"

I thrust a finger toward the car. "That's Boss Rooney's work — maybe not personally, but he had it done. You know about the Circular Union and the hassles they been giving Goldblatt's, right?"

Pribyl nodded, somewhat reluctantly; he liked me well enough, but I was a private detective. He didn't like having me in the middle of police business.

"Heller, we've been keeping the union headquarters under surveillance for six weeks now. I saw Rooney there today, myself, from the apartment across the way we rented."

"So did anyone leave the union hall tonight? Before the shooting, say around three?"

He shook his head glumly. "We've only been maintaining our watch during department-store business hours. The problem of night attacks is where hired hands like you come in."

"Okay." I sighed. "I won't blame you if you don't blame me."

"Deal."

"So what's next?"

"You can go on home." He glanced toward the Ford. "We'll take care of this."

"You want me to tell the family?"

"Were you close to them?"

"Not really. They're from my old neighborhood, is all."

"I'll handle it."

"You sure?"

"I'm sure." He patted my shoulder. "Go home."

I started to go, then turned back. "When are you going to pick up Rooney?"

"I'll have to talk to the State's Attorney, first. But my guess? Tomorrow. We'll raid the union hall tomorrow."

"Mind if I come along?"

"Wouldn't be appropriate, Heller."

"The kid worked for me. He got killed working for me."

"No. We'll handle it. Go home! Get some sleep."

"I'll go home," I said.

A chill breeze was whispering.

"But the sleep part," I said, "that I can't promise you."

✗ ✗ ✗

The next afternoon I was having a beer in a booth in the bar next to the deli below my office. Formerly a blind pig — a speakeasy that looked shuttered from the street (even now, you entered through the deli) — it was a business investment of fighter Barney Ross, as was reflected by the framed boxing photos decorating the dark, smoky little joint.

I grew up with Barney on the West Side. Since my family hadn't practiced Judaism in several generations, I was *shabbes goy* for Barney's very Orthodox folks, a kid doing chores and errands for them from Friday sundown through Saturday.

But we didn't become really good friends, Barney and me, till we worked Maxwell street as pullers — teenage street barkers who literally pulled customers into stores for bargains they had no interest in.

Barney, a roughneck made good, was a real Chicago success story. He owned this entire building, and my office — which, with its Murphy bed, was also my residence — was space he traded me for keeping an eye on the place. I was his nightwatchman, unless a paying job like Goldblatt's came along to take precedence.

The lightweight champion of the world was having a beer, too, in that back booth; he wore a cheerful blue and white sportshirt and a dour expression.

"I'm sorry about your young pal," Barney said.

"He wasn't a 'pal,' really. Just an acquaintance."

"I don't know that Douglas Park crowd myself. But to think of a kid, on his twenty-first birthday . . ." His mildly battered bulldog countenance looked woeful. "He have a girl?"

"Yeah."

"What's her name?"

"I don't remember."

"Poor little bastard. When's the funeral?"

"I don't know."

"You're going, aren't you?"

"No. I don't really know the family that well. I'm sending flowers."

He looked at me with as long a face as a round-faced guy could muster. "You oughta go. He was working for you when he got it."

"I'd be intruding. I'd be out of place."

"You should do kaddish for the kid, Nate."

A mourner's prayer.

"Jesus Christ, Barney, I'm no Jew. I haven't been in a synagogue more than half a dozen times in my life, and then it was social occasions."

"Maybe you don't consider yourself a Jew, with that Irish mug of yours your ma bequeathed you . . . but you're gonna have a rude awakening one of these days, boyo."

"What do you mean?"

"There's plenty of people you're just another 'kike' to, believe you me."

I sipped the beer. "Nudge me when you get to the point."

"You owe this kid kaddish, Nate."

"Hell, doesn't that go on for months? I don't know the lingo. And if you think I'm putting on some fuckin' beanie and . . ."

There was a tap on my shoulder. Buddy Gold, the bartender, an ex-pug, leaned in to say, "You got a call."

I went behind the bar to use the phone. It was Sergeant Lou Sapperstein at Central HQ in the Loop; Lou had been my boss on the pickpocket detail. I'd called him this morning with a request.

"Tubbo's coppers made their raid this morning, around nine," Lou said. Sapperstein was a hardnosed, balding cop of about forty-five and one of the few friends I had left on the PD.

"And?"

"And the union hall was empty, 'cept for a bartender. Pribyl and his partner Bert Gray took a whole squad up there, but Rooney and his boys had flew the coop."

"Fuck. Somebody tipped them."

"Are you surprised?"

"Yeah. Surprised I expected the cops to play it straight for a change. You wouldn't have the address of that union, by any chance?"

"No, but I can get it. Hold a second."

A sweet union scam like the Circular Distributors had Outfit written all over it — and Captain Tubbo Gilbert, head of the State Prosecutor's police, was known as the richest cop in Chicago. Tubbo was a bagman and police fixer so deep in Frank Nitti's pocket he had Nitti's lint up his nose.

Lou was back: "It's at 7 North Racine. That's Madison and Racine."

"Well, hell — that's spitting distance from Skid Row."

"Yeah. So?"

"So that explains the scam — that 'union' takes hobos and makes day laborers out of them. No wonder they charge daily dues. It's just bums handing out ad circulars . . ."

"I'd say that's a good guess, Nate."

I thanked Lou and went back to the booth where Barney was brooding about what a louse his friend Heller was.

"I got something to do," I told him.

"What?"

"My kind of kaddish."

✗ ✗ ✗

Less than two miles from the prominent department stores of the Loop they'd been fleecing, the Circular Distributors Union had their headquarters on the doorstep of Skid Row and various Hoovervilles. This Madison Street area, just north of Greek town, was a seedy mix of flophouses, marginal apartment buildings and storefront businesses, mostly bars. Union HQ was on the second floor of a two-story brick building whose bottom floor was a plumbing supply outlet.

I went up the squeaking stairs and into the union hall, a big high-ceilinged open room with a few glassed-in offices toward the front, to the left and right. Ceiling fans whirred lazily, stirring stale smoky air; folding chairs and cardtables were scattered everywhere on the scuffed wooden floor, and seated at some were unshaven, tattered "members" of the union. Across the far end stretched a bar, behind which a burly blond guy in rolled-up white-shirt sleeves was polishing a glass. More hobos leaned against the bar, having beers.

I ordered a mug from the bartender, who had a massive skull and tiny dark eyes and a sullen kiss of a mouth.

I salted the brew as I tossed him a nickel. "Hear you had a raid here this morning."

He ignored the question. "This hall's for union members only."

"Jeez, it looks like a saloon."

"Well, it's a union hall. Drink up and move along."

"There's a fin in it for you, if you answer a few questions."

He thought that over; leaned in. "Are you a cop?"

"No. Private."

"Who hired you?"

"Goldblatt's."

He thought some more. The tiny eyes narrowed. "Let's hear the questions."

"What do you know about the Gross kid's murder?"

"Not a damn thing."

"Was Rooney here last night?"

"Far as I know, he was home in bed asleep."

"Know where he lives?"

"No."

"You don't know where your boss lives."

"No. All I know is he's a swell guy. He don't have nothin' to do with these department store shakedowns the cops are tryin' to pin on him. It's union-busting, is what it is."

"Union busting." I had a look around at the bleary-eyed clientele in their patched clothes. "You have to be a union, first, 'fore you can get busted up."

"What's *that* supposed to mean?"

"It means this is a scam. Rooney pulls in winos, gets 'em day-labor jobs for $3.25 a day, then they come up here to pay their daily dues of a quarter, and blow the rest on beer or booze. In other words, first the bums pass out ad fliers, then they come here and just plain pass out."

"I think you better scram. Otherwise I'm gonna have to throw you down the stairs."

I finished the beer. "I'm leaving. But you know what? I'm not gonna give you that fin. I'm afraid you'd just drink it up."

I could feel his eyes on my back as I left, but I'd have heard him if he came out from around the bar. I was starting down the stairs when the door below opened and Sgt. Pribyl, looking irritated, came up to meet me on the landing, half-way. He looked more his usual dapper self, but his eyes were black-bagged.

"What's the idea, Heller?"

"I just wanted to come bask in the reflected glory of your triumphant raid this morning."

"What's that supposed to mean?"

"It means when Tubbo's boys are on the case, the Outfit gets advance notice."

He winced. "That's not the way it was. I don't know why Rooney and Berry and the others blew. But nobody in our office warned 'em off."

"Are you sure?"

He clearly wasn't. "Look, I can't have you messing in this. We're on the damn case, okay? We're maintaining surveillance from across the way . . . that's how we spotted you."

"Peachy. Twenty-four surveillance, now?"

"No." He seemed embarrassed. "Just day shift."

"You want some help?"

"What do you mean?"

"Loan me the key to your stakeout crib. I'll keep nightwatch. Got a phone in there?"

"Yeah."

"I'll call you if Rooney shows. You got pictures of him and the others you can give me?"

"Well . . ."

"What's the harm? Or would Tubbo lower the boom on you, if you really did your job?"

He sighed. Scratched his head and came to a decision. "This is unofficial, okay? But there's a possibility the door to that apartment's gonna be left unlocked tonight."

"Do tell."

"Third-floor — 3O1." He raised a cautionary finger. "We'll try this for one night . . . no showboating, okay? Call me if one of 'em shows."

"Sure. You tried their homes?"

He nodded. "Nothing. Rooney lives on North Ridgeland in Oak Park. Four kids. Wife's a pleasant, matronly type."

"Fat, you mean."

"She hasn't seen Rooney for several weeks. She says he's away from home a lot."

"Keeping a guard posted there?"

"Yeah. And that *is* twenty-four hour." He sighed, shook his head. "Heller, there's a lot about this case that doesn't make sense."

"Such as?"

"That maroon Plymouth. We never saw a car like that in the entire six weeks we had the union hall under surveillance. Rooney drives a blue LaSalle coupe."

"Any maroon Plymouths reported stolen?"

He shook his head, no. "And it hasn't turned up abandoned, either. They must still have the car."

"Is Rooney *that* stupid?"

"We can always hope," Pribyl said.

✗ ✗ ✗

I sat in an easy chair with sprung springs by the window in room 301 of the residential hotel across the way. It wasn't a flophouse cage, but it wasn't a suite at the Drake, either. Anyway, in the dark it looked fine. I had a flask of rum to keep me company, and the breeze fluttering the sheer, frayed curtains remained unseasonably cool.

Thanks to some photos Pribyl left me, I now knew what Rooney looked like: a good-looking, oval-faced smoothie, in his mid-forties, just starting to lose his dark, slicked-back hair; his eyes were hooded, his mouth soft, sensual, sullen. There were also photos of bespectacled, balding Berry and pockmarked, cold-eyed Herbert Arnold, V.P. of the union.

But none of them stopped by the union hall — only a steady stream of winos and bums went in and out.

Then, around seven, I spotted somebody who didn't fit the profile.

It was a guy I knew — a fellow private op, Eddie McGowan, a Pinkerton man, in uniform, meaning he was on nightwatchman duty. A number of the merchants along Madison must have pitched in for his services.

I left the stakeout and waited down on the street, in front of the plumbing supply store, for Eddie to come back out. It didn't take long — maybe ten minutes.

"Heller!" he said. He was a skinny, tow-haired guy in his late twenties with a bad complexion and a good outlook. "What no good are you up to?"

"The Goldblatt's shooting. That kid they killed was working with me."

"Oh! I didn't know! Heard about the shooting, of course, but didn't read the papers or anything. So you were involved in that? No kidding."

"No kidding. You on watchman duty?"

"Yeah. Up and down the street, here, all night."

"Including the union hall?"

"Sure." He grinned. "I usually stop up for a free drink, 'bout this time of night."

"Can you knock off for a couple of minutes? For another free drink?"

"Sure!"

Soon we were in a smoky booth in back of a bar and Eddie was having a boilermaker on me.

"See anything unusual last night," I asked, "around the union hall?"

"Well . . . I had a drink there, around two o'clock in the morning. *That* was a first."

"A drink? Don't they close earlier than that?"

"Yeah. Around eleven. That's all the longer it takes for their 'members' to lap up their daily dough."

"So what were you doing up there at two?"

He shrugged. "Well, I noticed the lights was on upstairs, so I unlocked the street level door and went up. Figured Alex . . . that's the bartender, Alex Davidson . . . might have forgot to turn out the lights, 'fore he left. The door up there was locked, but then Mr. Rooney opened it up and told me to come on in."

"Why would he do that?"

"He was feelin' pretty good. Looked like he was workin' on a bender. Anyway, he insists I have a drink with him. I says, sure. Turns out Davidson is still there."

"No kidding?"

"No kidding. So Alex serves me a beer. Henry Berry — he's the union's so-called business agent, mousy little guy with glasses — he was there, too. He was in his cups, also. So was Rooney's wife — she was there, and also feeling giddy."

I thought about Pribyl's description of Mrs. Rooney as a matronly woman with four kids. "His *wife* was there?"

"Yeah, the lucky stiff."

"Lucky?"

"You should see the dame! Good-lookin' tomato with big dark eyes and a nice shape on her."

"About how old?"

"Young. Twenties. It'd take the sting out of a ball and chain, I can tell you that."

"Eddie . . . here's a fin."

"Heller, the beer's enough!"

"The fin is for telling this same story to Sgt. Pribyl of the State's

Attorney's coppers."

"Oh. Okay."

"But do it tomorrow."

He smirked. "Okay. I got rounds to make, anyway."

So did I.

✗ ✗ ✗

At around eleven-fifteen, bartender Alex Davidson was leaving the union hall; his back was turned, as he was locking the street-level door, and I put my nine-millimeter in it.

"Hi, Alex," I said. "Don't turn around, unless you prefer being gut-shot."

"If it's a stick-up, all I got's a couple bucks. Take 'em and bug off!"

"No such luck. Leave that door unlocked. We're gonna step back inside."

He grunted and opened the door and we stepped inside.

"Now we're going up the stairs," I said, and we did, in the dark, the wooden steps whining under our weight. He was a big man; I'd have had my work cut out for me — if I hadn't had the gun.

We stopped at the landing where earlier I had spoken to Sgt. Pribyl. "Here's fine," I said.

I allowed him to face me in the near-dark.

He sneered. "You're that private dick."

"I'm sure you mean that in the nicest way. Let me tell you a little more about me. See, we're going to get to know each other, Alex."

"Fuck you."

I slapped him with the nine millimeter.

He wiped blood off his mouth and looked at me with hate, but also with fear. And he made no more smart-ass remarks.

"I'm the private dick whose twenty-one year-old partner got shot in the head last night."

Now the fear was edging out the hate; he knew he might die in this dark stairwell.

"I know you were here with Rooney and Berry and the broad, last night, serving up drinks as late as two in the morning," I said. "Now you're going to tell me the whole story — or you're the one who's getting tossed down the fucking stairs."

He was trembling, now; a big hulk of a man trembling with fear. "I didn't have anything to do with the murder. Not a damn thing!"

"Then why cover for Rooney and the rest?"

"You saw what they're capable of!"

"Take it easy, Alex. Just tell the story."

Rooney had come into the office about noon the day of the shooting; he had started drinking and never stopped. Berry and several other union "officers" arrived and angry discussions about being under surveillance by the State's Attorney's cops were accompanied by a lot more drinking.

"The other guys left around five, but Rooney and Berry, they just hung around drinking all evening. Around midnight, Rooney handed me a phone number he jotted on a matchbook, and gave it to me to call for him. It was a Berwyn number. A woman answered. I handed him the phone and he said to her, 'Bring one.' "

"One what?" I asked.

"I'm gettin' to that. She showed up around one o'clock — good-looking dame with black hair and eyes so dark they coulda been black, too."

"Who was she?"

"I don't know. Never saw her before. She took a gun out of her purse and gave it to Rooney."

"That was what he asked her to bring."

"I guess. It was a .38 revolver, a Colt I think. Anyway, Rooney and Berry were both pretty drunk; I don't know what *her* excuse was. So Rooney takes the gun and says, 'We got a job to pull at Goldblatt's. We're gonna throw some slugs at the windows and watchmen.' "

"How did the girl react?"

He swallowed. "She laughed. She said, 'I'll go along and watch the fun.' Then they all went out."

Jesus.

Finally I said, "What did you do?"

"They told me to wait for 'em. Keep the bar open. They came back in, laughing like hyenas. Rooney says to me, 'You want to see the way he keeled over?' And I says, 'Who?' And he says, 'The guard at Goldblatt's.' Berry laughs and says, 'We really let him have it.' "

"That kid was twenty-one, Alex. It was his goddamn birthday."

The bartender was looking down. "They laughed and joked about it 'til Berry passed out. About six in the morning, Rooney has me pile

Berry in a cab. Rooney and the twist slept in his office for maybe an hour. Then they came out, looking sober and kind of . . . scared. He warned me not to tell anybody what I seen, unless I wanted to trade my job for a morgue slab."

"Colorful. Tell me, Alex. You got that girl's phone number in Berwyn?"

"I think it's upstairs. You can put that gun away. I'll help you."

It was dark, but I could see his face well enough; the big man's eyes looked damp. The fear was gone. Something else was in its place. Shame? Something.

We went upstairs, he unlocked the union hall and, under the bar, found the matchbook with the number written inside: Berwyn 2981.

"You want a drink before you go?" he asked.

"You know," I said, "I think I'll pass."

✗ ✗ ✗

I went back to my office to use the reverse-listing phone book that told me Berwyn 2981 was Rosalie Rizzo's number; and that Rosalie Rizzo lived at 6348 West 13th Street in Berwyn.

First thing the next morning, I borrowed Barney's Hupmobile and drove out to Berwyn, the clean, tidy Hunky suburb populated in part by the late Mayor Cermak's patronage people. But finding a Rosalie Rizzo in this largely Czech and Bohemian area came as no surprise: Capone's Cicero was a stone's throw away.

The woman's address was a three-story brick apartment building, but none of the mailboxes in the vestibule bore her name. I found the janitor and gave him Rosalie Rizzo's description. It sounded like Mrs. Riggs to him.

"She's a doll," the janitor said. He was heavy-set and needed a shave; he licked his thick lips as he thought about her. "Ain't seen her since yesterday noon."

That was about nine hours after Stanley was killed.

He continued: "Her and her husband was going to the country, she said. Didn't expect to be back for a couple of weeks, she said."

Her husband.

"What'll a look around their apartment cost me?"

He licked his lips again. "Two bucks?"

Two bucks it was; the janitor used his passkey and left me to it. The well-appointed little apartment included a canary that sang in its gilded cage, a framed photo of slick Boss Rooney on an end table, and a closet containing two sawed-off shotguns and a repeating rifle.

I had barely started to poke around when I had company: a slender, gray-haired woman in a flowered print dress.

"Oh!" she said, coming in the door she'd unlocked.

"Can I help you?" I asked.

"Who are you?" Her voice had the lilt of an Italian accent.

Under the circumstances, the truth seemed prudent. "A private detective."

"My daughter is not here! She and her-a husband, they go to vacation. Up north some-a-where. I just-a come to feed the canary!"

"Please don't be frightened. Do you know where she's gone, exactly?"

"No. But . . . maybe my husband do. He is-a downstairs . . ."

She went to a window, threw it open and yelled something frantically down in Italian.

I eased her aside in time to see a heavy-set man jump into a maroon Plymouth with a silver swan on the radiator cap, and cream colored wheels, and squeal away.

And when I turned, the slight gray-haired woman was just as gone. Only she hadn't squealed.

✗ ✗ ✗

The difference, this time, was a license number for the maroon coupe; I'd seen it: 519-836. In a diner I made a call to Lou Sapperstein, who made a call to the motor vehicle bureau, and phoned back with the scoop: the Plymouth was licensed to Rosalie Rizzo, but the address was different — 2848 South Cuyler Avenue, in Berwyn.

The bungalow was typical for Berwyn — a tidy little frame house on a small perfect lawn. My guess was this was her folks' place. In back was a small matching, but unattached garage, on the alley. Peeking in the garage windows, I saw the maroon coupe and smiled.

"Is Rosalie in trouble again?"

The voice was female, sweet, young.

I turned and saw a slender, almost beautiful teenage girl with dark eyes and bouncy, dark shoulder-length hair. She wore a navy-blue sailor-ish playsuit. Her pretty white legs were bare.

"Are you Rosalie's sister?"

"Yes. Is she in trouble?"

"What makes you say that?"

"I just know Rosalie, that's all. That man isn't really her husband, is he? That Mr. Riggs."

"No."

"Are you here about her accident?"

"No. Where is she?"

"Are you a police officer?"

"I'm a detective. Where did she go?"

"Papa's inside. He's afraid he's going to be in trouble."

"Why's that?"

"Rosalie put her car in our garage yesterday. She said she was in an accident and it was damaged and not to use it. She's going to have it repaired when she gets back from vacation."

"What does that have to do with your papa being scared?"

"Rosalie's going to be mad as h at him, that he used her car." She shrugged. "He said he looked at it and it didn't look damaged to him, and if mama was going to have to look after Rosalie's g.d. canary, well he'd sure as h use *her* gas not his."

"I can see his point. Where did your sister go on vacation?"

"She didn't say. Up north someplace. Someplace she and Mr. Riggs like to go to, to . . . you know. To get away?"

✗ ✗ ✗

I called Sgt. Pribyl from a gas station where I was getting Barney's Hupmobile tank re-filled. I suggested he have another talk with bartender Alex Davidson, gave him the address of "Mr. and Mrs. Riggs," and told him where he could find the maroon Plymouth.

He was grateful but a little miffed about all I had done on my own.

"So much for not showboating," he said, almost huffily. "You've found everything but the damn suspects."

"They've gone up north somewhere," I said.

"Where up north?"

"They don't seem to've told anybody. Look, I have a piece of evidence you may need."

"What?"

"When you talk to Davidson, he'll tell you about a matchbook

Rooney wrote the girl's number on. I got the matchbook."

It was still in my pocket. I took it out, idly, and shut the girl's number away, revealing the picture on the matchbook cover: a blue moon hovered surrealistically over a white lake on which two blue lovers paddled in a blue canoe — Eagle River Lodge, Wisconsin.

"I suppose we'll need that," Pribyl's voice over the phone said, "when the time comes."

"I suppose," I said, and hung up.

✗ ✗ ✗

Eagle River was a town of 1,386 (so said the sign) just inside the Vilas County line at the junction of US 45 and Wisconsin State Highway 70. The country was beyond beautiful — green pines towering higher than Chicago skyscrapers, glittering blue lakes nestling in woodland pockets.

The lodge I was looking for was on Silver Lake, a gas station attendant told me. A beautiful dusk was settling on the woods as I drew into the parking of the large resort sporting a red city-style neon saying, DINING AND DANCE. Log-cabin cottages were flung here and there around the periphery like Paul Bunyan's tinker-toys. Each one was just secluded enough — ideal for couples, married or un-.

Even if Rooney and his dark-haired honey weren't staying here, it was time to find a room: I'd been driving all day. When Barney loaned me his Hupmobile, he'd had no idea the kind of miles I'd put on it. Dead tired, I went to the desk and paid for a cabin.

The guy behind the counter had a plaid shirt on, but he was small and squinty and Hitler-mustached, smoking a stogie, and looked more like a bookie than a lumberjack.

I told him some friends of mine were supposed to be staying here.

"We don't have anybody named Riggs registered."

"How 'bout Mr. and Mrs. Rooney?"

"Them either. How many friends you got, anyway?"

"Why, did I already catch the limit?"

Before I headed to my cabin, I grabbed some supper in the rustic restaurant. I placed my order with a friendly brunette girl of about nineteen with plenty of personality, and make-up. A road-company Paul Whiteman outfit was playing "Sophisticated Lady" in the adjacent dance hall, and I went over and peeked in, to look for familiar faces. A number of couples were cutting a rug, but not Rooney and Rosalie. Or Henry

Berry or Herbert Arnold, either. I went back and had my green salad and fried trout and well-buttered baked potato; I was full and sleepy when I stumbled toward my guest cottage under the light of a moon that bathed the woods ivory.

Walking along the path, I spotted something: snuggled next to one of the secluded cabins was a blue LaSalle coupe with Cook County plates.

Suddenly I wasn't sleepy. I walked briskly back to the lodge check-in desk and batted the bell to summon the stogie-chewing clerk.

"Cabin seven," I said. "I think that blue LaSalle is my friends' car."

His smirk turned his Hitler mustache Chaplinesque. "You want I should break out the champagne?"

"I just want to make sure it's them. Dark-haired doll and an older guy, good-looking, kinda sleepy-eyed, just starting to go bald?"

"That's them." He checked his register. "That's the Ridges." He frowned. "Are they usin' a phony name?"

"Does a bear shit in the woods?"

He squinted. "You sure they're friends of yours?"

"Positive. Don't call their room and tell 'em I'm here, though — I want to surprise them . . ."

✗ ✗ ✗

I knocked with my left hand; my right was filled with the nine millimeter. Nothing. I knocked again.

"Who is it?" a male voice said gruffly. *"What* is it?"

"Complimentary fruit basket from the management."

"Go away!"

I kicked the door open.

The lights were off in the little cabin, but enough moonlight came in with me through the doorway to reveal the pair in bed, naked. She was sitting up, her mouth and eyes open in a silent scream, gathering the sheets up protectively over white skin, her dark hair blending with the darkness of the room, making a cameo of her face. He was diving off the bed for the sawed-off shotgun, but I was there to kick it away, wishing I hadn't, wishing I'd let him grab it so I could have had an excuse to put one in his forehead, right where he'd put one in Stanley's.

Boss Rooney wasn't boss of anything, now: he was just a naked, balding, forty-four year old scam artist, sprawled on the floor. Kicking him would have been easy.

So I did; in the stomach.

He clutched himself and puked. Apparently he'd had the trout, too.

I went over and slammed the door shut, or as shut as it could be, half-off its hinges. Pointing the gun at her retching naked boy friend, I said to the girl, "Turn on the light and put on your clothes."

She nodded dutifully and did as she was told. In the glow of a nightstand lamp, I caught glimpses of her white, well-formed body as she stepped into her step-ins; but you know what? She didn't do a thing for me.

"Is Berry here?" I asked Rooney. "Or Arnold?"

"N . . . no," he managed.

"If you're lying," I said, "I'll kill you."

The girl said shrilly, "They aren't here!"

"You can put your clothes on, too," I told Rooney. "If you have another gun hidden somewhere, do me a favor. Make a play for it."

His hooded eyes flared. "Who the hell are you?"

"The private cop you *didn't* kill the other night."

He lowered his gaze. "Oh."

The girl was sitting on the bed, weeping; body heaving.

"Take it easy on her, will you?" he said, zipping his fly. "She's just a kid."

I was opening a window to ease the stench of his vomit.

"Sure," I said. "I'll say kaddish for her."

✗ ✗ ✗

I handcuffed the lovebirds to the bed and called the local law; they in turn called the State Prosecutor's office in Chicago, and Sergeants Pribyl and Gray made the long drive up the next day to pick up the pair.

It seemed the two cops had already caught Henry Berry — a tipster gave them the West Chicago Avenue address of a second-floor room he was holed up in.

I admitted to Pribyl that I'd been wrong about Tubbo tipping off Rooney and the rest about the raid.

"I figure Rooney lammed out of sheer panic," I said, "the morning after the murder."

Pribyl saw it the same way.

The following March, Pribyl arrested Herbert Arnold running a northside handbill distributing agency.

Rooney, Berry and Rosalie Rizzo were all convicted of murder; the two men got life, and the girl twenty years. Arnold hadn't been part of the kill-happy joyride that took Stanley Gross' young life, and got only one to five for conspiracy and extortion.

None of it brought Stanley Gross back, nor did my putting on a beanie and sitting with the Gross family, suffering through a couple of stints at a storefront synagogue on Roosevelt Road.

But it did get Barney off my ass.

THE PERFECT CRIME

She was the first movie star I ever worked for, but I wasn't much impressed. If I were that easily impressed, I'd have been impressed by Hollywood itself. And having seen the way Hollywood portrayed my profession on the so-called silver screen, I wasn't much impressed with Hollywood.

On the other hand, Thelma Todd was the most beautiful woman who ever wanted to hire my services, and that did impress me. Enough so that when she called me, that October, and asked me to drive out to her "sidewalk cafe" nestled under the Palisades in Montemar Vista, I went, wondering if she would be as pretty in the flesh as she was on celluloid.

I'd driven out Pacific Coast Highway that same morning, a clear cool morning with a blue sky lording it over a vast sparkling sea. Pelicans were playing tag with the breaking surf, flying just under the curl of the white-lipped waves. Yachts, like a child's toy boats, floated out there just between me and the horizon. I felt like I could reach out for one, pluck and examine it, sniff it maybe, like King Kong checking out Fay Wray's lingerie.

"Thelma Todd's Sidewalk Cafe," as a billboard on the hillside behind it so labeled the place, was a sprawling two-story hacienda affair, as big as a beached luxury liner. Over its central, largest-of-many archways, a third-story tower rose like a stubby lighthouse. There weren't many cars here — it was approaching ten a.m., too early for the luncheon crowd and even I didn't drink cocktails this early in the day. Not and tell, anyway.

She was waiting in the otherwise unpopulated cocktail lounge, where massive wooden beams in a traditional Spanish mode fought the chromium-and-leather furnishings and the chrome-and-glass-brick bar and came out a draw. She was a big blonde woman with more curves than the highway out front and just the right number of hills and valleys. Wearing a clingy summery white dress, she was seated on one of the bar stools, with her bare legs crossed; they weren't the best-looking legs on the planet, necessarily. I just couldn't prove otherwise. That good a detective I'm not.

"Nathan Heller?" she asked, and her smile dimpled her cheeks in a manner that made her whole heart-shaped face smile, and the world smile as well, including me. She didn't move off the stool, just extended her hand in a manner that was at once casual and regal.

I took the hand, not knowing whether to kiss it, shake it, or press it into a book like a corsage I wanted to keep. I looked at her feeling vaguely embarrassed; she was so pretty you didn't know where to look next, and felt like there was maybe something wrong with looking anywhere. But I couldn't help myself.

She had pale, creamy skin and her hair was almost white blonde. They called her the ice-cream blonde, in the press. I could see why.

Then I got around to her eyes. They were blue of course, cornflower blue; and big and sporting long lashes, the real McCoy, not your dimestore variety. But they were also the saddest eyes I'd ever looked into. The smile froze on my face like I was looking at Medusa, not a twenty-nine year-old former six-grade teacher from Massachusetts who won a talent search.

"Is something wrong?" she asked. Then she patted the stool next to her.

I sat and said, "Nothing's wrong. I never had a movie star for a client before."

"I see. Thanks for considering this job — for extending your stay, I mean."

I was visiting L.A. from Chicago because a friend — a fellow former pickpocket detail dick — had recently opened an office out here in sunny Southern Cal. Fred Rubinski needed an out-of-towner to pose as a visiting banker, to expose an embezzler; the firm had wanted to keep the affair in-house.

"Mr. Rubinski recommended you highly." Her voice had a low, throaty quality that wasn't forced or affected; she was what Mae West would've been if Mae West wasn't a parody.

"That's just because Fred hasn't been in town long enough to make any connections. But if Thelma Todd wants me to consider extending my stay, I'm willing to listen."

She smiled at that, very broadly, showing off teeth whiter than cameras can record. "Might I get you a drink, Mr. Heller?"

"It's a little early."

"I know it is. Might I get you a drink?"

"Sure."

"Anything special?"

"Anything that doesn't have a little paper umbrella in it is fine by me . . . . Make it rum and Coke."

"Rum and Coke." She fixed me up with that, and had the same herself. Either we had similar tastes or she just wasn't fussy about what she drank.

"Have you heard of Lucky Luciano?" she asked, returning to her bar stool.

"Heard of him," I said. "Haven't met him."

"What do you know about him?"

I shrugged. "Big-time gangster from back east. Runs casinos all over southern California. More every day."

She flicked the air with a long red fingernail, like she was shooing away a bug. "Well, perhaps you've noticed the tower above my restaurant."

"Sure."

"I live on the second floor, but the tower above is fairly spacious."

"Big enough for a casino, you mean."

"That's right," she said, nodding. "I was approached by Luciano, more than once. I turned him away, more than once. After all, with my location, and my clientele, a casino could make a killing."

"You're doing well enough legally. Why bother with ill?"

"I agree. And if I were to get into any legal problems, that would mean a scandal, and Hollywood doesn't need another scandal. Busby Berkley's trial is coming up soon, you know."

The noted director and choreographer, creator of so many frothy fantasies, was up on the drunk-driving homicide of three pedestrians, not far from this cafe.

"But now," she said, her bee-lips drawn nervously tight, "I've begun to receive threatening notes."

"From Luciano, specifically?"

"No. They're extortion notes, actually. Asking me to pay off Artie Lewis. You know, the bandleader?"

"Why him?"

"He's in Luciano's pocket. Gambling markers. And I used to go with Artie. He lives in San Francisco, now."

"I see. Well, have you talked to the cops?"

"No."

"Why not?"

"I don't want to get Artie in trouble."

"Have you talked to Artie?"

"Yes — he claims he knows nothing about this. He doesn't want my money. He doesn't even want me back — he's got a new girl."

I'd like to see the girl that could make you forget Thelma Todd.

"So," I said, "you want me to investigate. Can I see the extortion notes?"

"No," she said, shaking her white blonde curls like the mop of the gods, "that's not it. I burned those notes. For Artie's sake."

"Well, for Nate's sake," I said, "where *do* I come in?"

"I think I'm being followed. I'd like a bodyguard."

I resisted looking her over wolfishly and making a wisecrack. She was a nice woman, and the fact that hers was the sort of a body a private eye would pay to guard didn't seem worth mentioning. My fee did.

"Twenty-five a day and expenses," I said.

"Fine," she said. "And you can have any meals you like right here at the Cafe. Drinks, too. Run a tab and I'll pick it up."

"Swell," I grinned. "I was wondering if I'd ever run into a fringe benefit in this racket."

"You can be my chauffeur."

"Well . . ."

"You have a problem with that, Mr. Heller?"

"I have a private investigator's license, and a license to carry a gun . . . in Illinois, anyway. But I don't have a chauffeur's license."

"I think a driver's license will suffice." Her bee-stung lips were poised in a kiss of amusement. "What's the real problem, Mr. Heller?"

"I'm not wearing a uniform. I'm strictly plainclothes."

She smiled tightly, wryly amused, saying, "All right, hang onto your dignity . . . but you have to let me pay the freight on a couple of new suits for you. I'll throw 'em in on the deal."

"Swell," I said. I liked it when women bought me clothes.

So for the next two months, I stayed on in southern Cal, and Thelma Todd was my only client. I worked six days a week for her — Monday through Saturday. Sundays God, Heller and Todd rested. I drove her in her candy-apple red Packard convertible, a car designed for blondes with wind-blown hair and pearls. She sat in back, of course. Most days I took her to the Hal Roach Studio where she was making a musical with Laurel and Hardy. I'd wait in some dark pocket of the soundstage and watch her every move out in the brightness. In a black wig, lacy bodice, and clinging, gypsy skirt, Thelma was the kind of girl you took home to mother, and if mother didn't like her, to hell with mother.

Evenings she hit the club circuit, the Trocadero and the El Mocambo chiefly. I'd sit in the cocktail lounges and quietly drink and wait for her and her various dates to head home. Some of these guys were swishy types that she was doing the studio a favor appearing in public with; a couple others spent the night.

I don't mean to tell tales out of school, but this tale can't be told at all unless I'm frank about that one thing: Thelma slept around. Later, when the gossip rags were spreading rumors about alcohol and drugs, that was all the bunk. But Thelma was a friendly girl. She had generous charms and she was generous with them.

"Heller," she said, one night in early December when I was dropping her off, walking her up to the front door of the Cafe like always, "I think I have a crush on you."

She was alone tonight, having played girl friend to one of those Hollywood funny boys for the benefit of Louella Parsons and company. Alone but for me.

She slipped an arm around my waist. She had booze on her breath, but then so did I, and neither one of us was drunk. She was bathed gently in moonlight and Chanel Number Five.

She kissed me with those bee-stung lips, stinging so softly, so deeply.

I moved away. "No. I'm sorry."

She winced. "What's wrong?"

"I'm the hired help. You're just lonely tonight."

Her eyes, which I seldom looked into because of the depth of the sadness there, hardened. "Don't you ever get lonely, you bastard?"

"Never," I said.

She drew her hand back to slap me, but then she just touched my face, instead. Gentle as the ocean breeze, and it was gentle tonight, the breeze, so gentle.

"Goodnight, Heller," she said.

And she slipped inside, but left the door slightly ajar.

"What the hell," I said, and I slipped inside, too.

✗ ✗ ✗

An hour later, I drove her Packard to the garage that was attached to the bungalow above the restaurant complex; to do that I had to take Montemar Vista Road to Seretto Way, turning right. The Mediterranean-style stucco bungalow, on Cabrillo, like so many houses in Montemar Vista, climbed the side of the hill like a clinging vine. It was owned by Thelma Todd's partner in the Cafe, movie director/ producer Warren Eastman. Eastman had an apartment next to Thelma's above the restaurant, as well as the bungalow, and seemed to live back and forth between the two.

I wondered what the deal was, with Eastman and my client, but I never asked, not directly. Eastman was a thin, dapper man in his late forties, with a pointed chin and a small mustache and a window's peak that his slick black hair was receding around, making his face look diamond shaped. He often sat in the cocktail lounge with a bloody Mary in one hand and a cigarette in a holder in the other. He was always talking deals with movie people.

"Heller," he said, one night, motioning me over to the bar. He was seated on the very stool that Thelma had been, that first morning. "This is Nick DeCiro, the talent agent. Nick, this is the gumshoe Thelma hired to protect her from the big bad gambling syndicate."

DeCiro was another darkly handsome man, a bit older than Eastman, though he lacked both the mustache and receding hairline of the director. DeCiro wore a white suit with a dark sportshirt, open at the neck to reveal a wealth of black chest hair.

I shook DeCiro's hand. His grip was firm, moist, like a fistful of topsoil.

"Nicky here is your client's ex-husband," Eastman said, with a wag of his cigarette-in-holder, trying for an air of that effortless decadence that Hollywood works so hard at.

"Thelma and me are still pals," DeCiro said, lighting up a foreign cig with a shiny silver lighter that he then clicked shut with a meaningless flourish. "We broke up amicably."

"I heard it was over extreme cruelty," I said.

DeCiro frowned, and Eastman cut in glibly, "Don't believe everything you read in the papers, Heller. Besides, you have to get a divorce over something."

"But then you'd *know* that in your line of work," DeCiro said, an edge in his thin voice.

"Don't knock it," I said with my own edge. "Where would your crowd be without divorce dicks? Now, if you gents will excuse me . . ."

"Heller, Heller," Eastman said, touching my arm, "don't be so touchy."

I waited for him to remove his hand from my arm, then said, "Did you want something, Mr. Eastman? I'm not much for this Hollywood shit-chat."

"I don't like your manner," DeCiro said.

"Nobody does," I said. "But I don't get paid well enough for it to matter."

"Heller," Eastman said, "I was just trying to convince Nicky here that my new film is perfect for a certain client of his. I'm doing a mystery. About the perfect crime. The perfect murder."

"No such animal," I said.

"Oh, really?" DeCiro said, lifting an eyebrow.

"Murder and crime are inexact sciences. All the planning in the world doesn't account for the human element."

"Then how do you explain," Eastman said archly, "the hundreds of murders that go unsolved in this country?"

"Policework is a more exact science than crime or murder," I admitted, "but we have a lot of bent cops in this world — and a lot of dumb ones."

"Then there *are* perfect crimes."

"No. Just unsolved ones. And imperfect detectives. Good evening, gentlemen."

That was the most extensive conversation I had with either Eastman or DeCiro during the time I was employed by Miss Todd, though I said hello and they did the same, now and then, at the Cafe.

But Eastman was married to an actress named Miranda Diamond, a fiery Latin whose parents were from Mexico City, even if she'd been raised in the Bronx. She fancied herself the next Lupe Velez, and she was a similarly voluptuous dame, though her handsome features were as hard as a gravestone.

She cornered me at the Cafe one night, in the cocktail lounge, where I was drinking on the job.

"You're a dick," she said.

We'd never spoken before.

"I hope you mean that in the nicest way," I said.

"You're bodyguarding that bitch," she said, sitting next to me on a leather and chrome couch. Her nostrils flared; if I'd been holding a red cape, I'd have dropped it and run for the stands.

"Miss Todd is my client, yes, Miss Diamond."

She smiled. "You recognize me."

"Oh yes. And I also know enough to call you Mrs. Eastman, in certain company."

"My husband and I are separated."

"Ah."

"But I could use a little help in the divorce court."

"What kind of help?"

"Photographs of him and that bitch in the sack." She said "the" like "thee."

"That would help you."

"Yes. You see . . . my husband has similar pictures of me, with a gentleman, in a compromising position."

"Even missionaries get caught in that position, I understand." I offered her a cigarette, she took it, and I lit hers and mine. "And if you had similar photos, you could negotiate yourself a better settlement."

"Exactly. Interested?"

"I do divorce work — that's no problem. But I try not to sell clients out. Bad for business."

She smiled; she put her hand on my leg. "I could make it worth your while. Financially and . . . otherwise."

It wasn't even Christmas and already here was a second screen goddess who wanted to hop in the sack with me. I must have really been something.

"Listen, if you like me, just say so. But we're not making a business arrangement — I got a client, already."

Then she suggested I do to myself what she'd just offered to do for me. She was full of ideas.

So was I. I was pretty sure Thelma and Eastman were indeed having an affair, but it was of the on-again-off-again variety. One night they'd be affectionate, in that sickening Hollywood sweetie-baby way; the next night he would be cool to her; the next she would be cool to him. It was love, I recognized it, but the kind that sooner or later blows up like an overheated engine.

✗ ✗ ✗

Ten days before Christmas, Thelma was honored by Lupino Lane — the famous British comedian, so famous I'd never the hell heard of him — with a dinner at the Troc. At a table for twelve upstairs, in the swanky cream-and-gold dining room, Thelma was being feted by her show-biz friends, while I sat downstairs in the oak-paneled Cellar Lounge with other people not famous enough to sit upstairs, nursing a rum and Coke at the polished copper bar. I didn't feel like a polished copper, that was for sure. I was just a chauffeur with a gun, and a beautiful client who didn't need me.

That much was clear to me: in the two months I'd worked for Thelma, I hadn't spotted anybody following her except a few fans, and I couldn't blame them. I think I was just a little bit in love with the ice-cream blonde myself. We'd only had that one slightly inebriated night together — and neither of us had mentioned it since, or even referred to it. Maybe we were both embarrassed; I didn't figure either of us were exactly the type to be ashamed.

About half an hour into the evening, I heard a scream upstairs. A woman's scream, a scream that might have belonged to Thelma.

I took the stairs four at a time and had my gun in my hand when I entered the fancy dining room. Normally when I enter fancy dining rooms with a gun in my hand, all eyes are on me. Not this time.

Thelma was clawing at her ex-husband, who was laughing at her. She was being held back by Patsy Kelly, the dark-haired rubber-faced comedienne who was Thelma's partner in the two-reelers. DeCiro, in a white tux, had a starlet on his arm, a blonde about twenty with a neckline down to her shoes. The starlet looked frightened, but DeCiro was having a big laugh.

I put my gun away and took over for Patsy Kelly.

"Miss Todd," I said, gently, whispering into her ear, holding onto her two arms from behind, "don't do this."

She went limp for a moment, then straightened and said, with stiff dignity, "I'm all right, Nathan."

It was the only time she ever called me that.

I let go of her.

"What's the problem?" I asked. I was asking both Thelma Todd and her ex-husband.

"He embarrassed me," she said, without any further explanation.

And without any further anything, I said to DeCiro, "Go."

DeCiro twitched a smile. "I was invited."

"I'm uninviting you. Go."

His face tightened and he thought about saying or doing something. But my eyes were on him like magnets on metal and instead he gathered his date and her decolletage and took a powder.

"Are you ready to go home?" I asked Thelma.

"No," she said, with a shy smile, and she squeezed my arm, and went back to the table of twelve where her party of Hollywood types awaited. She was the guest of honor, after all.

Two hours, and two drinks later, I was escorting her home. She sat in the back of the candy-apple red Packard in her mink coat and sheer mauve-and-silver evening gown and diamond necklace and told me what had happened, the wind whipping her ice-blonde hair.

"Nicky got himself invited," she said, almost shouting over the wind. "Without my knowledge. Asked the host to reserve a seat next to me at the table. Then he wandered in late, with a date, that little *starlet,* which you may have noticed rhymes with harlot, and sat at another table, leaving me sitting next to an empty seat at a party in *my* honor. He sat there necking with that little tramp and I got up and went over and gave him a piece of my mind. It . . . got a little out of hand. Thanks for stepping in, Heller."

"It's what you pay me for."

She sat in silence for a while; only the wind spoke. It was a cold Saturday night, as cold as a chilled martini. I had asked her if she wanted the top up on the convertible, but she said no. She began to look behind us as we moved slowly down Sunset.

"Heller," she said, "someone's following us."

"I don't think so."

"Somebody's following us, I tell you!"

"I'm keeping an eye on the rear-view mirror. We're fine."

She leaned forward and clutched my shoulder. "Get moving! Do you want me to be kidnapped, or killed? It could be Luciano's gangsters, for God's sake!"

She was the boss. I hit the pedal. At speeds up to seventy miles per, we sailed west around the curves of Sunset; there was a service station at the junction of the boulevard and the coast highway, and I pulled in.

"What are you doing?" she demanded.

I turned and looked into the frightened blue eyes. "I'm going to get some gas, and keep watch. And see if anybody comes up on us, or suspicious goes by. Don't you worry. I'm armed."

I looked close at every car that passed by the station. I saw no one and nothing suspicious. Then I paid the attendant and we headed north on the coast highway. Going nice and slow.

"I ought to fire you," she said, pouting back there.

"This is my last night, Miss Todd," I said. "I'm getting homesick for Chicago. They got a better breed of dishonest people back there. Anyway, I like to work for my money. I feel I'm taking yours."

She leaned forward, clutched my shoulder again. "No, no, I tell you, I'm frightened."

"Why?"

"I . . . I just feel I still need you around. You give me a sense of security."

"Have you had any more threatening notes?"

"No." Her voice sounded very small, now.

"If you do, call Fred Rubinski, or the cops. Or both."

It was two a.m. when I slid the big car in, in front of the sprawling Sidewalk Cafe. I was shivering with cold; a sea breeze was blowing, Old Man Winter taking his revenge on California. I turned and looked at her again. I smiled.

"I'll walk you to the door, Miss Todd."

She smiled at me, too, but this time the smile didn't light up her face, or the world, or me. This time the smile was as sad as her eyes. Sadder.

"That won't be necessary, Heller."

I was looking for an invitation, either in her eyes or her voice; I couldn't quite find one. "Are you sure?"

"Yes. Do me one favor. Work for me next week. Be my chauffeur one more week, while I decide whether or not to replace you with another bodyguard, or . . . what."

"Okay."

"Go away, Heller. See you Monday."

"See you Monday," I said, and I watched her go in the front door of the Cafe. Then I drove the Packard up to the garage above, on the Palisades, and got in my dusty inelegant 1925 Marmon and headed back to the Roosevelt Hotel in Hollywood. I had a hunch Thelma Todd, for all her apprehensions, would sleep sounder than I would, tonight.

My hunch was right, but for the wrong reason.

✗ ✗ ✗

Monday morning, sunny but cool if no longer cold, I pulled into one of the parking places alongside the Sidewalk Cafe; it was around ten-thirty and mine was the only car. The big front door was locked. I knocked until the Spanish cleaning woman let me in. She said she hadn't seen Miss Todd yet this morning. I went up the private stairway off the kitchen that led up to the two apartments. The door at the top of the stairs was unlocked; beyond it were the two facing apartment doors. I knocked on hers.

"Miss Todd?"

No answer.

I tried for a while, then went and found the cleaning woman again. "Maria, do you have any idea where Miss Todd might be? She doesn't seem to be in her room."

"She might be stay up at Meester Eastmon's."

I nodded, started to walk away, then looked back and added as an afterthought, "Did you see her yesterday?"

"I no work Sunday."

I guess Maria, like God, Heller and Thelma Todd, rested on Sunday. Couldn't blame her.

I thought about taking the car up and around, then said to hell with it and began climbing the concrete steps beyond the pedestrian bridge that arched over the highway just past the Cafe. These steps, all two-hundred and eighty of them, straight up the steep hill, were the only direct access from the coast road to the bungalow on Cabrillo Street. Windblown sand had drifted over the steps and the galvanized handrail was as cold and wet as a liar's handshake.

I grunted my way to the top. I'd started out as a young man, had reached middle age by step one hundred and was now ready for the retirement home. I sat on the cold damp top step and poured sand out of my scuffed-up Florsheims, glad I hadn't bothered with a shine in the last few weeks. Then I stood and looked past the claustrophobic drop of the steps, to where the sun was reflecting off the sand and sea. The beach was blinding, the ocean dazzling. It was beautiful, but it hurt to look at. A seagull was flailing with awkward grace against the breeze like a fighter losing the last round. Suddenly Lake Michigan seemed like a pond.

Soon I was knocking on Eastman's front door. No answer. Went to check to see if my client's car was there, swinging up the black-studded blue garage door. The car was there, all right, the red Packard convertible, next to Eastman's Lincoln sedan.

My client was there, too.

She was slumped in front, sprawled across the steering wheel. She was still in the mink, the mauve-and-silver gown, and the diamond necklace she'd worn to the Troc Saturday night. But her clothes were rumpled, in disarray, like an unmade bed; and there was blood on the front of the gown, coagulated rubies beneath the diamonds. There was blood on her face, on her white, white face.

She'd always had pale creamy skin, but now it was as white as a wedding dress. There was no pulse in her throat. She was cold. She'd been dead a while.

I stood and looked at her and maybe I cried. That's my business, isn't it? Then I went out and up the side steps to the loft above the garage and roused the elderly fellow named Jones who lived there; he was the bookkeeper for the Sidewalk Cafe. I asked him if he had a phone, and he did, and I used it.

✗ ✗ ✗

I had told my story to the uniformed men four times before the men from Central Homicide showed. The detective in charge was Lieutenant Rondell, a thin, somber, detached man in his mid-forties with smooth creamy gray hair and icy eyes. His brown gabardine suit wasn't expensive but it was well-pressed. His green pork-pie lightweight felt hat was in his hand, in deference to the deceased.

Out of deference to me, he listened to my story as I told it for the fifth time. He didn't seem to think much of it.

"You're telling me this woman was murdered," he said.

"I'm telling you the gambling syndicate boys were pressuring her, and she wasn't caving in."

"And you were her bodyguard," Rondell said.

"Some bodyguard," said the other man from homicide, Rondell's brutish shadow, and cracked his knuckles and laughed. We were in the garage and the laughter made hollow echoes off the cement, like a basketball bouncing in an empty stadium.

"I was her bodyguard," I told Rondell tightly. "But I didn't work Sundays."

"And she had to go to Chicago to hire a bodyguard?"

I explained my association with Fred Rubinski, and Rondell nodded several times, seemingly accepting it.

Then Rondell walked over and looked at the corpse in the convertible. A photographer from Homicide was snapping photos; pops and flashes of light accompanied the detective's trip around the car as if he were a star at a Hollywood opening.

I went outside. The smell of death is bad enough when it's impersonal; when somebody you know has died, it's like having asthma in a steamroom.

Rondell found me leaning against the side of the stucco garage.

"It looks like suicide," he said.

"Sure. It's supposed to."

He lifted an eyebrow and a shoulder. "The ignition switch is turned on. Carbon monoxide."

"Car wasn't running when I got here."

"Long since ran out of gas, most likely. If what you say is true, she's been there since Saturday night . . . that is, early Sunday morning."

I shrugged. "She's wearing the same clothes, at least."

"When we fix time of death, it'll all come clear."

"Oh, yeah? See what the coroner has to say about that."

Rondell's icy eyes froze further. "Why?"

"This cold snap we've had, last three days. It's warmer this morning, but Sunday night, Jesus. That sea breeze was murder — if you'll pardon the expression."

Rondell nodded. "Perhaps cold enough to retard decomposition, you mean."

"Perhaps."

He pushed the pork pie back on his head. "We need to talk to this bird Eastman."

"I'll say. He's probably at his studio. Paramount. When he's on a picture, they pick him up by limo every morning before dawn."

Rondell went to use the phone in old man Jones' loft flat. I smoked my cigarette.

Rondell's brutish sidekick exited the garage and slid his arm around the shoulder of a young uniformed cop, who seemed uneasy about the attention.

"Ice cream blonde, huh?" the big flatfoot said. "I woulda liked a coupla of scoops of that myself."

I tapped the brute on the shoulder and he turned to me and said, "Huh?", stupidly, and I coldcocked him. He went down like a building.

But not out, though. "You're gonna pay for that, you bastard," he said, sounding like the school-yard bully he was. He touched the blood in the corner of his mouth, hauled himself up off the cement. "In this town, you go to goddamn jail when you hit a goddamn cop!"

"You'd need a witness, first," I said.

"I got one," he said, but when he turned to look, the young uniformed cop was gone.

I walked up to him and stood damn near belt buckle to belt buckle and smiled a smile that had nothing to do with smiling. "Want to go another round, see if a witness shows?"

He tasted blood and fluttered his eyes like a girl and said something unintelligible and disappeared back inside the garage.

Rondell came clopping down the wooden steps and stood before me and smiled firmly. "I just spoke with Eastman. We'll interview him more formally, of course, but the preliminary interrogation indicates a possible explanation."

"Oh?"

He was nodding. "Yeah. Apparently Saturday night he bolted the stairwell door around midnight. It's a door that leads to both apartments up top the Sidewalk Cafe. Said he thought Miss Todd had mentioned she was going to sleep over at her mother's that night."

"You mean, she couldn't get in?"

"Right."

"Well, hell, man, she would've knocked."

"Eastman says if she did, he didn't hear her. He says there was high wind and pounding surf all night; he figures that drowned out all other sounds."

I smirked. "Does he, really? So what's your scenario?"

"Well, when Miss Todd found she couldn't get into her apartment, she must've decided to climb the steps to the street above, walked to the garage and spent the rest of the night in her car. She must've have gotten cold, and switched on the ignition to keep warm, and the fumes got her."

I sighed. "A minute ago you were talking suicide."

"That's still a possibility."

"What about the blood on her face and dress?"

He shrugged. "She may have fallen across the wheel and cut her mouth, when she fell unconscious."

"Look, if she wanted to get warm, why would she sit in her open convertible? That Lincoln sedan next to her is unlocked and has the keys in it."

"I can't answer that — yet."

I was shaking my head. Then I pointed at him. "Ask the elderly gent upstairs if he heard her opening the garage door, starting up the Packard's cold engine sometime between two a.m. and dawn. Ask him!"

"I did. He didn't. But it was a windy night, and . . ."

"Yeah, and the surf was crashing something fierce. Right. Let's take a look at her shoes."

"Huh?"

I pointed down to my scuffed-up Florsheims. "I just scaled those two-hundred-and-eighty steps. This shoeshine boy's nightmare is the result. Let's *see* if she walked up those steps."

Rondell nodded and led me into the garage. The print boys hadn't been over the vehicle yet, so the Lieutenant didn't open the door on the rider's side, he just leaned carefully in.

Then he stood and contemplated what he'd seen. For a moment he seemed to have forgotten me, then he said, "Have a look yourself."

I had one last look at the beautiful woman who'd driven to nowhere in this immobile car.

She wore delicate silver dress heels; they were as pristine as

Cinderella's glass slippers.

✗ ✗ ✗

The Coroner at the inquest agreed with me on one point: "The high winds and very low cold prevailing that week-end would have preserved the body beyond the usual time required for decomposition to set in."

The inquest was, otherwise, a bundle of contradictions, and about as inconclusive as the virgin birth. A few new, sinister facts emerged. She had bruises *inside* her throat. Had someone shoved a bottle down her throat? Her alcohol level was high — .13 percent — much higher than the three or four drinks she was seen to have had at the Troc. And there *was* gas left in the car, it turned out — several gallons; yet the ignition switch was turned on . . . .

But the coroner's final verdict was that Thelma died by carbon monoxide poisoning, "breathed accidentally." Nonetheless, the papers talked suicide, and the word on the streets of Hollywood was "hush-up." Nobody wanted another scandal. Not after Mary Astor's diaries and Busby Berkley's drunk-driving fatalities.

I wasn't buying the coroner's verdict, either.

I knew that three people, on the Monday I'd found Thelma, had come forward to the authorities and reported having seen her on *Sunday,* long after she had "officially" died.

Miranda Diamond, Eastman's now ex-wife (their divorce had gone through, finally, apparently fairly amicably), claimed to have seen Thelma, still dressed in her Trocadero fineries, behind the wheel of her distinctive Packard convertible at the corner of Sunset and Vine Sunday, mid-morning. She was, Miranda told the cops, in the company of a tall, swarthy, nattily dressed young man whom Miranda had never seen before.

Mrs. Wallace Ford, wife of the famed director, had received a brief phone call from Thelma around four Sunday afternoon. Thelma had called to say she would be attending the Fords' cocktail party, and was it all right if she brought along "a new, handsome friend?"

Finally, and best of all, there was Warren Eastman himself. Neighbors had reported to the police that they heard Eastman and Thelma quarreling bitterly, violently, at the bungalow above the restaurant, Sunday morning, around breakfast time. Eastman said he had thrown her out, and that she had screamed obscenities and beaten on the door for ten minutes (and police did find kick marks on the shrub-secluded, hacienda-style door).

"It was a lover's quarrel," Eastman told a reporter. "I heard she had a new boy friend — some Latin fellow from San Francisco — and she denied it. But I knew she was lying."

Eastman also revealed, in the press, that Thelma didn't own any real interest in her Sidewalk Cafe; she had made no investment other than lending her name, for which she got fifty percent of the profits.

I called Rondell after the inquest and he told me the case was closed.

"We both know something smells," I said. "Aren't you going to do something?"

"Yes," he said.

"What?"

"I'm going to hang up."

And he did.

Rondell was a good cop in a bad town, an honest man in a system so corrupt the Borgias would've felt moral outrage; even a Chicago boy like me found it disgusting. But he couldn't do much about movie-mogul pressure by way of City Hall; Los Angeles had one big business and the film industry was it. And I was just an out-of-town private detective with a local dead client.

On the other hand, she'd paid me to protect her, and ultimately I hadn't. I had accepted her money, and it seemed to me she ought to get something for it, even if it was posthumous.

I went out the next Monday morning — one week to the day since I'd found the ice-cream blonde melting in that garage — and at the Cafe, sitting alone in the cocktail lounge, reading *Variety* and drinking a bloody Mary, was Warren Eastman. He was between pictures and just two stools down from where she had sat when she first hired me. He was wearing a blue blazer, a cream silk cravat, and white pants.

He lowered the paper and looked at me; he was surprised to see me, but it was not a pleasant surprise, even though he affected a toothy smile under the twitchy little mustache.

"What brings you around, Heller? I don't need a bodyguard."

"Don't be so sure," I said genially, sitting next to him.

He looked down his nose at me, through slitted eyes; his diamond-shaped face seemed handsome to some, I supposed, but to me it was a harshly angular thing, a hunting knife with hair.

"What exactly," he said, "do you mean by that?"

"I mean I know you murdered Thelma," I said.

He laughed and returned to his newspaper. "Go away, Heller. Find some schoolgirl who frightens easily if you want to scare somebody."

"I want to scare somebody all right. I just have one question . . . did your ex-wife help you with the murder itself, or was she just a supporting player?"

He put the paper down. He sipped the bloody Mary. His face was wooden but his eyes were animated.

I laughed gutturally. "You and your convoluted murder mysteries. You were so clever you almost schemed your way into the gas chamber, didn't you? With your masquerades and charades."

"What in the hell are you talking about?"

"You were smart enough to figure out that the cold weather would confuse the time of death. But you thought you could make the coroner think Thelma met her fate the *next* day — Sunday evening, perhaps. You didn't have an alibi for the early a.m. hours of Sunday. And that's when you killed her."

"Is it, really? Heller, I saw her Sunday morning, breakfast. I argued with her, the neighbors heard . . ."

"Exactly. They *heard* — but they didn't *see* a thing. That was something you staged, either with your ex-wife's help, or whoever your current starlet is. Some actress, the same actress who later called Mrs. Ford up to accept the cocktail party invite and further spread the rumor of the new lover from San Francisco. Nice touch, that. Pulls in the rumors of gangsters from San Francisco who threatened her; was the 'swarthy man' Miranda saw a torpedo posing as a lover? A gigolo with a gun? A member of Artie Lewis' dance band, maybe? Let the cops and the papers wonder. Well, it won't wash with me; I was with her for her last month. She had no new serious love in her life, from San Francisco or elsewhere. Your 'swarthy man' is the little Latin lover who wasn't there."

"Miranda *saw* him with her, Heller . . ."

"No. Miranda didn't see anything. She told the story you wanted her to tell; she went along with you, and you treated her right in the divorce settlement. You can afford to. You're sole owner of Thelma Todd's

Sidewalk Cafe, now. Lock, stock and barrel, with no messy interference from the star on the marquee. And now you're free to accept Lucky Luciano's offer, aren't you?"

That rocked him, like a physical blow. "What?"

"That's why you killed Thelma. She was standing in your way. You wanted to put a casino in upstairs; it would mean big money, very big money."

"I have money."

"Yes, and you spend it. You live very lavishly. I've been checking up on you. I know you intimately already, and I'm going to know you even better."

His eyes quivered in the diamond mask of his face. "What are you talking about?"

"You tried to scare her at first — extortion notes, having her followed; maybe you did this with Luciano's help, maybe you did it on your own. I don't know. But then she hired me, and you scurried off into the darkness to think up something new."

He sneered and gestured archly with his cigarette holder, the cigarette in which he was about to light up. "I'm breathlessly awaiting just what evil thing it was I conjured up next."

"You decided to commit the perfect crime. Just like in the movies. You would kill Thelma one cold night, knocking her out, shoving booze down her, leaving her to die in that garage with the car running. Then you would set out to make it seem that she was still alive — during a day when you were very handsomely, unquestionably alibied."

"You're not making any sense. The verdict at the inquest was accidental death . . ."

"Yes. But the time of death is assumed to have been the night *before* you said you saw her last. Your melodrama was too involved for the simple-minded authorities, who only wanted to hush things up. They went with the more basic, obvious, tidy solution that Thelma died an accidental death early Saturday morning." I laughed, once. "You were so cute in pursuit of the 'perfect crime' you tripped yourself, Eastman."

"Did I really," he said dryly. It wasn't a question.

"Your scenario needed one more rewrite. First you told the cops you slept at the apartment over the cafe Saturday night, bolting the door around midnight, accidentally locking Thelma out. But later you admitted seeing Thelma the next morning, around breakfast time — at the *bungalow*."

His smile quivered. "Perhaps I slept at the apartment, and went up for breakfast at the bungalow."

"I don't think so. I think you killed her."

"No charges have been brought against me. And none will."

I looked at him hard, like a hanging judge passing sentence. "I'm bringing a charge against you now. I'm charging you with murder in the first degree."

His smile was crinkly; he stared into the redness of his drink. Smoke from his cigarette-in-holder curled upward like a wreath. "Ha. A citizen's arrest, is it?"

"No. Heller's law. I'm going to kill you myself."

He looked at me sharply. "What? Are you mad . . ."

"Yes, I'm mad. In sense of being angry, that is. Sometime, within the next year, or two, I'm going to kill you. Just how, I'm not just sure. Might be me who does, might be one of my Chicago pals. Just when, well . . . perhaps tomorrow. Perhaps a month from tomorrow. Maybe next Christmas. I haven't decided yet."

"You can't be serious . . ."

"I'm deadly serious. Right now I'm heading home to the Windy City, to mull it over. But don't worry — I'll be seeing you."

And I left him there at the bar, the glass of bloody Mary mixing itself in his hand.

Here's what I did to Warren Eastman: I hired Fred Rubinski to spend two weeks shadowing him. Letting him see he was being tailed by an ugly intimidating-looking bastard, which Fred was. Letting him extrapolate from this that I was, through my surrogate, watching his every move. Making him jump at that shadow, and all the other shadows, too.

Then I pulled Fred off Eastman's case. Home in Chicago, I slept with my gun under my pillow for a while, in case the director got ambitious. But I didn't bother him any further.

The word in Hollywood was that Eastman was somehow — no one knew exactly how, but somehow — dirty in the Todd murder. And nobody in town thought it was anything but a murder. Eastman never got another picture. He went from one of the hottest directors in Hollywood, to the coldest. As cold as the weekend Thelma Todd died.

The Sidewalk Cafe stopped drawing a monied, celebrity crowd, but it did all right from regular-folks curiosity seekers. Eastman made some dough there, all right; but the casino never happened. A combination of the wrong kind of publicity, and the drifting away of the high-class clientele, must have changed Lucky Luciano's mind.

Within a year of Thelma Todd's death, Eastman was committed to a rest home, which is a polite way of saying insane asylum or madhouse. He was in and out of such places for the next four years, and then, one very cold, windy night, he died of a heart attack.

Did I keep my promise? Did I kill him?

I like to think I did, indirectly. I like to think that Thelma Todd got her money's worth from her chauffeur/bodyguard, who had not been there when she took that last long drive, on the night her sad blue eyes closed forever.

I like to think, in my imperfect way, that I committed the perfect crime.

NATURAL DEATH, INC.

She'd been pretty, once. She was still sexy, in a slutty way, if you'd had enough beers and it was just before closing time.

Kathleen O'Meara, who ran the dingy dive that sported her last name, would have been a well-preserved fifty, if she hadn't been forty. But I knew from the background materials I'd been provided that she was born in 1899, here in the dirt-poor Irish neighborhood of Cleveland known as the Angles, a scattering of brick and frame dwellings and businesses at the north end of 25th Street in the industrial flats.

Kathleen O'Meara's husband, Frank, had been dead barely a month now, but Katie wasn't wearing black: her blouse was white with red polka dots, a low-cut peasant affair out of which spilled well-powdered, bowling ball-size breasts. Her mouth was a heavily red-rouged chasm within which gleamed white storebought choppers; her eyes were lovely, within their pouches, long-lashed and money-green.

"What's your pleasure, handsome?" she asked, her soprano voice musical in a calliope sort of way, a hint of Irish lilt in it.

I guess I was handsome, for this crowd anyway, six feet, one-hundred-eighty pounds poured into threadbare mismatched suitcoat and pants, a wilted excuse for a fedora snugged low over my reddish brown hair, chin and cheeks stubbled with two days growth, looking back at myself in the streaked smudgy mirror behind the bar. A chilly March afternoon had driven better than a dozen men inside the shabby walls of O'Meara's, where a churning exhaust fan did little to stave off the bouquet of stale smoke and beer-soaked sawdust.

"Suds is all I can afford," I said.

"There's worse ways to die," she said, eyes sparkling.

"Ain't been reduced to canned heat yet," I admitted.

At least half of the clientele around me couldn't have made that claim; while those standing at the bar, with a foot on the rail, like me, wore the sweatstained workclothes that branded them employed, the men hunkered at tables and booths wore the tattered rags of the derelict. A skinny dark-haired dead-eyed sunken-cheeked barmaid in an off-white waitress uniform was collecting empty mugs and replacing them with foaming new ones.

The bosomy saloonkeeper set a sloshing mug before me."Railroad worker?"

I sipped; it was warm and bitter. "Steel mill. Pretty lean in Gary; heard they was hiring at Republic."

"That was last month."

"Yeah. Found that out in a hurry."

She extended a pudgy hand. "Kathleen O'Meara, at your service."

"William O'Hara," I said. Nathan Heller, actually. The Jewish last name came from my father, but the Irish mug that was fooling the saloonkeeper was courtesy of my mother.

"Two O's, that's us," she grinned; that mouth must have have been something, once. "My pals call me Katie. Feel free."

"Well, thanks, Katie. And my pals call me Bill." Nate.

"Got a place to stay, Bill?"

"No. Thought I'd hop a freight tonight. See what's shakin' up at Flint."

"They ain't hiring up there, neither."

"Well, I dunno, then."

"I got rooms upstairs, Bill."

"Couldn't afford it, Katie."

"Another mug?"

"Couldn't afford that, either."

She winked. "Handsome, you got me wrapped around your little pinkie, ain't ya noticed?"

She fetched me a second beer, then attended to the rest of her customers at the bar. I watched her, feeling both attracted and repulsed; what is it about a beautiful woman run to fat, gone to seed, that can still summon the male in a man?

I was nursing the second beer, knowing that if I had enough of these I might do something I'd regret in the morning, when she trundled back over and leaned on the bar with both elbows.

"A room just opened up. Yours, if you want it."

"I told ya, Katie, I'm flat-busted."

"But I'm not," she said with a lecherous smile, and I couldn't be sure whether she meant money or her billowing powdered bosoms. "I could use a helpin' hand around here. . . . I'm a widow lady, Bill, runnin' this big old place by her lonesome."

"You mean sweep up and do dishes and the like."

Her cute nose wrinkled as if a bad smell had caught its attention; a little late for that, in this joint. "My daughter does most of the drudgery." She nodded toward the barmaid, who was moving through the room like a zombie with a beer tray. "Wouldn't insult ya with woman's work, Bill . . . But there's things only a man can do."

She said "things" like "tings."

"What kind of things?"

Her eyes had a twinkle, like broken glass. "Things . . . Interested?"

"Sure, Katie."

And it was just that easy.

✗ ✗ ✗

Three days earlier, I had been seated at a conference table in the spacious dark-wood and pebbled-glass office of the Public Safety Director in Cleveland's City Hall.

"It's going to be necessary to swear you in as a part of my staff," Eliot Ness said.

I had known Eliot since we were both teenagers at the University of Chicago. I'd dropped out, finished up at a community college and gone into law enforcement; Eliot had graduated and became a private investigator, often working for insurance companies. Somewhere along the way, we'd swapped jobs.

His dark brown hair brushed with gray at the temples, Eliot's faintly freckled, boyish good looks were going puffy on him, gray eyes pouchy and marked by crow's feet. But even in his late thirties, the former Treasury agent who had been instrumental in Al Capone's fall was the youngest Public Safety Director in the nation.

When I was on the Chicago P.D., I had been one of the few cops Eliot could trust for information; and when I opened up the one-man A-1 Detective Agency, Eliot had returned the favor as my only trustworthy source within the law enforcement community. I had remained in Chicago and he had gone on to more government crimebusting in various corners of the midwest, winding up with this high profile job as Cleveland's "top cop"; since 1935, he had made national headlines cleaning up the police department, busting crooked labor unions and curtailing the numbers racket.

Eliot was perched on the edge of the table, a casual posture at odds with his three-piece suit and tie. "Just a formality," he explained. "I caught a little heat recently from the City Council for hiring outside investigators."

I'd been brought in on several other cases, over the past five or six years.

"It's an undercover assignment?"

He nodded. "Yes, and I'd love to tackle it myself, but I'm afraid at this point, even in the Angles, this puss of mine is too well-known."

Eliot, a boyhood Sherlock Holmes fan, was not one to stay behind his desk; even as Public Safety Director, he was known to lead raids, wielding an ax, and go undercover, in disguise.

I said, "You've never been shy about staying out of the papers."

I was one of the few people who could make a crack like that and not get a rebuke; in fact, I got a little smile out of the stone face.

"Well, I don't like what's been in the papers, lately," he admitted, brushing the stray comma of hair off his forehead, for what good it did him. "You know I've made traffic safety a priority."

"Sure. Can't jaywalk in this burg without getting a ticket."

When Eliot came into office, Cleveland was ranked the second un-safest city in America, after Los Angeles. By 1938, Cleveland was ranked the safest big city, and by 1939 the safest city, period. This reflected Eliot's instituting a public safety campaign through education and "warning" tickets, and reorganizing the traffic division, putting in two-way radios in patrol cars and creating a fleet of motorcycle cops.

"Well, we're in no danger of receiving any 'safest city' honors this year," he said, dryly. He settled into the wooden chair next to mine, folded his hands prayerfully. "We've already had thirty-two traffic fatalities this year. That's more than double where we stood, this time last year."

"What's the reason for it?"

"We thought it had to do with increased industrial activity."

"You mean, companies are hiring again, and more people are driving to work"

"Right. We've had employers insert 'drive carefully' cards in pay envelopes, we've made elaborate safety presentations . . . There's also an increase in teenage drivers, you know, kids driving to high school."

"More parents working, more kids with cars. Follows."

"Yes. And we stepped up educational efforts, at schools, accordingly. Plus, we've cracked down on traffic violators of all stripes — four times as many speeding arrests; traffic violations arrests up twenty-five-percent, intoxication arrests almost double."

"What sort of results are you having?"

"In these specific areas — industrial drivers, teenage drivers — very positive. These are efforts that went into effect around the middle of last year — and yet this year, the statistics are far worse."

"You wouldn't be sending me undercover if you didn't have the problem pinpointed."

He nodded. "My Traffic Analysis Bureau came up with several interesting stats: seventy-two percent of our traffic fatalities this year are age 45 or older. But only twenty percent of our population falls in that category. And thirty-six percent of those fatalities are 65 or up . . . a category that comprises only four percent of Cleveland's population."

"So more older people are getting hit by cars than younger people," I said with a shrug. "Is that a surprise? The elderly don't have the reflexes of young bucks like us."

"Forty-five isn't 'elderly,' " Eliot said, "as we'll both find out sooner than we'd like."

The intercom on Eliot's nearby rolltop desk buzzed and he rose and responded to it. His secretary's voice informed us that Dr. Jeffers was here to see him.

"Send her in," Eliot said.

The woman who entered was small and wore a white shirt and matching trousers, baggy oversize apparel that gave little hint of any shape beneath; though her heart-shaped face was attractive, she wore no make-up and her dark hair was cut mannishly short, clunky thick-lensed tortoise-shell glasses distorting dark almond-shaped eyes.

"Alice, thank you for coming," Eliot said, rising, shaking her hand. "Nate Heller, this is Dr. Alice Jeffers, assistant county coroner."

"A pleasure, Dr. Jeffers," I said, rising, shaking her cool, dry hand, as she twitched me a smile.

Eliot pulled out a chair for her opposite me at the conference table, telling her, "I've been filling Nate in. I'm just up to your part in this investigation."

With no further prompting, Dr. Jeffers said, "I was alerted by a morgue attendant, actually. It seemed we'd had an unusual number of hit-and-skip fatalities in the last six months, particularly in January, from a certain part of the city, and a certain part of community."

"Alice is referring to a part of Cleveland called the Angles," Eliot explained, "which is just across the Detroit Bridge, opposite the factory and warehouse district."

"I've been there," I said. The Angles was a classic waterfront area, where bars and whorehouses and cheap rooming houses serviced a clientele of workingmen and longshoremen. It was also an area rife with derelicts, particularly since Eliot burned out the Hoovervilles nestling in Kingsbury Run and under various bridges.

"These hit-and-skip victims were vagrants," Dr. Jeffers said, her eyes unblinking and intelligent behind the thick lenses, "and tended to be in their fifties or sixties, though they looked much older."

"Rummies," I said.

"Yes. With Director Ness's blessing, and Coroner Gerber's permission, I conducted several autopsies, and encountered individuals in advanced stages of alcoholism. Cirrhosis of the liver, kidney disease, general debilitation. Had they not been struck by cars, they would surely have died within a matter of years or possibly months or even weeks."

"Walking dead men."

"Poetic but apt. My contact at the morgue began keeping me alerted when vagrant 'customers' came through, and I soon realized that automobile fatalities were only part of the story."

"How so?" I asked.

"We had several fatal falls-down-stairs, and a surprising number of fatalities by exposure to the cold weather, death by freezing, by pneumonia. Again, I performed autopsies where normally we would not. These victims were invariably intoxicated at the times of their deaths, and in advanced stages of acute alcoholism."

I was thoroughly confused. "What's the percentage in bumping off bums? You got another psychopath at large, Eliot? Or is the Butcher back, changing his style?"

I was referring to the so-called Mad Butcher of Kingsbury Run, who had cut up a number of indigents here in Cleveland, Jack the Ripper style; but the killings had stopped, long ago.

"This isn't the Butcher," Eliot confidently. "And it isn't psychosis . . . it's commerce."

"There's money in killing bums?"

"If they're insured, there is."

"Okay, okay," I said, nodding, getting it, or starting to. "But if you overinsure some worthless derelict, surely it's going to attract the attention of the adjusters for the insurance company."

"This is more subtle than that," Eliot said. "When Alice informed me of this, I contacted the State Insurance Division. Their chief investigator, Gaspar Corso — who we'll meet with later this afternoon, Nate — dug through our 'drunk cards' on file at the Central Police Station, some 20,000 of them. He came up with information that corroborated Alice's, and confirmed suspicions of mine."

Corso had an office in the Standard Building — no name on the door, no listing in the building directory. Eliot, Dr. Jeffers and I met with Corso in the latter's small, spare office, wooden chairs pulled up around a wooden desk that faced the wall, so that Corso was swung around facing us.

He was small and compactly muscular — a former high school football star, according to Eliot — bald with calm blue eyes under black beetle eyebrows. A gold watch chain crossed the vest of his three-piece tweed.

"A majority of the drunks dying either by accident or 'natural causes,' " he said in a mellow baritone, "come from the West Side — the Angles."

"And they were over-insured?" I asked.

"Yes, but not in the way you might expect. Do you know what industrial insurance is, Mr. Heller?"

"You mean, burial insurance?"

"That's right. Small policies designed to pay funeral expenses and the like."

"Is that what these bums are being bumped off for? Pennies?"

A tiny half smile formed on the impassive investigator's thin lips. "Hardly. Multiple policies have been taken out on these individuals, dozens in some cases . . . each small policy with a different insurance company."

"No wonder no alarms went off," I said. "Each company got hit for peanuts."

"Some of these policies are for two-hundred-and-fifty dollars, never higher than a thousand. But I have one victim here . . ." He turned to his desk, riffled through some papers. ". . . who I determined, by crosschecking with various companies, racked up a $24,000 payout."

"Christ. Who was the beneficiary?"

"A Kathleen O'Meara," Eliot said. "She runs a saloon in the Angles, with a rooming house upstairs."

"Her husband died last month," Dr. Jeffers said. "I performed the autopsy myself . . . He was intoxicated at the time of his death, and was in an advanced stage of cirrhosis of the liver. Hit by a car. But there was one difference."

"Yes?"

"He was fairly well-dressed, and was definitely not malnourished."

✗ ✗ ✗

O'Meara's did not serve food, but a greasy spoon down the block did, and that's where Katie took me for supper, around seven, leaving the running of the saloon to her sullen skinny daughter, Maggie.

"Maggie doesn't say much," I said, over a plate of meat loaf and mashed potatoes and gray. Like Katie, it was surprisingly appetizing, particularly if you didn't look too closely and were half-bombed.

We were in a booth by a window that showed no evidence of ever having been cleaned; cold March wind rattled it and leached through.

"I spoiled her," Katie admitted. "But, to be fair, she's still grieving over her papa. She was the apple of his eye."

"You miss your old man?"

"I miss the help. He took care of the books. I got a head for business, but not for figures. Thing is, he got greedy."

"Really?"

"Yeah, caught him featherin' his own nest. Skimmin'. He had a bank account of his own he never told me about."

"You fight over that?"

"Naw. Forgive and forget, I always say." Katie was having the same thing as me, and she was shoveling meat loaf into her mouth like coal into a boiler.

"I'm, uh, pretty good with figures," I said.

Her licentious smile was part lip rouge, part gravy. "I'll just bet you are . . . Ever do time, Bill?"

"Some. I'm not no thief, though . . . I wouldn't steal a partner's money."

"What were you in for?"

"Manslaughter."

"Kill somebody, did you?"

"Sort of."

She giggled. "How do you 'sort of' kill somebody, Bill?"

"I beat a guy to death with my fists. I was drunk."

"Why?"

"I've always drunk too much."

"No, why'd you beat him to death? With your fists."

I shrugged, chewed meat loaf. "He insulted a woman I was with. I don't like a man that don't respect a woman."

She sighed. Shook her head. "You're a real gent, Bill. Here I thought chivalry was dead."

✗ ✗ ✗

Three evenings before, I'd been in a yellow-leather booth by a blue-mirrored wall in the Vogue Room of the Hollenden Hotel. Clean-shaven and in my best brown suit, I was in the company of Eliot and his recent bride, the former Ev McMillan, a fashion illustrator who worked for Higbee's department store.

Ev, slender attractive brunette, wore a simple cobalt blue evening dress with pearls; Eliot was in the three-piece suit he'd worn to work. We'd had prime rib and were enjoying after dinner drinks; Eliot was on his second, and he'd had two before dinner, as well. Martinis. Ev was only one drink behind him.

Personal chit-chat had lapsed back into talking business.

"It's goddamn ghoulish," Eliot said. He was quietly soused, as evidenced by his use of the word "goddamn" — for a tough cop, he usually had a Boy Scout's vocabulary.

"It's coldblooded, all right," I said.

"How does the racket work?" Ev asked.

"I shouldn't have brought it up," Eliot said. "It doesn't make for pleasant after-dinner conversation . . ."

"No, I'm interested," she said. She was a keenly intelligent young woman. "You compared it to a lottery . . . how so?"

"Well," I said, "as it's been explained to me, speculators 'invest' in dozens of small insurance policies on vagrants who were already drinking themselves to imminent graves . . . malnourished men crushed by dope and/or drink, sleeping in parks and in doorways in all kinds of weather."

"Men likely to meet an early death by so-called natural causes," Eliot said. "That's how we came to nickname the racket 'Natural Death, Inc.' "

"Getting hit by a car isn't exactly a 'natural' death," Ev pointed out.

Eliot sipped his martini. "At first, the speculators were just helping nature along by plying their investments with free, large quantities of drink . . . hastening their death by alcoholism or just making them more prone to stumble in front of a car."

"Now it looks like these insured derelicts are being shoved in front of cars," I said.

"Or the drivers of the cars are purposely running them down," Eliot said. "Dear, this really is unpleasant conversation; I apologize for getting into it . . ."

"Nonsense," she said."Who *are* these speculators?"

"Women, mostly," he said. "Harridans running West Side beer parlors and roominghouses. They exchange information, but they aren't exactly an organized ring or anything, which makes our work difficult. I'm siccing Nate here on the worst offender, the closest thing there is to a ringleader — a woman we've confirmed is holding fifty policies on various 'risks.' "

Ev frowned. "How do these women get their victims to go along with them? I mean, aren't the insured's signatures required on the policies?"

"There's been some forgery going on," Eliot said."But mostly these poor bastards are willingly trading their signatures for free booze."

Ev twitched a non-smile above the rim of her martini glass. "Life in slum areas breeds such tragedy."

The subject changed to local politics — I'd heard rumors of Eliot's running for mayor, which he unconvincingly pooh-poohed — and, a few drinks later, Eliot spotted some reporter friends of his, Clayton Fritchey and Sam Wild, and excused himself to go over and speak to them.

"If I'm not being out of line," I said to Mrs. Ness, "Eliot's hitting the sauce pretty hard himself. Hope you don't have any extra policies out on him."

She managed a wry little smile. "I do my best to keep up with him, but it's difficult. Ironic, isn't it? The nation's most famous Prohibition agent, with a drinking problem."

"*Is* it a problem?"

"Eliot doesn't think so. He says he just has to relax. It's a stressful job."

"It is at that. But, Ev — I've been around Eliot during 'stressful' times before . . . like when the entire Capone gang was gunning for him. And he never put it away like that, then."

She was studied the olive in her martini. "You were part of that case, weren't you?"

"What case? Capone?"

"No — the Butcher."

I nodded. I'd been part of the capture of the lunatic responsible for those brutal slayings of vagrants; and was one of the handful who knew that Eliot had been forced to make a deal with his influential political backers to allow the son of a bitch — who had a society pedigree — to avoid arrest, and instead be voluntarily committed to a madhouse.

"It bothers him, huh?" I said, and grunted a laugh. "Mr. Squeaky Clean, the 'Untouchable' Eliot Ness having to cut a deal like that."

"I think so," she admitted. "He never says. You know how quiet he can be."

"Well, I think he should grow up. For Christ sake, for somebody from Chicago, somebody who's seen every kind of crime and corruption, he can be as naive as a schoolgirl."

"An alcoholic schoolgirl," Ev said with a smirk, and a martini sip. ". . . You want me to talk to him?"

"I don't know. Maybe . . . I think this case, these poor homeless men being victimized again, got memories stirred up."

"Of the Butcher case, you mean."

"Yes . . . and Nate, we've been getting postcards from that crazy man."

"What crazy man? Capone?"

"No! The Butcher . . . threatening postcards postmarked the town where that asylum is."

"Is there any chance Watterson can get out?"

Lloyd Watterson: the Butcher.

"Eliot says no," Ev said. "He's been assured of that."

"Well, these killings aren't the work of a madman. This is murder for profit, plain and simple. Good old-fashioned garden variety evil."

"Help him clear this up," she said, and an edge of desperation was in her voice. "I think it would . . . might . . . make a difference."

Then Eliot was back, and sat down with a fresh martini in hand.

"I hope I didn't miss anything good," he said.

✗ ✗ ✗

My room was small but seemed larger due to the sparseness of the furnishings, metallic, institutional-gray clothes cabinet, a chair and a metal cot. A bare bulb bulged from the wall near the door, as if it had blossomed from the faded, fraying floral-print wallpaper. The wooden floor had a greasy, grimy look.

Katie was saying, "Hope it will do."

"You still haven't said what my duties are."

"I'll think of something. Now, if you need anything, I'm down the hall. Let me show you . . ."

I followed her to a doorway at the end of the narrow gloomy hallway. She unlocked the door with a key extracted from between her massive breasts, and ushered me into another world.

The livingroom of her apartment held a showroom-like suite of walnut furniture with carved arms, feet and base rails, the chairs and davenport sporting matching green mohair cushions, assembled on a green and blue wall-to-wall Axminster carpet. Pale yellow wallpaper with gold and pink highlights created a tapestry effect, while floral satin damask draperies dressed up the windows, venetian blinds keeping out prying eyes. Surprisingly tasteful, the room didn't look very lived in.

"Posh digs," I said, genuinely impressed.

"Came into some money recently. Spruced the joint up a little . . . Now, if you need me after hours, be sure to knock good and loud." She swayed over to a doorless doorway and nodded for me to come to her. "I'm a heavy sleeper."

The bedroom was similarly decked out with new furnishings — a walnut-veener double bed, dresser and nightstand and three-mirror vanity with modern lines and zebrawood design panels — against ladylike pink-and-white floral wallpaper. The vanity top was neatly arranged with perfumes and face powder and the like, their combined scents lending the room a feminine bouquet. Framed prints of airbrushed flowers hung here and there, a large one over the bed, where sheets and blankets were neatly folded back below lush overstuffed feather pillows, as if by a maid.

"I had this room re-done, too," she said. "My late husband, rest his soul, was a slob."

Indeed it was hard to imagine a man sharing this room with her. There was a daintiness that didn't match up with its inhabitant. The only sign that anybody lived here were the movie magazines on the bedstand in the glow of the only light, a creamy glazed pottery-base lamp whose gold parchment shade gave the room a glow.

The only person more out of place in this tidy, feminine suite than me, in my tattered secondhand store suit, was my blowsy hostess in her polka-dot peasant blouse and flowing dark skirt. She was excited and proud, showing off her fancy living quarters, bobbing up and down like an eager kid; it was cute and a little sickening.

Or maybe that was the cheap beer. I wasn't drunk but I'd had three glasses of it.

"You okay, Bill?" she asked.

"Demon meatloaf," I said.

"Sit, sit."

And I was sitting on the edge of the bed. She stood before me, looming over me, frightening and oddly comely, with her massive bosom spilling from the blouse, her red-rouged mouth, her half-lidded long-lashed green eyes, mother/goddess/whore.

"It's been lonely, Bill," she said, "without my man."

"Suh . . . sorry for your loss."

"I could use a man around here, Bill."

"Try to help."

"It could be sweet for you."

She tugged the peasant blouse down over the full, round, white-powdered melons that were her bosom, and pulled my head between them. Their suffocation was pleasant, even heady, and I was wondering whether I'd lost count of those beers when I fished in my trousers for my wallet for the lambskin.

I wasn't *that* far gone.

✗ ✗ ✗

I had never been with a woman as overweight as Kathleen O'Meara before, and I don't believe I ever was again; many a man might dismiss her as fat. But the sheer womanliness of her was overwhelming; there was so much of her, and she smelled so good, particularly for a saloonkeeper, her skin so smooth, her breasts and behind as firm as they were large and round, that the three nights I spent in her bed remain bittersweet memories. I didn't love her, obviously, nor did she me — we were using each other, in our various nasty ways.

But it's odd, how many times, over the years, the memory of carnality in Katie's bed pops unbidden into my mind. On more than one occasion, in bed with a slender young girlish thing, the image of womanly, obscenely voluptuous Katie would taunt me, as if saying, *Now I was a* real *woman!*

Katie was also a real monster. She waited until the second night, when I lay next to her in the recently purchased bed, in her luxuriant remodeled suite of rooms in a waterfront rooming house where her pitiful clientele slept on pancake-flat piss-scented mattresses, to invite me to be her accomplice.

"Someday I'll move from here," she said in the golden glow of the parchment lamp and the volcanic sex we'd just had. She was on her back, the sheet only half-covering the globes of her bosom; she was smoking, staring at the ceiling.

I was on my back, too — I wasn't smoking, cigarettes being one filthy habit I didn't partake of. "But, Katie — this place is hunky-dory."

"These rooms are nice, love. But little Katie was meant for a better life than the Angles can provide."

"You got a good business, here."

She chuckled. "Better than you know."

"What do you mean?"

She leaned on one elbow and the sheet fell away from the large, lovely bosoms. "Don't you wonder why I'm so good to these stumblebums?"

"You give a lot of free beer away, I noticed."

"Why do you suppose Katie does that?"

"'Cause you're a good Christian woman?"

She roared with laughter, globes shimmering like Jello. "Don't be a child! Have you heard of burial insurance, love?"

And she filled me in on the scheme — the lottery portion of it, at least, taking out policies on men who were good bets for quick rides to potter's field. But she didn't mention anything about helping speed the insured to even quicker, surer deaths.

"You disappointed in Katie?" she asked. "That I'm not such a good Christian woman?"

I grinned at her. "I'm tickled pink to find out how smart you are, baby. Was your old man in on this?"

"He was. But he wasn't trustworthy."

"Lucky for you he croaked."

"Lucky."

"Hey . . . I didn't mean to be coldhearted, baby. I know you miss him."

Her plump pretty face was as blank as a bisque baby's. "He disappointed me."

"How'd he die?"

"Got drunk and stepped in front of a car."

"Sorry."

"Don't pay for a dipso to run a bar, too much helpin' himself . . . I notice you don't hit the sauce so hard. You don't drink too much, and you hold what you do drink."

"Thanks."

"You're just a good joe, down on his luck. Could use a break."

"Who couldn't?"

"And I can use a man. I can use a partner."

"What do I have to do?"

"Just be friendly to these rummies. Get 'em on your good side, get 'em to sign up. Usually all it takes is a friendly ear and a pint of rotgut."

"And when they finally drink themselves into a grave, we get a nice payday."

"Yup. And enough nice paydays, we can leave the Angles behind. Retire rich while we're still young and pretty."

✗ ✗ ✗

His name was Harold Wilson. He looked at least sixty but when we filled out the application, he managed to remember he was forty-three.

He and I sat in a booth at O'Meara's and I plied him with cheap beers, which Katie's hollow-eyed daughter dutifully delivered, while Harold told me, in bits and pieces, the sad story that had brought him to the Angles.

Hunkered over the beer, he seemed small, but he'd been of stature once, physically and otherwise. In a face that was both withered and puffy, bloodshot powder-blue eyes peered from pouches, by turns rheumy and teary.

He had been a stock broker. When the Crash came, he chose to jump a freight rather than out a window, leaving behind a well-bred wife and two young daughters.

"I meant to go back," Harold said, in a baritone voice whose dignity had been sandpapered away, leaving scratchiness and quaver behind. "For years, I did menial jobs . . . seasonal work, janitorial work, chopping firewood, shoveling walks, mowing grass . . . and I'd save. But the money never grew. I'd either get jackrolled or spend it on . . ."

He finished the sentence by grabbing the latest foamy mug of warm beer from Maggie O'Meara and guzzling it.

I listened to Harold's sad story all afternoon and into the evening; he repeated himself a lot, and he signed three burial policies, one for $450, another for $750 and finally the jackpot, $1000. Death would probably be a merciful way out for the poor bastard, but even at this stage of his life, Harold Wilson deserved a better legacy than helping provide for Katie O'Meara's retirement.

Late in the evening, he said, "Did go back, once . . . to Elmhurst . . . Tha's Chicago."

"Yeah, I know, Harold."

"Thomas Wolfe said, 'Can't go home again.' Shouldn't go home again's more like it."

"Did you talk to them?"

"No! No. It was Chrissmuss. Sad story, huh? Looked in the window. Didn't expect to see 'em, my family; figured they'd lose the house."

"But they didn't? How'd they manage that?"

"Mary . . . that's my wife . . . her family had some money. Must not've got hurt as bad as me in the Crash. Figure they musta bought the house for her."

"I see."

"Sure wasn't her new husband. I recognized him; fella I went to high school with. A postman."

"A mail carrier?"

"Yeah. 'Fore the Crash, Mary, she woulda looked down on a lowly civil servant like that . . . But in Depression times, that's a hell of a good job."

"True enough."

The eyes were distant and runny. "My girls was grown. College age. Blonde and pretty, with boy friends, holdin' hands . . . The place hadn't changed. Same furniture. Chrissmuss tree where we always put it, in the front window . . . We'd move the couch out of the way and . . . anyway. Nothing different. Except in the middle of it, no me. A mailman took my place."

For a moment I thought he said "male man."

✗ ✗ ✗

O'Meara's closed at two a.m. I helped Maggie clean up, even though Katie hadn't asked me to. Katie was upstairs, waiting for me in her bedroom. Frankly, I didn't feel like doing my duty tonight, pleasant though it admittedly was. On the one hand, I was using Katie, banging this broad I was undercover, and undercovers, to get the goods on, which made me a louse; and on the other hand, spending the day with her next victim, Harold Wilson, brought home what an enormous louse she was.

I was helping daughter Maggie put chairs on tables; she hadn't said a word to me yet. She had her mother's pretty green eyes and she might have been pretty herself if her scarecrow thin frame and narrow, hatchet face had a little meat on them.

The room was tidied when she said, "Nightcap?"

Surprised, I said, "Sure."

"I got a pot of coffee on, if you're sick of warm beer."

The kitchen in back was small and neat and Maggie's living quarters were back here, as well. She and her mother did not live together; in fact, they rarely spoke, other than Katie issuing commands.

I sat at a wooden table in the midst of the small cupboard-lined kitchen and sipped the coffee Maggie provided in a chipped cup. In her white waitress uniform, she looked like a wilted nurse.

"That suit you're wearing," she said.

Katie had given me clothes to wear; I was in a brown suit and a yellow-and-brown tie, nothing fancy but a step or two up from the threadbare duds "Bill O'Hara" had worn into O'Meara's.

"What about 'em?"

"Those were my father's." Maggie sipped her coffee. "You're about his size."

I'd guessed as much. "I didn't know. I don't mean to be a scavenger, Miss O'Meara, but life can do that to you. The Angles ain't high society."

"You were talking to that man all afternoon."

"Harold Wilson. Sure. Nice fella."

"Ma's signing up policies on him."

"That's right. You know about that, do you?"

"I know more than you know. If you knew what I knew, you wouldn't be so eager to sleep with that cow."

"Now, let's not be disrespectful . . ."

"To you or the cow? . . . Mr. O'Hara, you seem like a decent enough sort. Careful what you get yourself into. Remember how my papa died."

"No one ever told me," I lied.

"He got run down by a car. I think he got pushed."

"Really? Who'd do a thing like that?"

The voice behind us said, "This is cozy."

She was in the doorway, Katie, in a red kimono with yellow flowers on it; you could've rigged out a sailboat with all that cloth.

"Mr. O'Hara helped me tidy up," Maggie said coldly. No fear in her voice. "I offered him coffee."

"Just don't offer him anything else," Katie snapped. The green eyes were hard as jade.

Maggie blushed, and rose, taking her empty cup and mine and depositing them awkwardly, clatteringly, in the sink.

In bed, Katie said, "Good job today with our investment, Bill."

"Thanks."

"Know what Harold Wilson's worth, now?"

"No."

"Ten thousand . . . Poor sad soul. Terrible to see him suffering like that. Like it's terrible for us to have to wait and wait, before we can leave all this behind."

"What are you sayin', love?"

"I'm sayin', were somebody to put that poor man out of his misery, they'd be doin' him a favor, is all I'm sayin'."

"You're probably right, at that. Poor bastard."

"You know how cars'll come up over the hill . . . 25th Street, headin' for the bridge? Movin' quick through this here bad part of a town?"

"Yeah, what about 'em?"

"If someone were to shove some poor soul out in front of a car, just as it was coming up and over, there'd be no time for stoppin'."

I pretended to digest that, then said, "That'd be murder, Katie."

"Would it?"

"Still . . . You might be doin' the poor bastard a favor, at that."

"And make ourselves $10,000 richer."

". . . You ever do this before, Katie?"

She pressed a hand to her generous bare bosom. "No! No. But I never had a man I could trust before."

✗ ✗ ✗

Late the next morning, I met with Eliot in a back booth at Mickey's, a dimly lit hole-in-the-wall saloon a stone's throw from City Hall. He was having a late breakfast — a bloody Mary — and I had coffee.

"How'd you get away from Kathleen O'Meara?" he wondered. He looked businesslike in his usual three-piece suit; I was wearing a blue number from the Frank O'Meara Collection.

"She sleeps till noon. I told her daughter I was taking a walk."

"Long walk."

"The taxi'll be on my expense account. Eliot, I don't know how much more of this I can stand. She sent the forms in and paid the premiums on Harold Wilson, and she's talking murder all right, but if you want to catch her in the act, she's plannin' to wait at least a month before we give Harold a friendly push."

"That's a long time for you to stay undercover," Eliot admitted, stirring his bloody Mary with its celery stalk. "But it's in my budget."

I sighed. "I never knew being a city employee could be so exhausting."

"I take it you and Katie are friendly."

"She's a ride, all right. I've never been so disgusted with myself in my life."

"It's that distasteful?"

"Hell, no, I'm having a whale of time, so to speak. It's just shredding what little's left of my self-respect, and shabby little code of ethics, is all. Banging a big fat murdering bitch and liking it." I shuddered.

"This woman is an ogre, no question . . . and I'm not talking about her looks. Nate, if we can stop her, and expose what's she done, it'll pave the way for prosecuting the other women in the Natural Death, Inc., racket . . . or at the very least scaring them out of it."

✗ ✗ ✗

That evening Katie and I were walking up the hill. No streetlights in this part of town, and no moon to light the way; lights in the frame and brick houses we passed, and the headlights of cars heading toward the bridge, threw yellow light on the cracked sidewalk we trundled up, arm in arm, Katie and me. She wore a yellow peasant blouse, always pleased to show off her treasure chest, and a full green skirt.

"Any second thoughts, handsome?"

"Just one."

She stopped; we were near the rise of the hill and the lights of cars came up and over and fell like prison searchlights seeking us out. "Which is?"

"I'm willing to do a dirty deed for a tidy dollar, don't get me wrong, love. It's just . . . didn't your husband die this same way?"

"He did."

"Heavily insured and pushed in front of his oncoming destiny?"

There was no shame, no denial; if anything, her expression — chin high, eyes cool and hard — spoke pride. "He did. And I pushed him."

"Did you, now? That gives a new accomplice pause."

"I guess it would. But I told you he cheated me. He salted money away. And he was seeing other women. I won't put up with disloyalty in a man."

"Obviously not."

"I'm the most loyal steadfast woman in the world . . . 'less you cross me. Frank O'Meara's loss is your gain . . . if you have the stomach for the work that needs doing."

A truck came rumbling up over the rise, gears shifting into low gear, and for a detective, I'm ashamed to admit I didn't know we'd been shadowed; but we had. We'd been followed, or anticipated; to this day

I'm not sure whether she came from the bushes or behind us, whether fate had helped her or careful planning and knowledge of her mother's ways. Whatever the case, Maggie O'Meara came flying out of somewhere, hurling her skinny stick-like arms forward, shoving the much bigger woman into the path of the truck.

Katie had time to scream, and to look back at the wild-eyed smiling face of her daughter washed in the yellow headlights. The big rig's big tires rolled over her, her girth presenting no problem, bones popping like twigs, blood streaming like water.

The trucker was no hit-and-skip guy. He came to a squealing stop and hopped out and trotted back and looked at the squashed shapeless shape, yellow and green clothing stained crimson, limbs, legs, turned to pulp, head cracked like a melon, oozing.

I had a twinge of sorrow for Katie O'Meara, that beautiful horror, that horrible beauty; but it passed.

"She just jumped right out in front of me!" the trucker blurted. He was a small, wiry man with a mustache, and his eyes were wild.

I glanced at Maggie; she looked blankly back at me.

"I know," I said. "We saw it, her daughter and I . . . poor woman's been despondent."

✗ ✗ ✗

I told the uniform cops the same story about Katie, depressed over the loss of her dear husband, leaping in front of the truck. Before long, Eliot arrived himself, topcoat flapping in the breeze as he stepped from the sedan that bore his special EN-1 license plate.

"I'm afraid I added a statistic to your fatalities," I admitted.

"What's the real story?" he asked me, getting me to one side. "None of this suicide nonsense."

I told Eliot that Katie had been demonstrating to me how she wanted me to push Harold Wilson, lost her footing and stumbled to an ironic death. He didn't believe me, of course, and I think he figured that I'd pushed her myself.

He didn't mind, because I produced such a great witness for him. Maggie O'Meara had the goods on the Natural Death racket, knew the names of every woman in her mother's ring, and in May was the star of eighty witnesses in the Grand Jury inquiry. Harold Wilson and many other of the "unwitting pawns in the death-gambling insurance racket" (as reporter Clayton Fritchey put it) were among those witnesses. So were Dr. Alice Jeffers, investigator Gaspar Corso and me.

That night, the night of Katie O'Meara's "suicide," after the police were through with us, Maggie had wept at her kitchen table while I fixed coffee for her, though her tears were not for her mother or out of guilt, but for her murdered father. Maggie never seemed to put together that her dad had been an accomplice in the insurance scheme, or anyway never allowed herself to admit it.

Finally, she asked, "Are you . . . are you really going to cover for me?"

That was when I told her she was going to testify.

She came out of it, fine; she inherited a lot of money from her late mother — the various insurance companies did not contest previous pay-outs — and I understand she sold O'Meara's and moved on, with a considerable nest egg. I have no idea what became of her, after that.

Busting the Natural Death, Inc., racket was Eliot's last major triumph in Cleveland law enforcement. The following March, after a night of dining, dancing and drinking at the Vogue Room, Eliot and Ev Ness were in an automobile accident, Eliot sliding into another driver's car. With Ev minorly hurt, Eliot — after checking the other driver and finding him dazed but all right — rushed her to a hospital and became a hit-and-run driver. He made some efforts to cover up and, even when he finally fessed up in a press conference, claimed he'd not been intoxicated behind that wheel; his political enemies crucified him, and a month later Eliot resigned as Public Safety Director.

During the war, Eliot headed up the government's efforts to control venereal disease on military bases; but he never held a law enforcement position again. He and Ev divorced in 1945. He married a third time, in 1946, and ran, unsuccessfully for mayor of Cleveland in '47, spending the rest of his life trying, without luck, to make it in the world of business, often playing on his reputation as a famed gangbuster.

In May, 1957, Eliot Ness collapsed in his kitchen shortly after he had arrived home from the liquor store, where he had bought a bottle of Scotch.

He died with less than a thousand dollars to his name — I kicked in several hundred bucks on the funeral, wishing his wife had taken out some damn burial insurance on him.

SCREWBALL

Not long ago Miami Beach had been a sixteen-hundred-acre stretch of jungle sandbar thick with mangroves and scrub palmetto, inhabited by wild birds, mosquitoes and snakes. Less than thirty years later, the wilderness had given way to plush hotels, high-rent apartment houses and lavish homes, with manicured terraces and swimming pools, facing a beach littered brightly with cabanas and sun umbrellas.

That didn't mean the place wasn't still infested with snakes, birds and bugs — just that it was now the human variety.

It was May 22, 1941, and dead; winter season was mid-December through April, and the summer's onslaught of tourists was a few weeks away. At the moment, the majority of restaurants and nightclubs in Miami Beach were shuttered, and the handful of the latter still doing business were the ones with gaming rooms. Even in off-season, gambling made it pay for a club to keep its doors open.

The glitzy showroom of Chez Clifton had been patterned on (though was about a third the size of) the Chez Paree back home in Chicago, with a similarly set up backroom gambling casino called (in both instances) the Gold Key Club. But where the Chez Paree was home to bigname stars and orchestras — Edgar Bergen and Charlie McCarthy, Ted Lewis, Martha Raye — the Chez Clifton's headliner was invariably its namesake: Pete Clifton.

A near ringer for Zeppo, the "normal" Marx Brother, Clifton was tall, dark and horsily handsome, his slicked-back, parted-at-the side hair as black as his tie and tux. He was at the microphone, leaning on it like a jokester Sinatra, the orchestra behind him, accompanying him occasionally on song parodies, the drummer providing the requisite rimshots, the boys laughing heartily at gags they'd heard over and over, prompting the audience.

Not that the audience needed help: the crowd thought Clifton was a scream. And, for a Thursday night, it was a good crowd, too.

"Hear about the guy that bought his wife a bicycle?" he asked innocently. "Now she's peddling it all over town."

They howled at that.

"Hear about the sleepy bride? . . . She couldn't stay away awake for a second."

Laughter all around me, I was settled in at a table for two — by myself — listening to one dirty joke after another. Clifton had always worked blue, back when I knew him; he'd been the opening act at the Colony Club showroom on Rush Street — a mob joint fronted by Nicky Dean, a crony of Al Capone's successor, Frank Nitti.

But tonight, every gag was filthy.

"Hear about the girl whose boyfriend didn't have any furniture? She was floored."

People were crying at this rapier wit. But not everybody liked it. The guy Clifton was fronting for, in particular.

"Nate," Frank Nitti had said to me earlier that afternoon, "I need you to deliver a message to your old pal Pete Clifton."

In the blue shade of an umbrella at a small white metal table, buttery sun reflecting off the shimmer of cool blue water, Nitti and I were sitting by the pool at Nitti's Di Lido Island estate, his palatial digs looming around us, rambling white stucco buildings with green-tile roofs behind bougainvillea-covered walls.

Eyes a mystery behind sunglasses, Nitti wore a blue-and-red Hawaiian print shirt, white slacks and sandals, a surprisingly small figure, his handsome oval face flecked with occasional scars, his slicked back black hair touched with gray and immaculately trimmed. I was the one who looked like a gangster, in my brown suit and darker brown fedora, having just arrived from Chicago, Nitti's driver having picked me up at the railroad station.

"I wouldn't call Clifton an 'old pal,' Mr. Nitti."

"How many times I gotta tell ya, call me 'Frank'? After what we been through together?"

I didn't like the thought of having been through anything "together" with Frank Nitti. But the truth was, fate and circumstance had on several key occasions brought Chicago's most powerful gangster leader into the path of a certain lowly Loop private detective — though, I wasn't as lowly as I used to be. The A-1 Agency had a suite of offices now, and I had two experienced ops and a pretty blonde secretary under me — or anyway, the ops were under me; the secretary wasn't interested.

But when Frank Nitti asked the President of the A-1 to hop a train to Miami Beach and come visit, Nathan Heller hopped and visited — the blow softened by the three hundred dollar retainer check Nitti's man Louis Campagna had delivered to my Van Buren Street office.

"I understand you two boys used to go out with showgirls and strippers, time to time," Nitti said, lighting up a Cuban cigar smaller than a billy club.

"Clifton was a cocky, good-looking guy, and the toast of Rush Street. The girls liked him. I liked the spillover."

Nitti nodded, waving out his match. "He's still a good-looking guy. And he's still cocky. Ever wonder how he managed to open up his own club?"

"Never bothered wondering. But I guess it is a little unusual."

"Yeah. He ain't famous. He ain't on the radio."

"Not with *that* material."

Nitti blew a smoke ring; an eyebrow arched. "Oh, you remember that? How blue he works."

I shrugged. "It was kind of a gimmick, Frank — clean-cut kid, looks like a matinee idol. Kind of a funny, startling contrast with his off-color material."

"Well, that's what I want you to talk to him about."

"Afraid I don't follow, Frank . . ."

"He's workin' too blue. Too goddamn fuckin' filthy."

I winced. Part of it was the sun reflecting off the surface of the pool; most of it was confusion. Why the hell did Frank Nitti give a damn if some two-bit comic was telling dirty jokes?

"That foulmouth is attracting the wrong kind of attention," Nitti was saying. "The blue noses are gettin' up in arms. Ministers are givin' sermons, columnists are frownin' in print. There's this 'Citizens Committee for Clean Entertainment.' Puttin' political pressure on. Jesus Christ! The place'll get raided — shut down."

I hadn't been to Chez Clifton yet, though I assumed it was running gambling, wide-open, and was already on the cops' no-raid list. But if anti-smut reformers made an issue out of Clifton's immoral monologues, the boys in blue would *have* to raid the joint — and the gambling baby would go out the window with the dirty bathwater.

"What's your interest in this, Frank?"

Nitti's smile was mostly a sneer. "Clifton's got a club 'cause he's got a silent partner."

"You mean . . . *you*, Frank? I thought the Outfit kept out of the Florida rackets . . ."

It was understood that Nitti, Capone and other Chicago mobsters with homes in Miami Beach would not infringe on the hometown gambling syndicate. This was said to be part of the agreement with local politicos to allow the Chicago Outfit to make Miami Beach their home away from home.

"That's why I called you down here, Nate. I need somebody to talk to the kid who won't attract no attention. Who ain't directly connected to me. You're just an old friend of Clifton's from outa town."

"And what do you want me to do, exactly?"

"Tell him to clean up his fuckin' act."

✗ ✗ ✗

So now I was in the audience, sipping my rum and Coke, the walls ringing with laughter, as Pete Clifton made such deft witticisms as the following: "Hear about the doll who found a tramp under her bed? She got so upset, her stomach was on the bum all night."

Finally, to much applause, Clifton turned the entertainment over to the orchestra, and couples filled the dancefloor to the strains of "Nice Work if You Can Get It." Soon the comic had filtered his way through the admiring crowd to join me at my table.

"You look good, you rat bastard," Clifton said, flashing his boyish smile, extending his hand, which I took and shook. "Getting any since I left Chicago?"

"I wet the wick on occasion," I said, sitting as he settled in across from me. All around us patrons were sneaking peeks at the star performer who had deigned to come down among them.

"I didn't figure you'd ever get laid again, once I moved on," he said, straightening his black tie. "How long you down here for?"

"Couple days."

He snapped his fingers, pointed at me and winked. "Tell you what, you're goin' boating with me tomorrow afternoon. These two cute skirts down the street from where I live, they're both hot for me — you can take one of 'em offa my hands."

Smiling, shaking my head, I said, "I thought maybe you'd have found a new hobby, by now, Pete."

"Not me." He fired up a Lucky Strike, sucked in smoke, exhaled it like dragon breath from his nostrils. "I never found a sweeter pastime than doin' the dirty deed."

"Doing dames ain't the only dirty deed you been doing lately, Pete."

"Whaddya mean?"

"Your act." I gestured with my rum-and-Coke. "I've seen cleaner material on outhouse walls."

He grinned toothily. "You offended? Getting prudish in your old age, Heller? Yeah, I've upped the ante, some. Look at this crowd, weeknight, off season. They love it. See, it's my magic formula: everybody loves sex; and everybody loves a good dirty joke."

"Not everybody."

The grin eased off and his forehead tightened. "Wait a minute . . . This isn't a social call, is it?"

"No. It's nice seeing you again, Pete . . . but no. You think you know who sent me — and you're right. And he wants you to back off the smut."

"You kidding?" Clifton smirked and waved dismissively. "I found a way to mint money, here. And it's making me a star."

"You think you can do that material on the radio, or in the movies? Get serious."

"Hey, everybody needs an angle, a trademark, and I found mine."

"Pete, I'm not here to discuss it. Just to pass the word along. You can ignore it if you like." I sipped my drink, shrugged. "Take your dick out and conduct the orchestra with it, far as I'm concerned."

Clifton leaned across the table. "Nate, you heard those laughs. You see the way every dame in this audience is lookin' at me? There isn't a quiff in this room that wouldn't get on her back for me, or down on her damn knees."

"Like I said, ignore it if you like. But my guess is, if you do keep working blue — and the Chez Clifton gets shut down — your silent partner'll get noisy."

The comic thought about that, drawing nervously on the Lucky. In his tux, he looked like he fell off a wedding cake. Then he said, "What would you do, Nate?"

"Get some new material. Keep some of the risque stuff, sure — but don't be so Johnny One-note."

Some of the cockiness had drained out of him; frustration colored his voice, even self-pity. "It's what I do, Nate. Why not tell Joe E. Lewis not to do drunk jokes. Why not tell Eddie Cantor not to pop his eyes out?"

"'Cause somebody'll pop *your* eyes out, Pete. I say this as a friend, and as somebody who knows how certain parties operate. Back off."

He sighed, sat back. I didn't say anything. The orchestra was playing "I'll Never Smile Again," now.

"Tell Nitti I'll . . . tone it down."

I saluted him with my nearly empty rum-and-Coke glass. "Good choice."

And that was it. I had delivered my message. He had another show to do, and I didn't see him again till the next afternoon, when — as promised — he took me out on his speedboat, a sleek mahogany nineteen-foot Gar Wood runabout whose tail was emblazoned *Screwball*.

And, as promised, we were in the company of two "cute skirts," although that's not what they were wearing. Peggy Simmons, a slender pretty pugnose blonde, and Janet Windom, a cow-eyed bosomy brunette, were in white shorts that showed off their nice, nicely tanned legs. Janet, who Pete had claimed, wore a candy-striped top; Peggy, who had deposited herself next to me on the leather seat, wore a pink longsleeve angora sweater.

"Aren't you warm in that?" I asked her, sipping a bottle of Pabst. I was in a shortsleeve sportshirt and chinos, my straw fedora at my feet, away from the wind.

"Not really. I get chilled in the spray." She had a high-pitched voice that seemed younger than her twenty-two years, though the lines around her sky-blue eyes made her seem older. Peggy laughed and smiled a lot, but those eyes were sad, somehow.

I had been introduced to Peggy as a theatrical agent from Chicago. She was a model and dancer, and apparently Clifton figured this lie would help me get laid; this irritated me — being burdened with a fiction of someone else's creation, and the notion I needed help in that regard. But I hadn't corrected it.

Janet, it seemed, was also interested in show business; a former dentist's assistant, she was a couple years older than Peggy. They had roomed together in New York City and came down here a few months ago, seeking sun and fame and fortune.

The afternoon was pleasant enough. Clifton sat at the wheel with Janet cuddling next to him, and Peggy and I sat in the seat behind them. She was friendly, holding my hand, putting her head on my shoulder, though we barely knew each other. We drank in the sun-drenched, invigorating gulf-stream air, as well as our bottled beers, and enjoyed the view — royal palms waving, white-capped breakers peaking, golden sands glistening with sunlight.

The runabout had been bounding along, which — with the engine noise — had limited conversation. But pretty soon Clifton charted us up and down Indian Creek, a tranquil, seawalled lagoon lined with palm-fringed shores and occasional well-manicured golf courses, as well as frequent private piers and landing docks studded with gleaming yachts and lavish houseboats.

"Have you found any work down here?" I asked the fresh-faced, sad-eyed girl.

She nodded. "Some cheesecake modeling Pete lined up. Swimsuits and, you know . . . art studies."

Nudes.

"What are you hoping for?"

"Well, I am a good dancer, and I sing a little, too. Pete says he's going to do a big elaborate show, soon, with a chorus line and everything."

"And he's going to use both you and Janet?"

She nodded.

"Any thoughts beyond that, Peggy? You've got nice legs, but show business is a rough career."

Her chin crinkled as she smiled, but desperation tightened her eyes. "I'd be willing to take a Chicago booking."

Though we weren't gliding as quickly over the water now, the engine noise was still enough to keep my conversation with Peggy private while Pete and Janet laughed and kissed and chugged their beers.

"I'm not a booking agent, Peggy."

She drew away just a little. "No?"

"Pete was . . . I don't know what he was doing."

She shrugged again, smirked. "Pete's a goddamn liar, sometimes."

"I know some people who book acts in Chicago, and would be glad to put a word in . . . but don't be friendly with me on account of that."

She studied me and her eyes didn't seem as sad, or as old, suddenly. "What do you know? The vanishing American."

"What?"

"A nice guy."

And she cuddled next to me, put a hand on my leg.

Without looking at me, she asked, "Why do *you* think I came to Florida, Nate?"

"It's warm and sunny."

"Yes."

"And . . ." I nodded toward either side of us, where the waterway entrances of lavish estates, trellised with bougainvillea and allamanda, seemed to beckon. ". . . there's more money here than you can shake a stick at."

She laughed. "Yes."

By four o'clock we were at the girls' place, in a six-apartment building on Jefferson Street, a white-trimmed-pink geometric affair among many other such streamlined structures of sunny yellow, flamingo pink and sea green, with porthole windows and racing stripes and *bas relief* zig-zags. The effect was at once elegant and insubstantial, like a movie set. Their one-bedroom apartment was on the second of two floors; the furnishings had an *art moderne* look, too, though of the low-cost Sears showroom variety.

Janet fixed us drinks and we sat in the little pink and white living room area and made meaningless conversation for maybe five minutes. Then Clifton and Janet disappeared into that one bedroom, and Peggy and I necked on the couch. The lights were low, when I got her sweater and bra off her, but I noticed the needle tracks on her arms, just the same.

"What's wrong?" she asked.

"Nothing . . . What are you on? H?"

"What do you mean? . . . Not H."

"What?"

"M."

Morphine.

She folded her arms over her bare breasts, but it was her arms she was hiding.

"I was blue," she said, defensively, shivering suddenly. "I needed something."

"Where'd you get it?"

"Pete has friends."

Pete had friends, all right. And I was one of them.

"Put your sweater on, baby."

"Why? Do I . . . do I make you sick?"

And she began to cry.

So I made love to her there on the couch, sweetly, tenderly, comforting her, telling her she was beautiful, which she was. She needed the attention, and I didn't mind giving it to her, though I was steaming at that louse Clifton.

Our clothes relatively straightened, Peggy having freshened in the bathroom, we were sitting, chatting, having Cokes on ice like kids on a date, when Clifton — in the pale yellow sportshirt and powder-blue slacks he'd gone boating in — emerged from the bedroom, arm around Janet, who was in a terrycloth robe.

"We better blow, Nate," he told me with a grin, and nuzzled the giggling Janet's neck. She seemed to be on something, too. "I got a nine o'clock show to do."

It was a little after seven.

We made our goodbyes and drove the couple of blocks in his white Lincoln Zephyr convertible.

"Do I take care of you," he asked with a grin, as the shadows of the palms lining the streets rolled over us, "or do I take care of you?"

"You're a pal," I said.

We were slipping past more of those movie theater-like apartment houses, pastel chunks of concrete whose geometric harshness was softened by well-barbered shrubs. The three-story building on West Jefferson, in front of which Clifton drew his Lincoln, was set back a ways, a walk cutting through a golf green of a lawn to the pale yellow cube whose blue cantilevered sunshades were like eyebrows.

Clifton's apartment was on the third floor, a two bedroom affair with pale yellow walls and a parquet floor flung with occasional oriental carpets. The furnishings were in the *art moderne* manner, chrome and leather and well-varnished light woods, none of it from Sears.

I sat in a pastel green easy chair whose lines were rounded; it was as comfortable as an old shoe but considerably more stylish.

"How do those unemployed showgirls afford a place like that?" I wondered aloud.

Clifton, who was making us a couple of rum-and-Cokes over at the wet bar, said, "Did you have a good time?"

"I like Peggy. If I lived around here, I'd try to straighten her out."

"Oh yeah! Saint Heller. I thought you did straighten her out — on that couch."

"Are you pimping for those girls?"

"No!" He came over with a drink in either hand. "They're not pros."

"But you fix them up with friends and other people you want to impress."

He shrugged, handing me the drink. "Yeah. So what? Party girls like that are a dime a dozen."

"Where are you getting the dope?"

That stopped him for a moment, but just a moment. "It makes 'em feel good; what's the harm?"

"You got 'em hooked and whoring for you, Pete. You're one classy guy."

Clifton smirked. "I didn't see you turning down the free lay."

"You banging 'em both?"

"Never at the same time. What, you think I'm a pervert?"

"No. I think you're a prick."

He just laughed at that. "Listen, I got to take a shower. You coming down to the club tonight, or not?"

"I'll come. But Pete — where are you getting the dope you're giving those girls?"

"Why do you care?"

"Because I don't think Frank Nitti would like it. He doesn't do business with people in that racket. If he knew you were involved . . ."

Clifton frowned. "You going to tell him?"

"I didn't say that."

"Maybe I don't give a shit if you do. Maybe I got a possible new investor for my club, and Frank Nitti can kiss my ass."

"Would you like me to pass that along?"

A grimace drained all the boyishness from his face. "What's wrong with you, Heller? Since when did you get moral? These gangsters are like women — they exist to be used."

"Only the gangsters don't discard as easily."

"I ain't worried." He jerked a thumb at his chest. "See, Heller, I'm a public figure — they don't bump off public figures; it's bad publicity."

"Tell Mayor Cermak — he got hit in Florida."

He blew me a Bronx cheer. "I'm gonna take a shower. You want a free meal down at the club, stick around . . . but leave the sermons to Billy Sunday, okay?"

"Yeah. Sure."

I could hear him showering, singing in there, "All or Nothing at All." Had we really been friends, once? I had a reputation as something of a randy son of a bitch myself; but did I treat woman like Clifton did? The thought make me shudder.

On the oblong glass coffee table before me, a white phone began to ring. I answered it.

"Pete?" The voice was low-pitched, but female — a distinctive, throaty sound.

"No, it's a friend. He's in the shower, getting ready for his show tonight."

"Tell him to meet me out front in five minutes."

"Well, let me check with him and see if that's possible. Who should I say is calling?"

There was a long pause.

Then the throaty purr returned: "Just tell him the wife of a friend."

"Sure," I said, and went into the bathroom and reported this, over the shower needles, through the glass door, to Clifton, who said, "Tell her I'll be right down."

Within five minutes, Clifton — his hair still wet — moved quickly through the living room; he had thrown on the boating clothes from this afternoon.

"This won't take long." He flashed the boyish grin. "These frails can't get enough of me."

"You want me to leave?"

"Naw. I'll set somethin' up with her for later. I don't think she has a friend, though — sorry, pal."

"That's okay. I try to limit myself to one doped-up doxie a day."

Clifton smirked and waved at me dismissively as he headed out, and I sat there for maybe a minute, then decided I'd had it. I plucked my straw fedora off the coffee table and trailed out after him, hoping to catch up with him and make my goodbyes.

The night sky was cobalt and alive with stars, a sickle-slice of moon providing the appropriate deco touch. The sidewalk stretched out before me like a white ribbon, toward where palms mingled with street lights. A Buick was along the curb and Pete was leaning against the window, like a car hop taking an order.

That sultry, low female voice rumbled through the night like pretty thunder: *"For God's sake, Pete, don't do it! Please don't do it!"*

As Pete's response — laughter — filled my ears, I stopped in my tracks, not wanting to intrude. Then Pete, still chuckling, making a dismissive wave, turned toward me, and walked. He was giving me a cocky smile when the first gunshot cracked the night.

I dove and rolled and wound up against a sculpted hedge that separated Clifton's apartment house from the hunk of geometry next door. Two more shots rang out, and I could see the orange muzzle flash as the woman shot through the open car window.

For a comic, Pete was doing a hell of a dance; the first shot had caught him over the right armpit, and another plowed through his neck in a spray of red, and he twisted around to face her to accommodate another slug.

Then the car roared off, and Pete staggered off the sidewalk and pitched forward onto the grass, like a diver who missed the pool.

I ran to his sprawled figure, and turned him over. His eyes were wild with dying.

"Them fuckin' dames ain't . . . ain't so easy to discard, neither," he said, and laughed, a bloody froth of a laugh, to punctuate his last dirty joke.

People were rushing up, talking frantically, shouting about the need for the police to be called and such like. Me, I was noting where the woman had put her last shot.

She caught him right below the belt.

✗ ✗ ✗

After a long wait in a receiving area, I was questioned by the cops in an interview room at the Dade County Courthouse in Miami. Actually, one of them, Earl Carstensen — Chief of Detectives of the Miami Beach Detective Bureau — was a cop; the other guy — Ray Miller — was chief investigator for the State Attorney's office.

Carstensen was a craggy guy in his fifties and Miller was a skinny balding guy with wirerim glasses. The place was air-conditioned and they brought me an iced tea, so it wasn't exactly the third degree.

We were all seated at the small table in the soundproofed cubicle. After they had established that I was a friend of the late Pete Clifton, visiting from Chicago, the line of questioning took an interesting turn.

Carstensen asked, "Are you aware that 'Peter Clifton' was not the deceased's real name?"

"I figured it was a stage name, but it's the only name I knew him by."

"He was born Peter Tessitorio," Miller said, "in New York. He had a criminal background — two burglary raps."

"I never knew that."

Carstensen asked, "You're a former police officer?"

"Yeah. I was a detective on the Chicago P.D. pickpocket detail till '32."

Miller asked, "You spent the afternoon with Clifton, in the company of two girls?"

"Yeah."

"What are their names?"

"Peggy Simmons and Janet Windom. They live in an apartment house on Jefferson . . . I don't know the address, but I can point you, if you want to talk to them."

The two men exchanged glances.

"We've already picked them up," Miller said. "They've been questioned, and they're alibiing each other. They say they don't know anybody who'd want to kill Clifton."

"They're just a couple of party girls," I said.

Carstensen said, "We found a hypo and bottle of morphine in their apartment. Would you know anything about that?"

I sighed. "I noticed the tracks on the Simmons' kid's arms. I gave Pete hell, and he admitted to me he was giving them the stuff. He also indicated he had connections with some dope racketeer."

"He didn't give you a name?" Miller asked.

"No."

"You've never heard of Leo Massey?"

"No."

"Friend of Clifton's. A known dope smuggler."

I sipped my iced tea. "Well, other than those two girls, I don't really know any of Clifton's associates here in Miami."

An eyebrow arched in Carstensen's craggy puss. "You'd have trouble meeting Massey — he's dead."

"Oh?"

"He was found in Card Sound last September. Bloated and smellin' to high heavens."

"What does that have to do with Pete Clifton?"

Miller said, "Few days before Massey's body turned up, that speedboat of his — the *Screwball* — got taken out for a spin."

I shrugged. "That's what a speedboat's for, taking it out for a spin."

"At midnight? And not returning till daybreak?"

"You've got witness to that effect?"

Miller nodded.

"So Pete was a suspect in Massey's murder?"

"Not exactly," the State Attorney's investigator said. "Clifton had an alibi — those two girls say he spent the night with 'em."

I frowned in confusion. "I thought you had a witness to Clifton takin' his boat out . . ."

Carstensen said, "We have a witness at the marina to the effect that the boat was taken out, and brought back — but nobody saw who the captain was."

Now I was getting it. "And Pete said somebody must've borrowed his boat without his permission."

"That's right."

"So, what? You're making this as a gangland hit? But it was a woman who shot him."

Miller asked, "Did you see that, Mr. Heller?"

"I heard the woman's voice — I didn't actually see her shoot him. Didn't actually see her at all. But it seemed like she was agitated with Pete."

Other witnesses had heard the woman yelling at Pete; so the cops knew I hadn't made up this story.

"Could the woman have been a decoy?" Carstensen asked. "Drawn

Clifton to that car for some man to shoot?"

"I suppose. But my instinct is, Pete's peter got him bumped. If I were you, fellas, I'd go over that apartment of his and look for love letters and the like; see if you can find a little black book. My guess is — somebody he was banging banged him back."

They thanked me for my help, told me to stick around for the inquest on Tuesday, and turned me loose. I got in my rental Ford and drove to the Biltmore, went up to my room, ordered a room service supper, and gave Frank Nitti a call.

"So my name didn't come up?" Nitti asked me over the phone.

"No. Obviously, I didn't tell 'em you hired me to come down here; but they didn't mention you, either. And the way they were giving out information, it would've come up. They got a funny way of interrogating you in Florida — they spill and you listen."

"Did they mention a guy named McGraw?"

"No, Frank. Just this Leo Massey."

"McGraw's a rival dope smuggler," Nitti said thoughtfully. "I understand he stepped in and took over Massey's trade after Massey turned up a floater."

"What's that got to do with Clifton?"

"Nothin' much — just that my people tell me McGraw's a regular at the Chez Clifton. Kinda chummy with our comical late friend."

"Maybe McGraw's the potential investor Clifton was talking about — to take your place, Frank."

Silence. Nitti was thinking.

Finally, he returned with, "Got another job for you, Nate."

"I don't know, Frank — I probably oughta keep my nose clean, do my bit at the inquest and scram outa this flamingo trap."

"Another three C's in it for you, kid — just to deliver another message. No rush — tomorrow morning'll be fine."

Did you hear the one about the comic who thought he told killer jokes? He died laughing.

"Anything you say, Frank."

✗ ✗ ✗

Eddie McGraw lived at the Delano, on Collins Avenue, the middle of a trio of towering hotels rising above Miami Beach like Mayan temples got out of hand. McGraw had a penthouse on the eleventh floor, and I had to bribe the elevator attendant to take me there.

It was eleven a.m. I wasn't expecting trouble. My nine millimeter Browning was back in Chicago, in a desk drawer in my office. But I wasn't unarmed — I had the name *Frank Nitti* in my arsenal.

I knocked on the door.

The woman who answered was in her late twenties — a brunette with big brown eyes and rather exaggerated features, pretty in a cartoonish way. She had a voluptuous figure, wrapped up like a present in a pink chiffon dressing gown.

"Excuse me, ma'am. Is Mr. McGraw home?"

She nodded. The big brown eyes locked onto me coldly, though her voice was a warm contralto: "Who should I say is calling?"

"I'm a friend of Pete Clifton's."

"Would you mind waiting in the hall?"

"Not at all."

She shut the door, and a few seconds later, it flew back open, revealing a short but sturdy looking guy in a red sportshirt and gray slacks. He was blond with wild thatches of overgrown eyebrow above sky-blue eyes; when you got past a bulbous nose, he kind of looked like James Cagney.

"I don't do business at my apartment," he said. His voice was high-pitched and raspy. He started to shut the door and I stopped it with my hand.

He shoved me, and I went backward, but I latched onto his wrist, and pushed his hand back, and pulled him forward, out into the hall, until he was kneeling in front of me.

"Frank Nitti sent me," I said, and released the pressure on his wrist.

He stood, ran a hand through slicked back blond hair that didn't need straightening, and said, "I don't do business with Nitti."

"I think maybe you should. You know about Pete's killing?"

"I saw the morning paper. I liked Pete. He was funny. He was an all right guy."

"Yeah, he was a card. Did he by any chance sell you an interest in the Chez Clifton?"

McGraw frowned at me; if he'd been a dog, he'd have growled. "I told you . . . what's your name, anyway?"

"Heller. Nate Heller."

"I don't do business at my apartment. My wife and me, we got a life separate from how I make my living. Got it?"

"Did Pete sell you an interest in the Chez Clifton?"

He straightened his collar, which also didn't need it. "As a matter of fact, he did."

"Then you were wrong about not doing business with Frank Nitti."

McGraw sneered. "What's that supposed to mean?"

"Mr. Nitti would like to discuss that with you himself." I handed him a slip of paper. "He's in town, at his estate on Di Lido Island. He'd like to invite you to join him there for lunch today."

"Why should I?"

I laughed once, a hollow thing. "Mr. McGraw, I don't care what you do, as long as you don't put your hands on me again. I'm just delivering a message. But I will tell you this — I'm from Chicago, and when Frank Nitti invites you for lunch, you go."

McGraw thought about that. Then he nodded and said, "Sorry about the rough stuff."

"I apologize for bothering you at home. But you don't keep an office, and you're unlisted."

"Yeah, well, nature of my business."

"Understood."

I held out my hand. He studied it for a moment, then shook it.

"Why don't you give Mr. Nitti a call, at that number, and confirm your luncheon engagement."

He nodded and disappeared inside the apartment.

Half an hour later, I knocked on the door again. Returning had cost me another fin to the elevator boy.

Mrs. McGraw, still in her pink chiffon robe, opened the door and said, "I'm afraid my husband has stepped out."

"I know he has," I said, brushing past her into the apartment, beautifully appointed in the usual Miami-tropical manner.

"Leave at once!" she demanded, pointing past the open door into the hall.

"No," I said, and shut the door. "I recognized your voice, Mrs. McGraw. It's very distinctive. I like it."

"What are you talking about?" But her wide eyes and the tremor in her tone told me she was afraid she already knew.

I told her, anyway. "I'm the guy who answered the phone last night, at Pete's. That's when I first heard that throaty purr of yours. I also heard you warn him — right before he turned his back on you and you shot him."

She was clutching herself, as if she were cold. "I don't know what you're talking about. Please leave!"

"I'm not going to stay long. Turn around."

"What?"

"Turn around and put your hands on that door."

"Why?"

"I'm gonna frisk you, lady. I don't figure you have a gun hidden away on you, but I'd like to make sure."

"No!"

So I took her by the wrist, sort of like I had her husband, and twisted her arm around her back and shoved her against the door. I frisked her all over. She was a little plump, but it was one of the nicer frisks I ever gave.

No gun — several concealed weapons, but no gun.

She stood facing me now, her back to the door, trembling. "Are you . . . are you a cop?"

"I'm just a friend of Pete's."

She raised a hand to her face, fingers curling there, like the petals of a wilting flower. "Are you here to turn me in?"

"We'll see."

Now she looked at me in a different way, something flaring in her dark eyes. "Oh. You're here to . . . deal."

"Maybe. Can we sit down over there?" I gestured to the living room — white walls, white carpet, glass tables, white chairs and couch, a white fireplace with a big mirror with flamingos etched in it.

I took an easy chair across from the couch, where she sat, arms folded, legs crossed — nice legs, muscular, supple, tan against the pink chiffon. She seemed to be studying me, trying to get a bead on me.

"I'd like to hear your side of it."

Her chin titled. "You really think you can make a positive identification, based just on my voice?"

"Ask Bruno Hauptmann. He went to the chair on less."

She laughed but it wasn't very convincing. "You didn't see me."

"Do you have an alibi? Is your husband in on it?"

"No! Of course not."

"Your side of it. Let's have it."

She looked at the floor. "Your . . . friend . . . was a terrible man."

"I noticed."

That surprised her. Looking right at me, she asked, "You did?"

"Pete used women like playthings. They weren't people to him. Is that what he did to you?"

She nodded; her full mouth was quivering — if this was an act, it was a good one.

Almost embarrassed, she said, "I thought he was charming. He was good-looking, clever and . . . sexy, I guess."

"You've been having an affair with him."

One nod.

Well, that didn't surprise me. Just because McGraw was his business partner, and a hood at that, wouldn't stop Pete Clifton from going after a good-looking doll like Mrs. McGraw.

"Can I smoke?" she asked. She indicated her purse on the coffee table. I checked inside it, found no gun, plucked out the pack of Luckies — Pete's brand — and tossed it to her. Also her lighter.

"Thanks," she said, firing up. "It was just . . . a fling. Stupid god-damn fling. Eddie was neglecting me, and . . . it's an old story. Anyway, I wanted to stop it, but . . . Pete wanted more. Not because . . . he loved me or anything. Just because . . . do you know what he said to me?"

"I can imagine."

"He said, 'Baby, you're one sweet piece of ass. You don't have to like me to satisfy me.' "

I frowned at her. "I don't know if I'm following this. If you wanted to break it off, how could he —"

"He blackmailed me."

"With what? He couldn't tell your husband about the affair without getting himself in a jam."

She heaved a sigh. "No . . . but Pete coulda turned my husband in for . . . for something he had on him."

And now I knew.

Clifton had loaned McGraw the *Screwball* for disposal of the body of Leo Massey, the rival dope smuggler, which put Clifton in a position to finger McGraw.

"Okay," I said, and stood.

She gazed up at me, astounded. "What do you mean . . . 'okay'?"

"Okay, I understand why you killed him."

I walked to the door, and she followed, the sound of her slippers whispering through the thick carpet.

She stopped me at the door, a hand on my arm; she was very close to me, and smelled good, like lilacs. Those brown eyes were big enough to dive into.

Her throaty purr tickled the air between us. "You're not going to turn me in?"

"Why should I? I just wanted to know if there were any ramifications for my client or me, in this thing, and I don't see any."

"I thought Pete was your friend."

"Hell, he was your lover, and look what you thought of him."

Her eyes tightened. "What do you want from me?"

"Nothing. You had a good reason to do it. I heard you warn him."

"You're very kind . . ." She squeezed my arm, moved closer, to where her breasts were pressed gently against me. "My husband won't be home for a while . . . we could go to my bedroom and —"

I drew away. "Jesus, lady! Isn't screwin' around what got you into trouble in the first place?"

And I got the hell out of there.

✗ ✗ ✗

I said just enough at the inquest to get it over with quick, and was back in Chicago by Wednesday night.

I don't know whether Frank Nitti and Eddie McGraw wound up doing business together. I do know the Chez Clifton closed down and re-opened under another name, the Beach Club. But Nitti put his Di Lido Island estate up for sale and sold it, shortly after that. So maybe he just got out while the getting was good.

Mrs. McGraw — whose first name I never knew — was never charged with Pete Clifton's murder, which remains unsolved on the Miami Beach P.D.'s books. The investigation into the Clifton killing, however, did lead the State Attorney's Office to nailing McGraw on the Massey slaying; McGraw got ninety-nine years, which is a little much, considering all he did was kill another dope smuggler. The two party girls, Peggy and Janet, were charged with harboring narcotics, which was dropped in exchange for their cooperation in the McGraw/Massey inquiry.

Pete Clifton really was a prick, but I always thought of him, over the ensuing years, when so many dirty-mouthed comics — from Lenny Bruce to George Carlin — made it big.

Maybe Clifton got the last laugh, after all.

SHOOT-OUT ON SUNSET

The Sunset Strip — the center of Hollywood's nightlife — lay near the heart of Los Angeles, or would have if L.A. had a heart. I'm not waxing poetic, either: postwar L.A. (circa late summer 1949) sprawled over some 452 square miles, but isolated strips of land within the city limits were nonetheless not part of the city. Sunset Boulevard itself ran from downtown to the ocean, around twenty-five miles; west on Sunset, toward Beverly Hills — roughly a mile and a half, from Crescent Heights Boulevard to Doheny Drive — the Strip threaded through an unincorporated area surrounded by (but not officially part of) the City of Angels.

Prime nightspots like the Trocadero, Ciro's, the Mocambo, and the Crescendo shared the glittering Strip with smaller, hipper clubs and hideaway restaurants like Slapsy Maxie's, the Little New Yorker and the Band Box. Seediness and glamour intermingled, grit met glitz, as screen legends, power brokers and gangsters converged in West Hollywood for a free-spirited, no-holds-barred good time.

The L.A. police couldn't even make an arrest on the Strip, which was under the jurisdiction of County Sheriff Eugene Biscailuz, who cheerfully ignored both the city's cops and its ordinances. Not that the L.A. coppers would have made any more arrests than the sheriff's deputies: the Vice Squad was well-known to operate chiefly as a shakedown racket. A mighty bookmaking operation was centered on the Sunset Strip, and juice was paid to both the county sheriff and the city vice squad. This seemed unfair to Mickey Cohen.

The diminutive, dapper, vaguely simian Cohen was a former Ben "Bugsy" Siegel associate who had built his bookie empire on the bodies of his competitors. Rivals with such colorful names as Maxie Shaman, Benny "the Meatball" Gambino, and Tony Trombino were just a few of the violently deceased gangsters who had unwillingly made way for Mickey; and the Godfather of Southern California — Jack Dragna — could only grin and bear it and put up with Cohen's bloody empire building. Cohen had the blessing of the east coast Combination —

Luciano, Meyer Lanksy, the late Siegel's crowd — and oldtime Prohibition-era mob boss Dragna didn't like it. A West Coast mob war had been brewing for years.

I knew Cohen from Chicago, where in the late thirties he was strictly a smalltime gambler and general-purpose hoodlum. Our paths had crossed several times since — never in a nasty way — and I rather liked the street-smart, stupid-looking Mick. He was nothing if not colorful: owned dozens of suits, wore monogrammed silk shirts and made-to-order shoes, drove a $15,000 custom-built blue Caddy, lived with his pretty little wife in a $150,000 home in classy Brentwood, and suffered a cleanliness fetish that had him washing his hands more than Lady MacBeth.

A fixture of the Sunset Strip, Mick strutted through clubs spreading dough around like advertising leaflets. One of his primary hangouts was Sherry's, a cocktail lounge slash restaurant, a favorite film-colony rendezvous whose nondescript brick exterior was offset by an ornate interior.

My business partner Fred Rubinski was co-owner of Sherry's. Fireplug Fred — who resembled a slightly better-looking Edward G. Robinson — was an ex-Chicago cop who had moved out here before the war to open a detective agency. We'd known each other in Chicago, both veterans of the pickpocket detail, and I too had left the Windy City PD to go private, only I hadn't gone west, young man.

At least, not until after the war. The A-1 Detective Agency — of which I, Nathan Heller, was president — had (over the course of a decade-and-change) grown from a one-man hole-in-the-wall affair over a deli on Van Buren to a suite of offices in the Monadnock Building rife with operatives, secretaries and clients. Expansion seemed the thing, and I convinced my old pal Fred to throw in with me. So, starting in late '46, the Los Angeles branch operated out of the Bradbury Building at Third and Broadway, with Fred — now vice president of the A-1 — in charge, while I of course kept the Chicago offices going.

Only it seemed, more and more, I was spending time in California. My wife was an actress, and she had moved out here with our infant son, after the marriage went quickly south. The divorce wasn't final yet, and in my weaker moments, I still had hopes of patching things up, and was looking at finding an apartment or small house to rent, so I could divide my time between L.A. and Chicago. In July of '49, however, I was in a bungalow at the Beverly Hills Hotel, for whom the A-1 handled occasional security matters, an arrangement which included the perk of free lodgings.

Like Cohen, Fred Rubinski attempted to make up for his homeliness with natty attire, such as the blue suit with gray pinstripes and the gray-and-white silk tie he wore, as he sat behind his desk in his Bradbury Building office, a poolcue Havana shifting from corner to corner of his thick lips.

"Just do it as a favor to me, Nate," Fred said.

I was seated across from him, in the client chair, ankle on a knee. "You don't do jobs for Cohen — why should I?"

Fred patted the air with his palms; blue cigar smoke swirled around him like a wreath. "You don't have to do a job for him — just hear him out. He's a good customer at Sherry's and I don't wanna cross him."

"You also don't want to do jobs for him."

A window air conditioner was chugging; hot day. Fred and I had to speak up over it.

"I use the excuse that I'm too well-known out here," my partner said. "Also, the Mickster and me are already considered to be cronies, 'cause of Sherry's. He knows the cops would use that as an excuse to come down on me, hard, if suddenly I was on Mickey Cohen's retainer."

"But you're not asking me to do this job."

"No. Absolutely not. Hell, I don't even know what it is."

"You can guess."

"Well . . . I suppose you know he's been kind of a clay pigeon, lately. Several attempts on his life, probably by Dragna's people . . . Mick probably wants a bodyguard."

"I don't do that kind of work anymore. Anyway, what about those Seven Dwarfs of his?"

That was how Cohen's inner circle of lieutenants/strong-arms were known — Neddie Herbert, Davy Ogul, Frank Niccoli, Johnny Stompanato, Al Snyder, Jimmy Rist, and the late Hooky Rothman, who about a year ago had got his face shot off when guys with shotguns came barging right into Cohen's clothing shop. I liked my face right where it was.

"Maybe it's not a bodyguard job," Fred said with a shrug. "Maybe he wants you for something else."

I shifted in the chair. "Fred, I'm trying to distance myself from these mobsters. My connections with the Outfit back home, I'm still trying to live down — it's not good for the A-1 . . ."

"Tell him! Just don't insult the man . . . don't piss him off."

I got up, smoothing out my suit. "Fred, I was raised right. I hardly ever insult homicidal gangsters."

"You've killed a few, though."

"Yeah," I said from the doorway, "but I didn't insult them."

The haberdashery known poshly as Michael's was a two-story brick building in the midst of boutiques and nighteries at 8804 Sunset Boulevard. I was wearing a tan tropical worsted sportcoat and brown summer slacks, with a rust-color tie and two-tone Florsheims, an ensemble that had chewed up a hundred bucks in Marshall Field's men's department, and spit out pocket change. But the going rates inside this plush shop made me look like a piker.

Within the highly polished walnut walls, a few ties lay on a central glass counter, sporting silky sheens and twenty-five buck price tags. A rack of sportshirts ran seventy-five per, a stack of dress shirts ran in the hundred range. A luxurious brown robe on a headless manikin — a memorial to Hooky Rothman? — cost a mere two-hundred bucks, and the sportcoats went for two-hundred up, the suits three to four. Labels boasted: "Tailored Exclusively for Mickey Cohen."

A mousy little clerk — a legit-looking joker with a wispy mustache, wearing around five cee's worth of this stuff — looked at me as if a hobo had wandered into the shop.

"May I help you?" he asked, stuffing more condescension into four words than I would have thought humanly possible.

"Tell your boss Nate Heller's here," I said casually, as I poked around at the merchandise.

This was not a front for a bookmaking joint: Cohen really did run a high-end clothing store; but he also supervised his other, bigger business — which was extracting protection money from bookmakers, reportedly $250 per week per phone — out of here, as well. Something in my manner told the effete clerk that I was part of the backroom business, and his patronizing manner disappeared.

His whispered-into-a-phone conversation included my name, and soon he was politely ushering me to the rear of the store, opening a steel-plated door, gesturing me into a walnut-paneled, expensively-appointed office.

Mayer Harris Cohen — impeccably attired in a double-breasted light gray suit, with a gray and green paisley silk tie — sat behind a massive mahogany desk whose glass-topped surface bore three phones, a small clock with pen-and-pencil holder, a vase with cut flowers, a notepad and no other sign of work. Looming over him was an ornately framed hand-colored photograph of FDR at his own desk, cigarette holder at a jaunty angle.

Standing on either side, like Brillcreamed bookends, were two of Cohen's dark-eyed Dwarfs: Johnny Stompanato, a matinee-idol handsome hood who I knew a little; and hook-nosed Frank Niccoli, who I knew even less. They were as well-dressed as their boss.

"Thanks for droppin' by, Nate," Cohen said, affably, not rising. His thinning black hair was combed close to his egg-shaped skull; with his broad forehead, blunt nose and pugnacious chin, the pint-sized gangster resembled a bull terrier.

"Pleasure, Mickey," I said, hat in my hands.

Cohen's dark eyes flashed from bodyguard to bodyguard. "Fellas, some privacy?"

The two nodded at their boss, but each stopped — one at a time — to acknowledge me, as they headed to a side door, to an adjacent room (not into the shop).

"Semper fi, mac," Stompanato said, flashing his movie-star choppers. He always said this to me, since we were both ex-Marines.

"Semper fi," I said.

Niccoli stopped in front of me and smiled, but it seemed forced. "No hard feelings, Heller."

"About what?"

"You know. No hard feelings. It was over between us, anyway."

"Frank, I don't know what you're talking about."

His hard, pockmarked puss puckered into an expression that, accompanied by a dismissive wave, implied "no big deal."

When the bodyguards were gone, Cohen gestured for me to sit on the couch against the wall, opposite his desk. He rose to his full five six, and went to a console radio against the wall and switched it on — Frankie

Laine was singing "Mule Train"... loud. Then Cohen trundled over and sat next to me, saying quietly, barely audible with the blaring radio going, "You can take Frankie at his word."

At first I thought he was talking about Frankie Laine, then I realized he meant Niccoli.

"Mick," I said, whispering back, not knowing why but following his lead, "I don't know what the hell he's talking about."

Cohen's eyes were wide — he almost always had a startled deer look. "You're dating Didi Davis, right?"

Didi was a starlet I was seeing, casually; I might have been trying to patch up my marriage, but I wasn't denying myself the simple pleasures.

"Yeah, I met her a couple weeks ago at Sherry's."

"Well, Nate, she used to be Frankie's girl."

Cohen smelled like a barber shop got out of hand — reeking heavily of talcum powder and cologne, which seemed a misnomer considering his perpetual five o'clock shadow.

"I didn't know that, Mick. She didn't say anything . . ."

A whip cracked on the radio, as "Mule Train" wound down.

Cohen shrugged. "It's over. She got tired of gettin' slapped around, I guess. Anyway, if Frankie says he don't hold no grudge, he don't hold no grudge."

"Well, that's just peachy." I hated it when girls forgot to mention their last boyfriend was a hoodlum.

Vaughn Monroe was singing "Ghost Riders in the Sky" on the radio — in full nasal throttle. And we were still whispering.

Cohen shifted his weight. "Listen, you and me, we never had no problems, right?"

"Right."

"And you know your partner, Fred and me, we're pals."

"Sure."

"So I figured I'd throw some work your way."

"Like what, Mick?"

He was sitting sideways on the couch, to look at me better; his hands were on his knees. "I'm gettin' squeezed by a pair of vice cops — Delbert Potts and Rudy Johnson, fuckers' names. They been tryin' to sell me recordings."

"Frankie Laine? Vaughn Monroe?"

"Very funny — these pricks got wire recordings of me, they say, business transactions, me and who-knows-who discussing various illegalities . . . I ain't heard anything yet. But they're trying to shake me down for twenty gee's — this goes well past the taste they're gettin' already, from my business."

Now I understood why he was whispering, and why the radio was blasting.

"We're not talking protection," I said, "but straight blackmail."

"On the nose. I want two things, Heller — I want my home and my office, whadyacallit, checked for bugs . . ."

"Swept."

"Huh?"

"Swept for bugs. That's what it's called, Mick."

"Yeah, well, that's what I want — part of what I want. I also want to put in my own wiretaps and bugs and get those two greedy bastards on my recordings of them shakin' me down."

"Good idea — create a standoff."

He twitched a smile, apparently pleased by my approval. "You up for doing that?"

"It's not my specialty, Mick — but I can recommend somebody. Guy named Vaus, Jim Vaus. Calls himself an 'electronics engineering consultant.' He's in Hollywood."

The dark eyes tightened but retained their deer-in-the-headlights quality. "You've used this guy?"

"Yeah . . . well, Fred has. But what's important is: the cops use him, too."

"They don't have their own guy?"

"Naw. They don't have anybody like that on staff — they're a backward bunch. Jim's strictly freelance. Hell, he may be the guy who bugged you for the cops."

"But can he be trusted?"

"If you pay him better than the LAPD — which won't be hard — you'll have a friend for life."

"How you wanna handle this, Nate? Through your office, or will this, what's-his-name, Vaus, kick back a little to you guys, or —"

"This is just a referral, Mick, just a favor . . . I think I got one of his cards . . ."

I dug the card out of my wallet and gave it to Cohen, whose big brown eyes were dancing with sugarplumbs.

"This is great, Nate!"

I felt relieved, like I'd dodged a bullet: I had helped Cohen without having to take him on as a client.

So I said, "Glad to have been of service," and began to get up, only Cohen stopped me with a small but firm hand on my forearm.

Bing Crosby was singing "Dear Hearts and Gentle People" on the radio — casual and easygoing and loud as hell.

"What's the rush, Nate? I got more business to talk."

Sitting back down, I just smiled and shrugged and waited for the pitch.

It was a fastball: "I need you should bodyguard me."

"Jesus, Mick, with guys like Stompanato and Niccoli around? What the hell would you need me for?"

He was shaking his head; he had a glazed expression. "These vice cops, they got friends in the sheriff's office. My boys been gettin' rousted regularly — me, too. Half the time when we leave this place, we get shoved up against the wall and checked for concealed weapons."

"Oh. Is that what happened to Happy Meltzer?"

"On the nose again! Trumped-up gun charge. And these vice cops are behind it — and maybe Jack Dragna, who's in bed with the sheriff's department. Dragna would like nothin' better than to get me outa of the picture, without makin' our mutual friends back east sore."

"Hell, Mick, how do you see me figuring in this?"

"You're a private detective — licensed for bodyguard work. Licensed to carry a weapon! Shit, man, I need somebody armed standin' at my side, to keep me from gettin' my ass shot off! Just a month ago, somebody took a blast at me with a shotgun, and then we found a bomb under my house, and . . ."

He rattled on, as I thought about his former bodyguard, Hooky Rothman, getting his face shot off, in that posh shop just beyond the metal-lined door.

"I got friends in the Attorney General's office," he was saying, "and they tell me they got an inside tip that there's a contract out on yours truly — there's supposed to be two triggers in from somewheres on the east coast, to do the job. I need somebody with a gun, next to me."

"Mickey," I said, "I have to decline. With all due respect."

"You're not makin' me happy, Nate."

"I'm sorry. I'm in no position to help out. First off, I don't live out here, not fulltime, anyway. Second, I have a reputation of mob connections that I'm trying to live down."

"You're disappointing me . . ."

"I'm trying to get my branch office established out here, and you and Fred being friends — you hanging out at Sherry's — that's as far as our relationship, personal or professional, can go."

He thought about that. Then he nodded and shrugged. "I ain't gonna twist your arm . . . Two grand a week, just for the next two weeks?"

That might have tempting, if Cohen hadn't already narrowly escaped half a dozen hit attempts.

"You say you got friends in the Attorney General's office?" I asked.

"Yeah. Fred Howser and me are like this." He held up his right hand, forefinger and middlefinger crossed.

If the attorney general himself was on Cohen's pad, then those wire recordings the vice cops had might implicate Howser . . .

"Mick, ask Howser to assign one of his men to you as a bodyguard."

"A cop?"

"Who better? He'll be armed, he'll be protecting a citizen, and anyway, a cop to a hoodlum is like garlic to a vampire. Those triggers'll probably steer clear, long as a state investigator is at your side."

Cohen was thinking that over; then he began to nod.

"Not a bad idea," he said. "Not a bad idea at all."

I stood. "No consulting fee, Mick. Let's stay friends — and not do business together."

He snorted a laugh, stood and went over and shut off the radio, cutting off Mel Torme singing "Careless Hands." Then he walked me to the steel-lined door and — when I extended my hand — shook with me.

As I was leaving, I heard him, in the private bathroom off his office, tap running, as he washed up — removing my germs.

✗ ✗ ✗

I had a couple stops to make, unrelated to the Cohen appointment, so it was late afternoon when I made it back to the Beverly Hills Hotel. Entering my bungalow — nothing fancy, just a marble fireplace, private patio and furnishings no more plush than the palace at Versailles — I heard something . . . someone . . . in the bedroom. Rustling around in there.

My nine millimeter was in my suitcase, and my suitcase was in the bedroom. And I was just about to exit, to find a hotel dick or maybe call a cop, when my trained detective's nose sniffed a clue; and I walked across the living room, and pushed the door open.

Didi Davis gasped; she was wearing glittery earrings — just glittery earrings, and the Chanel Number Five I'd nosed — and was poised, pulling back the covers, apparently about to climb into bed. She looked like a French maid who forgot her costume.

"I wanted to surprise you," she said. She was a lovely brunette, rather tall — maybe five nine — with a willowy figure that would have seemed skinny if not for pert breasts and an impertinent dimpled behind. She was tanned all over. Her hair was up. It wasn't alone.

"I thought you were working at Republic today," I said, undoing my tie.

She crawled under the covers and the sheets made inviting, crinkly sounds. "Early wrap . . . I tipped a bellboy who let me in."

Soon I was under covers, equally naked, leaning on a pillow. "You know, I run with kind of a rough crowd — surprises like this can backfire."

"I just wanted to do something sweet for you," she said.

And she proceeded to do something sweet for me.

Half an hour later, still in the bedroom, we were getting dressed when I brought up the rough crowd she ran with.

"Why didn't you mention you used to date Frank Niccoli?"

She was fastening a nylon to her garter belt, long lovely leg stretched out as if daring me to be mad at her. "I don't know — Nate, you and I met at Sherry's, after all. You hang around with those kind of people. What's the difference?"

"The difference is, suppose he's a jealous type. Niccoli isn't your average ex-beau — he's a goddamn thug. Is it true he smacked you around?"

She was putting on her other nylon, fastening it, smoothing it; this kind of thing could get boring in an hour or two. "That's why I walked out on him. I warned him and he said he wouldn't do it again, and then a week later, he did it again."

"Has he bothered you? Confronted you in public? Called you on the phone?"

"No. It's over. He knows it, and I know it . . . now you know it. Okay, Nate? Do I ask you questions about your ex-wife?"

Didi didn't know my wife wasn't officially my ex, yet; nor that I was still hoping to rekindle those flames. She thought I was a great guy, unaware that I was a heel who would never marry another actress, but would gladly sleep with one.

"Let's drop it," I said.

"What a wonderful idea." She stood, easing her slip down over her nyloned legs, and was shimmying into her casual light-blue dress when the doorbell rang. Staying in a bungalow at the Beverly Hills, incidentally, was the only time I can recall a hotel room having a doorbell.

"I'm not expecting company," I told her, "but stay in here, would you? And keep mum?"

"I need to put my make-up on —"

The bell rang again — pretty damn insistent.

I got my nine millimeter out of the suitcase, stuffed it in my waistband, slipped on my sportjacket and covered it. "Just sit down — there's some magazines by the bed. We don't need to advertise."

She saw the common sense of that, and nodded. No alarm had registered in her eyes at the sight of the weapon; but then she'd been Niccoli's girl, hadn't she?

I shut her in there and went to answer the door.

I'd barely cracked the thing open when the two guys came barging in, the first one in brushing past me, the second slamming the door.

I hadn't even had a chance to say, "Hey!" when the badge in the wallet was thrust in my face.

"Lieutenant Delbert Potts," he said, putting the wallet away. He was right on top of me and his breath was terrible: it smelled like anchovies taste. "L.A. vice squad. This is my partner, Sergeant Rudy Johnson."

Potts was a heavy-set character in an off-the-rack brown suit that looked slept in; hatless, he had greasy reddish-blond hair and his drink-reddened face had a rubbery softness. His eyes were bloodshot, his nose as misshapen as a blob of putty somebody had stuck there carelessly, his lips thick and plump and vaguely obscene.

Johnson was thin and dark — both his features and his physique — and his navy suit looked tailored. He wore a black snapbrim that had set him back a few bucks.

"Fancy digs, Mr. Heller," Potts said, prowling the place, his thick-lipped smile conveying disgust. He had a slurry voice — he reminded me of a loathsome Arthur Godfrey, if that wasn't redundant.

"I do some work for the hotel," I said. "They treat me right when I'm out here."

"You goin' back to Chicago soon?" Johnson asked, right next to me. He had a reedy voice and his eyes seemed sleepy unless you noticed the sharpness under the half-lids.

"Not right away."

I'd never met this pair, yet they knew my name and knew I was from Chicago. And they hadn't taken me up on my offer to sit down.

"You might re-consider," Potts said. He was over at the wet bar, checking out the brands.

"Help yourself," I said.

"We're on duty," Johnson said.

"Fellas — what's this about?"

Potts wandered back over to me and thumped me on the chest with a thick finger. "You stopped by Mickey Cohen's today."

"That's right. He wanted me to do a job for him — I turned him down."

The bloodshot eyes tightened. "You turned him down? Are you sure?"

"I have a real good memory, Lieutenant. I remember damn near everything that happened to me, all day."

"Funny." That awful breath was warm in my face — fishy smell. "You wouldn't kid a kidder, would you?"

Backing away, I said, "Fellas — make your point."

Potts kept moving in on me, his breath in my face, like a foul furnace, his finger thumping at my chest. "You and your partner . . . Rubinski . . . you shouldn't be so thick with that little kike."

"Which little kike?"

Johnson said, "Mickey Cohen."

I looked from one to the other. "I already told you guys — I turned him down. I'm not working for him."

Potts asked, "What job did he want you for?"

"That's confidential."

He swung his fist into my belly — I did not see it coming, nor did I expect a slob like him to have such power. I dropped to my knees and thought about puking on the oriental carpet — I also thought about the gun in my waistband.

Slowly, I got to my feet. And when I did, the nine millimeter was in my hand.

"Get the fuck out of my room," I said.

Both men backed away, alarm widening their seen-it-all eyes. Potts blurted, "You can be arrest for —"

"This is licensed, and you clowns barged into my room and committed assault on me."

Potts had his hands up; he seemed nervous but he might have been faking, while he looked for an opening. "I shouldn'ta swung on ya. I apologize — now, put the piece away."

"No." I motioned toward the door with the Browning. "You're about to go, gents . . . but first — here's everything you need to know: I'm not working for Cohen, and neither is Fred."

The two exchanged glances, Johnson shaking his head.

"Why don't you put that away," Pott said, with a want-some-candy-little-girl smile, "and we'll just talk."

"We have talked. Leave."

I pressed forward and the two backed up — toward the door.

"You better be tellin' the truth," Potts said, anger swimming in his rheumy eyes.

I opened the door for them. "What the hell have you been eating, Potts? Your breath smells like hell."

The cop's blotchy face reddened, but his partner let out a sharp, single laugh. "Sardine sandwiches — it's all he eats on stakeouts."

That tiny moment of humanity between Johnson and me ended the interview; then they were out the door, and I shut and nightlatched it. I watched them through the window as they moved through the hotel's garden-like grounds, Potts taking the lead, clearly pissed-off, the flowering shrubs around him doing nothing to soothe him.

In the bedroom, Didi was stretched out on the bed, on her back, head to one side, fast asleep.

I sat next to her, on the edge of the bed, and this woke her with a start. "What? Oh . . . I must've dropped off. What was that about, anyway?"

"The Welcome Wagon," I said. "Come on, let's get an early supper."

And I took her to the Polo Lounge, where she chattered on and on about the picture she was working (with Roy Rogers and Dale Evans) and I said not much. I was thinking about those two bent cops, and how I'd pulled a gun on them.

✗ ✗ ✗

No retaliation followed my encounter with the two vice squad boys. They had made their point, and I mine. But I did take some precautionary measures: for two days I tailed the bastards, and (with my Speed Graphic, the divorce dick's best friend) got two rolls of film on them receiving pay-offs, frequently in the parking lot of their favorite coffee shop, Googie's, on Sunset at Crescent Heights.

I had no intention of using these for blackmail purposes — I just wanted some ammunition, other than the nine millimeter variety, with which to deal with these bent sons of bitches. On the other hand, I had taken to wearing my shoulder-holstered nine millimeter, in case things got interesting.

And for over a week, things weren't interesting — things were nicely dull. I had run into Cohen at Sherry's several times and he was friendly — and always in the company of a rugged-looking, ruggedly handsome investigator from the Attorney General's office, sandy-haired Harry Cooper . . . which rhymed with Gary Cooper, who the dick was just as tall as.

Mick had taken my advice — he now had an armed bodyguard, courtesy of the state of California. His retinue of a Dwarf or two also accompanied him, of course, just minus any artillery. Once or twice, Niccoli had been with him — he'd just smiled and nodded at me (and Didi), polite, no hard feelings.

On Tuesday night, July 19, I took Didi to see *Annie Get Your Gun* at the Greek Theater; Gertrude Niesen had just opened in the show, and she and it were terrific. Then we had a late supper at Ciro's, and hit a few jazz clubs. We wound up, as we inevitably did, at Sherry's for pastries and coffee.

Fred greeted us as we came in and joined us in a booth, Didi — who looked stunning in a low-cut spangly silver gown, her brunette hair piled high — and I were on one side, Fred on the other. A piano tinkling Cole Porter fought with clanking plates and after-theater chatter.

I ordered us up a half-slice of cheesecake for Didi (who was watching her figure — she wasn't alone), a Napoleon for me, and coffee for both of us. Fred just sat there with his hands folded, prayerfully, shaking his head.

"Gettin' too old for this," he said, his pouchy puss even pouchier than usual, a condition his natty navy suit and red silk tie couldn't make up for.

"What are you doing, playing host in the middle of the night?" I asked him. "You're an owner, for Christ's sake! Seems like lately, every time I come in here, in the wee hours, you're hovering around like a mother hen."

"You're not wrong, Nate. Mickey's been comin' in almost every night, and with that contract hanging over his head, I feel like . . . for the protection of my customers . . . I gotta keep an eye on things."

"Is he here tonight?"

"Didn't you see him, holding court over there?"

Over in the far corner of the modern, brightly-lighted restaurant — where business was actually a little slow tonight — a lively Cohen was indeed seated at a large round table with Cooper, Johnny Stompanato, Frank Niccoli and another of the Dwarfs, Neddie Herbert. Also with the little gangster were several reporters from the *Times,* and Florabel Muir and her husband, Denny. Florabel, a moderately attractive redhead in her late forties, was a Hollywood columnist for the *New York Daily News.*

Our order arrived, and Fred slid out of the booth, saying, "I better circulate."

"Fred, what, you think somebody's gonna open up with a chopper in here? This isn't a New Jersey clam house."

"I know . . . I'm just a nervous old woman."

Fred wandered off, and Didi and I nibbled at our desserts; we were dragging a little — it was after three.

"You okay?" I asked her.

"What?"

"You seem a little edgy."

"Really? Why would I be?"

"Having Niccoli sitting over there."

"No. That's over."

"What did you see in that guy, anyway?"

She shrugged. "He was nice, at first. I heard he had friends in pictures."

"You're already under contract. What do you need —"

"Nate, are we going to argue?"

I smiled, shook my head. "No. It's just . . . guys like Niccoli make me nervous."

"But he's been very nice to both of us."

"That's what makes me nervous."

Our mistake was using the restrooms: they were in back, and to use them, we'd had to pass near Cohen and his table. That's how we got invited to join the party — the two *Times* reporters had taken off, and chairs were available.

I sat next to Florabel, with Niccoli right next to me; and Didi was beside Cooper, the state investigator, who sneaked occasional looks down Didi's cleavage. Couldn't blame him and, anyway, detectives are always gathering information.

Florabel had also seen *Annie Get Your Gun,* and Cohen had caught a preview last week.

"That's the best musical to hit L.A. in years," the little gangster said. He was in a snappy gray suit with a blue and gray tie.

For maybe five minutes, the man who controlled bookie operations in Los Angeles extolled the virtues of Rodgers and Hammerstein's latest confection.

"Can I quote you in my column?" Florabel asked. She was wearing a cream-color suit with satin lapels, a classy dame with a hard edge.

"Sure! That musical gets the Mickey Cohen seal of approval."

Everyone laughed, as if it had been witty — me, too. I like my gangsters to be in a good mood.

"Mickey," the columnist said, sitting forward, "who do you think's been trying to kill you?"

"I really haven't the slightest idea. I'm as innocent as the driven snow."

"Yeah, but like Mae West said, you drifted."

He grinned at her — tiny rodent teeth. "Florabel, I love ya like a sister, I can talk to you about things I can't even tell my own wife."

Who was not present, by the way.

"You're in a neutral corner," he was saying, "like a referee. There's nothin' I can do for you, except help you sell papers, and you ain't got no axes to grind with me."

"That's true — so why not tell me what you really think? Is Jack Dragna behind these attempts?"

"Even for you, Florabel, that's one subject on which I ain't gonna spout off. If I knew the killers were in the next room, I wouldn't go public with it."

"Why not?"

"People like me, we settle things in our own way."

She gestured. "How can you sit in an open restaurant, Mick, with people planning to kill you?"

"Nobody's gonna do nothin' as long as you people are around. Even a crazy man wouldn't take a chance shooting where a reporter might get hit . . . or a cop, like Cooper here."

I was just trying to stay out of it, on the sidelines, but this line of reasoning I couldn't let slide. "Mickey," I said, "you really think a shooter's going to ask to see Florabel's press pass?"

Cohen thought that was funny, and almost everybody laughed — except me and Cooper.

Several at the table were nibbling on pastries; Didi and I had some more coffee. At one point, Niccoli got up to use the men's room, and Didi and I exchanged whispered remarks about how cordial he'd been to both of us. Florabel, still looking for a story, started questioning the slender, affable Neddie Herbert, who had survived a recent attempt on his life.

Herbert, who went back twenty years with Cohen, had dark curly hair, a pleasant-looking grown-up Dead-End Kid with a Brooklyn accent. He had been waylaid in the wee hours on the sidewalk in front of his apartment house.

"Two guys with .38s emptied their guns at me from the bushes." Herbert was grinning like a college kid recalling a frathouse prank. "Twelves slugs, the cops recovered — not one hit me!"

"How is that possible?" Florabel asked.

"Ah, I got a instinct for danger — I didn't even see them two guys, but I sensed 'em right before I heard 'em, and I dropped to the sidewalk right before they started shooting. I crawled up onto the stairway, outa range, while their bullets were fallin' all around."

"Punks," Cohen said.

"If they'da had any guts," Herbert said, "they'da reloaded and moved in close, to get me — but they weaseled and ran."

Fred came over to the table, and — after some small talk — said, "It's almost four, folks — near closing time. Mind if I have one of the parking lot attendants fetch your car, Mick?"

"That'd be swell, Fred."

I said, "Fetch mine, too, would you, Fred?"

And as Rubinski headed off to do that, Cohen grabbed the check, fending off a few feeble protests, and everybody gathered their things. This seemed like a good time for Didi and me to make our exit, as well.

Sherry's was built up on a slope, so there were a couple steps down from the cashier's counter to an entryway that opened right out to the street. Cohen strutted down and out, through the glass doors, with Neddie Herbert and the six-three Cooper right behind him. Niccoli and Stompanato were lingering inside, buying chewing gum and cigarettes. Florabel and her husband were lagging, as well, talking to some woman who I gathered was the Mocambo's press agent.

Then Didi and I were standing on the sidewalk just behind Cohen and his bodyguards, under the Sherry's canopy, out in the fresh, crisp night air . . . actually, early morning air. The normally busy Strip was all but deserted, only the occasional car gliding by. Just down a ways, the flashing yellow lights of sawhorses marking road construction blinked lazily.

"I love this time of night," Didi said, hugging my arm, as we waited behind Cohen and his retinue for the attendants to bring our cars. "So quiet . . . so still . . ."

And it was a beautiful night, bright with starlight and neon, palm trees peeking over a low-slung mission-style building across the way, silhouetted against the sky like a decorative wallpaper pattern. Directly across from us, however, a vacant lot with a Blatz beer billboard and a smaller FOR INFORMATION CONCERNING THIS PROPERTY PLEASE CALL sign did spoil the mood, slightly.

Didi — her shoulders and back bare, her silvery gown shimmering with reflected light — was fussing in her little silver purse. "Damn — I'm out of cigarettes."

"I'll go back and get you some," I said.

"Oh, I guess I can wait . . ."

"Don't be silly. What is it you smoke?"

"Chesterfields."

I went back in and up the three or four steps and bought the smokes. Florabel was bending over, picking up all the just-delivered morning editions, stacked near the cashier; her husband was still yakking with that dame from the Mocambo. Stompanato was flirting with a pretty waitress; Niccoli was nowhere in sight.

I headed down the short flight of steps and was coming out the glass doors just as Cohen's blue Caddy drew up, and the young string-tied attendant got out, and the night exploded.

It wasn't thunder, at least not God's variety: this was a twelve-gauge boom accompanied by the cracks of a high-power rifle blasting, a deadly duet echoing across the pavement, shotgun bellow punctuated by the sharp snaps of what might have been an M-1, the sound of which took me back to Guadalcanal. As the fusillade kicked in, I reacted first and best, diving for the sidewalk, yanking at Didi's arm as I pitched past, pulling her down, the glass doors behind me shattering in a discordant song. My sportcoat was buttoned, and it took a couple seconds to get at the nine millimeter under my shoulder, and during those slow-motion moments I saw Mickey get clipped, probably by the rifle.

Cohen dropped to one knee, clawing at his right shoulder with his left hand, blood oozing through his fingers, streaming down his expensive suit. Neddie Herbert's back had been to the street — he was turned toward his boss when the salvo began — and a bullet, courtesy of the rifle, blew through him, even as shotgun pellets riddled his legs. Herbert — the man who'd just been bragging about his instincts for danger — toppled to the sidewalk, screaming.

The Attorney General's dick, Cooper, had his gun out from under his shoulder when he caught a belly-full of buckshot and tumbled to the cement, yelling, "Shit! Fuck!" Mickey Cohen, on his knees, was saying, I swear to God, "This is a new goddamn suit!"

The rifle snapping over the shotgun blasts continued, as I stayed low and checked Didi who was shaking in fear, a crumpled moaning wreck;

her bare back was red-pocked from two pellets, which seemed not to have entered her body, probably bouncing off the pavement and nicking her — but she was scared shitless.

Still, I could tell she was okay, and — staying low, using the Caddy as my shield — I fired the nine millimeter toward that vacant lot, where orange muzzle flash emanated from below that Blatz billboard. The safety glass of the Caddy's windows spiderwebbed and then burst into tiny particles as the shotgunning continued, and I ducked down, noting that the rifle fire had ceased. Had I nailed one of them?

Then the shotgun stopped, too, and the thunder storm was over, leaving a legacy of pain and terror: Neddie Herbert was shrieking, yammering about not being able to feel his legs, and Didi was weeping, her long brunette hair come undone, trailing down her face and her back like tendrils. Writhing on the sidewalk like a bug on its back, big rugged Cooper had his revolver in one hand, waving it around in a punch-drunk manner; his other hand was clutching his bloody stomach, blood bubbling through his fingers.

I moved out from behind the Caddy, stepping out into the street, gun in hand — ready to dive back if I drew any fire.

But none came.

I wanted to run across there and try to catch up with the bastards, but I knew I had to stay put, at least for a while; if those guys had a car, they might pull around and try to finish the job. And since I had a gun — and hadn't been wounded — I had to stand guard.

Now time sped up: I saw the parking lot attendant, who had apparently ducked under the car when the shooting started, scramble out from under and back inside the restaurant, glass crunching under his feet. Niccoli ran out, with Stompanato and Fred Rubinski on his tail; Niccoli got in the Caddy, and Cohen — despite his limp bloody arm — used his other arm to haul the big, bleeding Cooper up into the backseat. Stompanato helped and climbed in back with the wounded cop.

Fred yelled, "Don't worry, Mick — ambulances are on the way! We'll take care of everybody!"

And the Caddy roared off.

Neddie Herbert couldn't be moved; he was alternately whimpering and screaming, still going on about not being able to move his legs. Some waitresses wrapped checkered tablecloths around the suffering

Neddie, while I helped Didi inside; she said she was cold and I gave her my sportjacket to wear.

Florabel came up to me, her left hand out of sight, behind her; she held out her right palm to show me a flattened deer slug about the size of a half dollar.

"Pretty nasty," she said.

"You get hit, Florabel?"

"Just bruised — where the sun don't shine. Hell, I thought it was fireworks, and kids throwing rocks."

"You reporters have such great instincts."

As a waitress tended to Didi, Fred took me aside and said, "Real professional job."

I nodded. "Shotgun to cause chaos, that 30.06 to pinpoint Cohen . . . only they missed."

"You okay, Nate?"

"Yeah — I don't think I even got nicked. Scraped my hands on the sidewalk, is all. Get me a flashlight, Fred."

"What?"

"Sheriff's deputies'll show up pretty soon — I want a look across the way before they get here."

Fred understood: the sheriff's office was in Jack Dragna's pocket, so their work might be more cover-up than investigation.

The vacant lot across the street, near the Blatz billboard, was not what I'd expected, and I immediately knew why they'd chosen this spot. Directly off the sidewalk, an embankment fell to a sunken lot, with cement stairs up the slope providing a perfect place for shooters to perch out of sight. No street or even alley back here, either: just the backyards of houses asleep for the night (lights in those houses were blazing now, however). The assassins could sit on the stairs, unseen, and fire up over the sidewalk, from ideal cover.

"Twelve-gauge," Fred commented, pointing to a scattering of spent shells in the grass near the steps.

My flashlight found something else. "What's this?"

Fred bent next to what appeared to be a sandwich — a half-eaten sandwich . . .

"Christ!" Fred said, lifting the partial slice of white bread. "Who eats this shit?"

An ambulance was screaming; so was Neddie Herbert.

"What shit?" I asked.

Fred shuddered. "It's a fucking sardine sandwich."

✗ ✗ ✗

The shooting victims were transferred from the emergency room of the nearest hospital to top-notch Queen of Angels, where the head doctor was Cohen's personal physician. An entire wing was roped off for the Cohen party, with a pressroom and listening posts for both the LAPD and County Sheriff's department.

I stayed away. Didi's wounds were only superficial, so she was never admitted, anyway. Cohen called me from the hospital to thank me for my "quick thinking"; all I had done was throw a few shots in the shooters' direction, but maybe that had kept the carnage to a minimum. I don't know.

Neddie Herbert got the best care, but he died anyway, a week later, of uremic poisoning: gunshot wounds in the kidney are a bitch. At that point, Cohen was still in the hospital, but rebounding fast; and the State Attorney's man, Cooper, was fighting for his life with a bullet in the liver and internal hemorrhaging from wounds in his intestines.

Fred and I both kept our profiles as low as possible — this kind of publicity for his restaurant and our agency was not exactly what we were looking for.

The night after Neddie Herbert's death in the afternoon, I was waiting in the parking lot of Googie's, the coffee shop at Sunset and Crescent Heights. Googie's was the latest of these atomic-type cafes popping up along the Strip like futuristic mushrooms: a slab of the swooping red-painted structural steel roof rose to jut at an angle toward the street, in an off-balance exclamation point brandishing the neon *googie's,* and a massive picture window looked out on the Strip as well as the nearby Hollywood hills.

I'd arrived in a blue Ford that belonged to the A-1; but I was standing alongside a burgundy Dodge, an unmarked car used by the two vice cops who made Googie's their home away from home. Tonight I wasn't taking pictures of their various dealings with bookmakers, madams, fellow crooked cops or politicians. This was something of a social call.

I'd been here since just before midnight; and we were into the early morning hours now — in fact, it was after two a.m. when Lieutenant

Delbert Potts and Sergeant Rudy Johnson strolled out of the brightly illuminated glass-and-concrete coffee shop, into the less illuminated parking lot. Potts was in another rumpled brown suit — or maybe the same one — and, again, Johnson was better-dressed than his slob partner, his slender frame well-served by a dark gray suit worthy of Michael's haberdashery.

Hell, maybe Cohen provided Johnson's wardrobe as part of the regular pay-off — at least till Delbert and Rudy got greedy and went after that twenty grand for the recordings they'd made of Mickey.

I dropped down into a crouch as they approached, pleased that no other customers had wandered into the parking lot at the same time as my friends from the vice squad. Tucked between the Dodge and the car parked next to it, I was as unseen as Potts and Johnson had been, when they'd crouched on those steps with their shotgun and rifle, waiting for Mickey.

Potts and Johnson were laughing about something — maybe Neddie Herbert's death — and the fat one was in the lead, fishing in his pants pocket for his car keys. He didn't see me as I rose from the shadows, swinging an underhand fist that sank six inches into his flabby belly.

Like a matador, I pushed past him, while shoving him to the pavement, where he began puking, and grabbed Johnson by one lapel and slammed his head into the rear rider's side window. He slid down the side of the car and sat, maybe not unconscious, but good and dazed. Neither one protested — the puking fat one, or the stunned thin one — as I disarmed them, pitching their revolvers into the darkness, where they skittered across the cement like crabs. I checked their ankles for hideout guns, but they were clean. So to speak.

Potts was still puking when I started kicking the shit out of him. I didn't go overboard: just five or six good ones, cracking two or three ribs. Pretty soon he stopped throwing up and began to cry, wallowing down there between the cars in his own vomit. Johnson was coming around, and tried to crawl away, but I yanked him back by the collar and slammed him into the hubcap of the Dodge.

Johnson had blood all over his face, and was spitting up a bloody froth, as well as a tooth or two, and he was blubbering like a baby.

Glancing over my shoulder, I saw a couple in their twenties emerging from Googie's; they walked to the car, on the other side of the lot. They were talking and laughing — presumably not about Neddie Herbert's death — and went to their Chevy convertible and rolled out of the lot.

I kicked Potts in the side and shook Johnson by the lapels, just to get their attention, and they wept and groaned and moaned while I gave them my little speech, which I'd been working on in my head while I waited for them in the parking lot.

"Listen to me, you simple fuckers — you can shoot at Mickey Cohen and his Dwarfs all you want. I really do not give a flying shit. But you shot at me and my date, and a copper too, and that pisses me off. Plus, you shot up the front of my partner's restaurant."

Potts tried to say something, but it was unintelligible; "mercy" was in there, somewhere. Johnson was whimpering, holding up his blood-smeared hands like this was a stick-up.

"Shut-up," I said, "both of you . . . I don't care what you or Dragna or any gangster or bent fucking cop does out here in Make-believe-ville. I live in Chicago, and I'm going back tomorrow. If you take any steps against me, or Fred Rubinski, or if you put innocent people in the path of your fucking war again, I will talk to my Chicago friends . . . and you will have an accident. Maybe you'll get run down by a milk truck, maybe a safe'll fall on you. Maybe you'll miss a turn off a cliff. My friends are creative."

Through his bloody bubbles, Johnson said, "Okay, Heller . . . okay!"

"By the way, I have photos of you boys taking pay-offs from a fine cross section of L.A.'s sleazy citizenry. Anything happens to me — if I wake up with a goddamn hangnail — those photos go to Jim Richardson at the *Examiner,* with a duplicate batch to Florabel Muir. Got it?"

Nobody said anything. I kicked Potts in the ass, and he yelped, "Got it!"

"Got it, got it, got it!" Johnson said, backing up against the hubcap, patting the air with his palms.

"We're almost done — just one question . . . Was Stompanato in on it, or was Niccoli your only tip-off man?"

Johnson coughed, getting blood on his chin. "Ni-Niccoli . . . just Niccoli."

"He wanted you to take out the Davis dame, right? That was part of the deal?"

Johnson nodded. So did Potts, who was on his belly, and to see me had to look over his shoulder, puke rolling down his cheeks like a bad complexion that had started to melt.

Just the sight of them disgusted me, and my handed drifted toward my nine millimeter in the shoulder holster. "Or fuck . . . maybe I should kill you bastards . . ."

They both shouted "no!" and Potts began to cry again.

Laughing to myself, I returned to the agency's Ford. These L.A. cops were a bunch of pansies; if this were Chicago, I'd have been dead by now.

✗ ✗ ✗

In the aftermath of the shoot-out at Sherry's, various political heads rolled, including Attorney General Fred Howser's, and several trials took place (Cohen acquitted on various charges), as well as a Grand Jury inquiry into police and political corruption. Potts and Johnson were acquitted of corruption charges, and despite much talk in the press of damning wire recordings in the possession of both sides, no such recordings were entered as evidence in any trial, though Cohen's lawyer was murdered on the eve of a trial in which those recordings were supposed to figure.

And the unsuccessful attempts on Cohen's life continued, notably a bombing of his house, which he and his wife and his bull terrier survived without scratches. But no more civilians were put in harm's way, and no repercussions were felt by either Fred Rubinski or myself.

A few months after Mickey Cohen got out of the hospital, his longtime crony Frank Niccoli — who he'd known since Cleveland days — turned up missing. Suspicions that Niccoli may have been a stool pigeon removed by Mickey himself were offset by Cohen losing $25,000 bail money he'd put up for Niccoli on an unrelated beef.

The next summer, I ran into Cohen at Sherry's — or actually, I was just coming out of Sherry's, a date on my arm; another cool, starlit night, around two a.m., the major difference this time being the starlet was a blonde. Mickey and Johnny Stompanato and two more Dwarfs were on their way in. We paused under the canopy.

The rodent grin flashed between five-o'clock-shadowed cheeks. "Nate! Here we are at the scene of the crime — like old times."

"I hope not, Mickey."

"You look good. You look swell."

"That's a nice suit, Mickey."

"Stop by Michael's — I'll fix you up . . . on the house. Still owe you a favor for whispering in my ear about . . . you know."

"Forget it."

He leaned in, sotto voce. "New girl?"

"Pretty new."

"You hear who Didi Davis is dating these days?"

"No."

"That State's Attorney cop — Cooper!"

I smiled. "Hadn't heard that."

"Yeah, he finally got the bullet removed outa his liver, the other day. My doc came up with some new treatment, makes liver cells replace themselves or somethin'. . . . All on my tab, of course."

My date tightened her grip on my arm; maybe she recognized Cohen and was nervous about the company I was keeping.

So I said, "Well, Mick, better let you and your boys go on in for your coffee and pastries . . . before somebody starts shooting at us again."

He laughed heartily and even shook hands with me — which meant he would have to go right in and wash up — but first, leaning in close enough for me to whiff his expensive cologne, he said, "Be sure to say hello to Frankie, since you're in the neighborhood."

"What do you mean?"

Actually, I knew he meant Frankie Niccoli, but wasn't getting the rest of his drift . . . .

Cohen nodded down the Strip. "Remember that road construction they was doin', the night we got hit? There's a nice new stretch of concrete there, now. You oughta try it out."

And Mickey and his boys went inside.

As for me, my latest starlet at my side, I had the parking lot attendant fetch my wheels, and soon I was driving right over that fresh patch of pavement, with pleasure.

STRIKE ZONE

My buddy Bill Veeck made many a mark in the world of big league baseball, owning his first club at twenty-eight, winning pennants, setting attendance records. Two of Bill's teams beat the Yankees in their heyday — the '48 Cleveland Indians and the '59 White Sox; only one other team managed that feat, the '54 Indians, which was mostly made up of Veeck's former players.

And, of course, Bill Veeck was a character as colorful as his exploding-paint-factory sportshirts — one of his many trademarks was a refusal to wear coat and tie — a hard-drinking, chainsmoking extrovert with a wooden leg and a penchant for ignoring such quaint customs as doctors' orders and a good night's sleep. Veeck thought nothing of commuting from Cleveland to New York, to hang out with show biz pals like Frank Sinatra and Skitch Henderson at the Copa, or to fly at the drop of a cap out to Hollywood for a game of charades with Hope and Crosby.

"Baseball is too grim, too serious," he liked to say. "It should be fun. Most owners are bunch of damn stuffed shirts."

Many of Veeck's stunts and promotions and just plain wild ideas indeed had irritated the stuffed shirts of baseball. During World War Two, when the draft had drained the game of so much talent, Veeck told Commissioner Kenesaw Mountain Landis that he planned to buy the Phillies and fill the team with black ball players (another buyer was quickly found). Still, Veeck did manage to put the first black player in the American League, Larry Doby, and even brought the legendary Negro Leagues pitcher, Satchel Paige, into the majors.

Nonetheless, Bill Veeck was resigned to the fact that — no matter what his other accomplishments, whether noble or absurd — he would go down in baseball history as the guy who brought a midget into the majors.

✗ ✗ ✗

Back in June of '61, when Veeck called the A-1 Detective Agency, saying he had a job for me, I figured it would have something to do with his recent resignation as president of the White Sox. A partner had bought out both Bill and his longtime associate, Hank Greenberg, and I wondered if it'd been a squeeze play.

Maybe Bill needed some dirt dug up on somebody. Normally, at that stage of my career anyway, I would have left such a shabby task to one of the agency's many operatives, rather than its president and founder — both of which were me.

I had known Veeck for something like fifteen years, however, and had done many an odd job for him. And besides, my policy was when a celebrity asked for Nate Heller, the celebrity got Nate Heller.

And Bill Veeck was, if nothing else, a celebrity.

The afternoon was sunny with a breeze, but blue skies were banished in the shadow of the El, where Miller's nestled, an undistinguished Greek-run American-style restaurant that Veeck had adopted as his favorite Loop hangout, for reasons known only to him. Any time Veeck moved into a new office, his first act was to remove the door — another of his trademarks — and Miller's honored their famous patron by making one of Veeck's discarded doors their own inner front one, with an explanatory plaque, and the inevitable quote: "My door is always open — Bill Veeck."

At a little after three p.m., Miller's was hardly hopping, its dark front windows adding to the under-the-El gloom. Bill was seated in his usual corner booth, his wooden leg extended into the aisle. I threaded through the empty formica tables and, after a handshake and hello, slid in opposite him.

"Well, you look like hell," I told him.

He exploded with laughter, almost losing his corner-of-the-mouth cigarette. "At last an honest man. Everybody else tells me I look in the pink — I'm getting the same kind of good reviews as a well-embalmed corpse."

Actually, a well-embalmed corpse looked better than Veeck: his oblong face was a pallid repository for pouchy eyes, a long lumpy nose and that wide, full-lipped mouth, which at the moment seemed disturbingly slack. His skin — as leathery and well-grooved as a catcher's mitt — hung loose on him, and was startlingly white. I had never seen him without a tan. Though I was ten years older, Veeck in his mid-forties looked sixty. A hard sixty.

"It's a little late to be looking for dirt on Allyn, isn't it?" I asked him, after a waitress brought Veeck a fresh bottle of Blatz and a first one for me.

Arthur Allyn had bought the White Sox and was the new president.

"This isn't about that," Veeck said gruffly, waving it off. "Art's a pal. This sale clears the way for Hank to relocate in L.A. When I get feeling better, Hank'll take me in as a full partner."

"Then what is this about, Bill?"

"Maybe I just want to hoist one with you, in honor of an old friend."

"Oh . . . Eddie Gaedel. I guess I should have known."

We clinked beer bottles.

I had seen Eddie's obit in yesterday's paper — and the little story the *Trib* ran in sports. Eddie had died of natural causes, the coroner had said, and bruises on his body were "probably suffered in a fall."

"I want you to look into it," Veeck said.

"Into what?"

"Eddie's death."

"Why? If it was natural causes."

"Eddie's mother says it was murder."

I sipped my beer, shook my head. "Well, those 'bruises' could have come from a beating he got, and deserved — Eddie always was a mouthy little bastard. A week after that game in St. Louis, ten years ago, he got arrested in Cincinnati for assaulting a cop, for Christ's sake."

Veeck swirled his beer and looked down into it with bleary eyes — in all the years I'd known this hard-drinking S.O.B., I'd never once seen him with bloodshot eyes . . . before.

"His mother says it's murder," Veeck repeated. "Run over to the South Side and talk to her — if what she says gets your nose twitchin', look into it . . . If it's just a grieving mother with some crazy idea about how her 'baby' died, then screw it."

"Okay. Why is this your business, Bill?"

"When you spend six months bouncing back and forth between your apartment and the Mayo Clinic, you get to thinking . . . putting your affairs in order. Grisly expression, but there it is."

"What is it? The leg again?"

"What's left of it. The latest slice took my knee away, finally. That makes seven operations. Lucky seven."

"Semper fi, mac," I said, and we clinked bottles again. We'd both been Marines in the South Pacific, where I got malaria and combat fatigue, and he had his leg run over by an anti-tank gun on the kickback. Both of us had spent more time in hospitals than combat.

"My tour was short and undistinguished," he said. "At least you got the Bronze Star."

"And a Section Eight."

"So I lost half a leg, and you lost half your marbles. We both got a better deal than a lot of guys."

"And you want me to see what kind of deal Eddie Gaedel got?"

"Yeah. Seems like the least I could do. You know, I saw him, not that long ago. He did a lot of stunts for me, over the years. Last year I dressed him up as a martian and ran him around the park. Opening day this year, I had midget vendors working the grandstand, giving out cocktail wieners in little buns, and shorty beers."

"And Eddie was one of the vendors."

"Yeah. Paid him a hundred bucks — same as that day back in '51."

That day when Eddie Gaedel — 3' 7", sixty-five pounds — stepped up to the plate for the St. Louis Browns, batting for Frank Saucier.

"Funny thing is," Veeck said, lighting up a fresh cigarette, "how many times I threatened to kill that little bastard myself. I told him, I've got a man up in the stands with a high-powered rifle, and if you take a swing at any pitch, he'll fire."

"You got the mother's address?"

"Yeah . . . yeah, I got it right here." He took a slip of paper out of his sportshirt pocket but didn't hand it to me. "Only she's not there right now."

"Where is she?"

"Visitation at the funeral home. Service is tomorrow morning."

"Why don't I wait, then, and not bother her . . ."

The gravel voice took on an edge. " 'Cause I'd like you to represent me. Pay her and Eddie your respects . . . plus, your detective's nose might sniff something."

"What, formaldehyde?"

But I took the slip of paper, which had the funeral home address as well as Mrs. Gaedel's.

He was saying, "Do you know the *New York Times* put Eddie's obit on the front page? The front goddamn page . . . And that's the thing,

Nate, that's it right there: my name is in Eddie's obit, big as baseball. And you know what? You know damn well, time comes, Eddie'll be in mine."

I just nodded; it was true.

The pouchy eyes tightened — bloodshot maybe, but bright and hard and shiny. "If somebody killed that little bastard, Nate, find out who, and why, and goddamnit, do something about it."

I squinted through the floating cigarette smoke. "Like go to the cops?"

Veeck shrugged; his wrinkled puss wrinkled some more. "You're the one pitching. Hurl it any damn way you want to."

✗ ✗ ✗

Of course this had all begun about ten years before — in the summer of '51 — when Veeck called me and asked if I knew any midgets who were "kinda athletic and game for anything."

"Why don't you call Marty Craine," I said, into the phone, leaning back in my office chair, "or some other booking agent."

"Marty's come up blank," Veeck's voice said through the long-distance crackle. "Can't you check with some of those lowlife pals of yours at the South State bump-and-grind houses? They take shows out to the carnivals, don't they?"

"You want an athletic midget," I said, "I'll find you an athletic midget."

So I had made a few calls, and wound up accompanying Eddie Gaedel on the train to Cleveland, for some as yet unexplained Bill Veeck stunt. Eddie was in his mid-twenties but had that aged, sad-eyed look common to his kind; he was pleasant enough, an outgoing character who wore loud sportshirts and actually reminded me of a pintsize Veeck.

"You don't know what the hell this is about?" he kept asking me in his highpitched squawk, an oversize cigar rolling from one corner to the other of his undersize mouth.

"No," I said. We had a private compartment and Gaedel's incessant cigar smoking provided a constant blue haze. "I just know Bill wants this kept mum — I wasn't to tell anybody but you, Eddie, that we're going to Cleveland to do a job for the Browns."

"You follow baseball, Nate?"

"I'm a boxing fan myself."

"I hope *I* don't have to know nothing about baseball."

"Veeck didn't say you had to know baseball — just you had to be athletic."

Gaedel was a theatrical midget who had worked in various acrobatic acts.

"Ask the dames," Gaedel said, chortling around the pool-cue Havana, "if Eddie Gaedel ain't athletic."

That was my first clue to Eddie's true personality, or anyway the Eddie that came out after a few drinks. In the lounge car, after he threw back one, then another Scotch on the rocks like a kid on a hot day downing nickel Cokes, I suddenly had a horny Charlie McCarthy on my hands.

I was getting myself a fresh drink, noticing out the corner of an eye as Eddie sidled up to a pair of attractive young women — a blonde and brunette travelling together, probably college students, sweaters and slacks — and set his drink on their little silver deco table. He looked first at the blonde, then at the brunette, as if picking out just the right goodie in a candy-store display case.

Then he put his hand on the blonde's thigh and leered up at her.

"My pal and me got a private compartment," he said, gesturing with his cigar like an obscenely suggestive wand, "if you babes are up for a little four-way action."

The blonde let out a yelp, brushing off Eddie's hand like a big bug. The brunette was frozen in Fay Wray astonishment.

Eddie grabbed his crotch and grinned. "Hey doll, you don't know what you're missin' — I ain't as short as you think."

Both women stood and backed away from the little man, pressing up against the windows, pretty hands up and clawed, their expressions about the same as if a tarantula had been crawling toward them.

I got over there before anybody else could — several men stood petrified, apparently weighing the urge to play Saint George against looking like a bully taking on such a pintsized dragon.

Grabbing him by the collar of his red shirt, I yanked the midget away from the horrified girls, saying, "Excuse us, ladies . . . Jesus, Eddie, behave yourself."

And the little guy spun and swung a hard sharp fist up into my crotch. I fell to my knees and looked right into the contorted face of Eddie

Gaedel, a demented elf laughing and laughing at the pitiful sight that was me.

A white-jacketed conductor was making his alarmed way toward us when my pain subsided before Eddie's kneeslapping laughter, giving me the window of opportunity to twist the little bastard's arm behind him and drag him out of the lounge, through the dining car, getting lots of dirty looks from passengers along the way for this cruelty, and back to our compartment, tossing him inside like the nasty little ragdoll he was.

He picked himself up, a kind of reassembling action, and came windmilling at me, his highpitched scream at once ridiculous and frightening.

I clipped him with a hard right hand and he collapsed like a string-snipped puppet. Out cold on the compartment floor. Well, if you have to be attacked by an enraged horny drunken midget, better that he have a glass jaw.

He slept through the night, and at breakfast in the dining car apologized, more or less.

"I'm kind of an ugly drunk," he admitted, buttering his toast.

"For Christ's sakes, Eddie, you only had two drinks."

"Hey, you don't have to be fuckin' Einstein to figure with my body size, it don't take much. Anyway, I won't tell Mr. Veeck my bodyguard beat the crap out of me."

"Yeah. Probably best we both forget the little incident."

He frowned at me, toast crumbs flecking his lips. " 'Little' incident? Is that a remark?"

"Eat your poached eggs, Eddie."

In Veeck's office, the midget sat in a wooden chair with his legs sticking straight out as the Hawaiian-shirted owner of the St. Louis Browns paced excitedly — though due to Bill's wooden leg, it was more an excited shuffle. I watched from the sidelines, leaning against a file cabinet.

Suddenly Veeck stopped right in front of the seated midget and thrust an Uncle Bill Wants You finger in his wrinkled little puss.

"Eddie, how would like to be a big-league ballplayer?"

"Me?" Eddie — wearing a yellow shirt not as bright as the sun — squinted up at him. "I been to maybe two games in my life! Plus, in case you ain't noticed, I'm a goddamn midget!"

"And you'd be the only goddamn midget in the history of the game." Tiny eyes bright and big as they could be, Veeck held up two hands that seemed to caress an invisible beach ball. "Eddie, you'll appear before thousands — your name'll go in the record books for all time!"

Eddie's squint turned interested. "Yeah?"

"Yeah. Eddie, my friend . . . you'll be immortal."

"Immortal. Wow. Uh . . . what does it pay?"

"A hundred bucks."

Eddie was nodding now — a hundred bucks was even better than immortality.

"So what *do* you know about baseball?" Veeck asked him.

"I know you're supposed to hit the white ball with the bat. And then you run somewhere."

Veeck snatched a little toy bat from his desk; then he crouched over as far as his gimpy leg would allow, and assumed the stance.

"The pitcher's gotta throw that white ball in your strike zone, Eddie."

"What the hell is that?"

"It's the area between the batter's armpits and the top of his knees . . . . Let's see your strike zone."

Eddie scrambled off the chair and took the toy bat, assuming the position.

"How's that, Mr. Veeck?"

"Crouch more. See, since you're only gonna go to bat once in your career, whatever stance you assume at the plate, that's your natural stance."

Eddie, clutching the tiny bat, crouched. His strike zone was maybe one and a half inches. Then he took an awkward, lunging swing.

"No!" Veeck said. "Hell, no!"

Eddie, still in his crouch, looked at Veeck curiously.

Veeck put his arm around the little guy. "Eddie, you just stay in that crouch. You just stand there and take four balls. Then you'll trot down to first base and we'll send somebody in to run for you."

"I don't get it."

Veeck explained the concept of a walk to Eddie, whose face fell, his dreams of glory fading.

"Eddie," Veeck said pleasantly, "if you so much as look like you're gonna swing, I'm gonna shoot you dead."

Eddie shrugged. "That sounds fair."

✗ ✗ ✗

On a hot Sunday in August, a crowd of twenty thousand — the largest attendance the chronically losing Browns had managed in over four years — came out to see Bill Veeck's latest wild stunt. The crowd, which was in a great, funloving mood, had no idea what that stunt would be; but as this doubleheader with the Tigers marked the fiftieth anniversary of the American League, the fans knew it would be something more than just the free birthday cake and ice cream being handed out.

Or the opening game itself, which the Browns, naturally, lost.

The half-time show began to keep the implied Veeck promise of zaniness, with a parade of antique cars, two couples in Gay Nineties attire pedalling a bicycle-built-for-four around the bases, and a swing combo with Satchel Paige himself on drums inspiring jitterbugging in the aisles. A three-ring circus was assembled, with a balancing act at first base, trampoline artists at second and a juggler at third.

Throughout all this, I'd been babysitting Eddie Gaedel in Veeck's office. Gaedel was wearing a Browns uniform that had been made up for Bill DeWitt, Jr., the nine year-old son of the team's former owner/current advisor. The number sewn onto the uniform was actually a fraction: 1/8; and kid's outfit or not, the thing was tent-like on Eddie.

We could hear the muffled roar of the huge crowd, and Eddie was nervous. "I don't feel so good, Nate."

The little guy was attempting to tie the small pair of cleats Veeck had somehow rustled up for him.

"You'll do fine, Eddie."

"I can't tie these fuckin' things! Shit!"

So I knelt and tied the midget's cleats. I was getting a hundred bucks for the day, too.

"These bastards hurt my feet! I don't think I can go on."

"There's twenty thousand people in that park, but there's one whose ass I know I can kick, Eddie, and that's you. Get going."

Soon we were under the stands, moving down the ramp, toward the seven-foot birthday cake out of which Veeck planned to have Eddie jump. Big Bill Durney, Veeck's travelling secretary, helped me lift the midget under the arms, so we could ease him onto the board inside the hollowed-section of the cake.

"What the hell am I?" Eddie howled, as he dangled between us. No one had told him about this aspect of his appearance. "A stripper?"

"When you feel the cake set down," I said, "jump out, and run around swingin' and clowning. Then run to the dugout and wait your turn at bat."

"This is gonna cost that bastard Veeck extra! I'm an AGVA member, y'know!"

And we set him down in there, handed him his bat, and covered him over with tissue paper, through which his obscenities wafted.

But when the massive cake was rolled out onto the playing field by two of the fans' favorite Browns, Satch Paige and Frank Saucier, and plopped down on the pitcher's mound, Eddie Gaedel rose to the occasion. As the stadium announcer introduced "a brand-new Brownie," Eddie burst through the tissue paper and did an acrobatic tumble across the wide cake, landing on his cleats nimbly, running to home, swinging the bat all the way, eating up the howls of laughter and the spirited applause from the stands.

Then Eddie headed for the dugout, and the various performers were whisked from the field for the start of the second game. The fans were having a fine time, though perhaps some were disappointed that the midget-from-the-cake might be the big Veeck stunt of the day; they had hoped for more.

They got it.

Frank Saucier was the leadoff batter for the Browns, but the announcer boomed, "For the Browns, number 1/8 — Eddie Gaedel, batting for Saucier!"

And there, big as life, so to speak, was Eddie Gaedel, swimming in the child's uniform, heading from the dugout with that small bat still in hand, swinging it, limbering up, hamming it up.

Amazed laughter rippled through the crowd as the umpire crooked a finger at Veeck's manager, Zack Taylor, who jogged out with the signed contract and a carbon of the telegram Veeck had sent major league headquarters adding Eddie to the roster.

By this time I had joined Veeck in the special box up on the roof, where visiting dignitaries could enjoy the perks of a bar and restaurant. Veeck was entertaining a crew from Falstaff Breweries, the Browns' radio sponsors, who were ecstatic with the shenanigans down on the diamond. Newspaper photographers were swarming onto the field, capturing the manager of the Tigers, Red Rolfe, complaining to the umpire, while pitcher Bob Cain and catcher Bob Swift just stood at their respective positions, occasionally shrugging at each other, obviously waiting for this latest Bill Veeck gag to blow over.

But it didn't blow over: after about fifteen minutes of discussion, argument and just plain bitching, the umpire shooed away the photogs and — with clear reluctance — motioned the midget to home plate.

"Look at the expression on Cain's puss!" Veeck exploded at my shoulder.

Even at this distance, the disbelief on the pitcher's face was evident, as he finally grasped that this joke was no joke: he had to pitch to a midget.

"He can't hurl underhand," Veeck was chortling, "'cause submarine pitches aren't legal. Look at that! Look at Swift!"

The catcher had dropped to his knees, to give his pitcher a better target.

"Shit!" Veeck said. His tone had turned on a dime. All around us, the Falstaff folks were having a gay old time; but Veeck's expression had turned as distressed as Cain's. "Will you look at that little bastard, Nate . . ."

Eddie Gaedel — who Veeck had spent hours instructing in achieving the perfect, unpitch-to-able crouch — was standing straight and, relatively speaking, tall, feet straddled DiMaggio-style, tiny bat held high.

"Have you got your gun, Nate? That little shit's gonna swing . . ."

"Naw," I said, a hand on Veeck's shoulder, "he's just playing up to the crowd."

Who were playing up to him, cheering, egging him on.

Then pitcher Cain came to Veeck's rescue by really pitching to the midget, sending two fast balls speeding past Eddie before he could even think to swing.

"I wouldn't worry now," I said to Veeck.

Cain had started to laugh; he was almost collapsing with laughter, which the crowd aped, and he could barely throw at all as he tossed two more looping balls, three and then four feet over Eddie's head.

The littlest Brown trotted to his base as the crowd cheered and cameras clicked; then he stood with one foot on the bag as if he were thinking of stealing, which got a huge, roaring laugh.

Finally pinch runner Jim Delsing came over and Gaedel surrendered the base to him, giving the big man a comradely pat on the butt.

The crowd was going wild, Veeck grinning like a monkey, as I made my exit, to go down and meet my midget charge in Veeck's office. Eddie had his clothes changed — he was wearing a bright green and yellow shirt that made Veeck's taste seem mild — and I warned him that the reporters would be lying in wait.

"Veeck says it's your call," I said. "I can sneak you out of here —"

"Hell no!" Eddie was sitting on the floor, tying his shoes — he didn't need any help, this time. "It's great publicity! Man, I felt like Babe Ruth out there."

"Eddie, you're now what most every man in the country wishes he could be."

"Yeah? What's that?"

"A former major-leaguer."

Since Veeck had been talking about using Gaedel again, the little guy really warmed up to the reporters waiting outside the stadium, telling them "two guys I'd really like to face on the mound are Bob Feller and Dizzy Trout."

But it didn't work out that way. First off, despite the midget ploy, the Browns lost 6-2 to the Tigers, anyway. And before Veeck could put Gaedel into a White Sox game in Eddie's hometown of Chicago a month later, the baseball commissioner banned midgets from baseball.

Veeck had responded to Commissioner Harridge by saying, "Fine, but first you gotta establish what a midget is — is it three foot six, like Eddie? If it's five six, great! We can get rid of Phil Rizzuto!"

The commissioner's ban was not only complete, but retroactive: Eddie didn't even make it into the record books, the Gaedel name nowhere to be seen in the official 1951 American League batting records — though the base-on-balls was in Cain's record, and a pinch-running appearance in Delsing's.

Nonetheless, this stuffed-shirt revisionist history did no good at all: record book or not, Eddie was immortal over Bill Veeck's stunt, and so was Bill Veeck.

Immortal in the figurative sense, of course. Their fame didn't stop

Veeck from staring death in the face, nor, apparently, had it spared little Eddie Gaedel from murder.

✗ ✗ ✗

The Keurtz Funeral Home was one of those storefront numbers, with a fancy faux-stone facade in the midst of pawn shops and bars. This was on the South Side, Ashland and 48th, the business district of a working-class neighborhood of two-flats and modest frame houses, a hard pitch away from Comiskey Park.

I left my car three blocks down, on a side street, mulling over what I'd learned from several phone calls to contacts in the Coroner's Office and the Homicide Bureau. The death had never been considered a possible homicide, so there'd been virtually no investigation.

A midget had died in his sleep, a not uncommon occurrence, considering the limited life expectancy of little people. Yes, there'd been some bruises, but Gaedel was known as a rough customer, a barroom brawler, with several assaults on his record. The unspoken but strongly implied thread was that if Gaedel hadn't died of natural causes, he'd earned whatever he'd gotten.

The alcove of the funeral home was filled with smoke and midgets. This was not surprising, the smoke anyway, being fairly typical for a Chicago storefront funeral parlor — no smoking was allowed in the visitation areas, so everybody crowded out in the entryway and smoked and talked.

Seeing all those small, strange faces turned toward me, as I entered, was unsettling: wrinkled doll faces, frowning at my six-foot presence, the men in suits and ties, the women in Sunday best, like children playing dress up. I took off my hat, nodded at them as a group, and they resumed their conversations, a highpitched chatter, like half a dozen Alvin and the Chipmunks records were playing simultaneously.

The dark-panelled visitation area was large, and largely empty, and just inside the door was the tiny coffin with Eddie peacefully inside. He wore a conservative suit and tie, hands folded; it was the only time I hadn't seen Eddie in a loud sportshirt, with the exception of that kid-size Browns uniform. Quite a few flowers were on display, many with Catholic trappings, a horseshoe arrangement ribboned MY FAVORITE BATTER — BILL VEECK prominent among them.

The folding chairs would have seated several hundred, but only two were occupied. Over to the right, a petite but normal-sized woman in black dabbed her eyes with a hanky as a trio of midgets — two men and a woman — stood consoling her. Eddie's mother, no doubt.

The female midget was maybe four feet and definitely quite lovely, a shapely blue-eyed blonde lacking pinched features or ungainly limbs, a miniature beauty in a blue satin prom dress. She was upset, weeping into her own hanky.

In the back sat a human non-sequitur, a slim, rangy mourner in his late thirties, with rugged aging-American-boy good looks — anything but a midget. His expression somber, his sandy hair flecked with gray, he looked familiar to me, though I couldn't place him.

Since Eddie's mom was occupied, I wandered back to the full-size mourner and he stood, respectfully, as I approached.

"Nate Heller," I said, extending a hand. "I take it you were a friend of Eddie's, too. Sorry I can't place you . . ."

"Bob Cain," he said, shaking my hand.

"The pitcher!"

His smile was embarrassed. "That's right. You're a friend of Bill Veeck's, aren't you?"

"Yeah. I've done a number of jobs for Bill . . . including body-guarding Eddie for that stunt, way back when."

Cain smiled again, a bittersweet expression. Then he moved over one and gestured to the empty chair, saying, "Sit down, won't you?"

We sat and talked. I was aware that Cain, after a contract squabble shortly following the midget incident, had been traded at Veeck's request to the Browns. Cain played the '52 and '53 seasons for him.

"Bill's a great guy," Cain said. "One owner who treated the players like human beings."

"Even if he did embarrass you?"

"That's just part of the Veeck package. Funny thing is, in the time I played for him, Bill never mentioned the midget thing. But I always wondered if he'd traded for me to make it up to me, or something. Anyway, I had a fine career, Mr. Heller."

"Nate."

"Beat the Yankees fifteen oh, in my first major league start. Pitched a one-hitter against Feller. I had a lot of good experiences in baseball."

"But you'll be remembered for pitching to a midget."

"At least I'll be remembered. It's part of baseball history, Nate — there'll never be another midget in the game . . . just Eddie."

"Did you stay in touch with the little guy?"

"Naw . . . I haven't seen him since I pitched against him. But when I read about this, I just had to pay my respects, as a good Christian, you know — to a man who was so important in my life."

"Are you still in the game, Bob?"

"Not since '56 . . . got a calcium deposit on my wrist, and couldn't get my pitch back. I drove up from Cleveland for this — felt kind of . . . obligated."

I didn't hear anything but sincerity in his words and his voice; but I would check up on Cain's whereabouts — and see if he'd driven up from Cleveland before or after Eddie's murder.

The petite blonde was standing at the casket, lingering there, staring down at Eddie, weeping softly into her hanky. The two men had gone back out to the alcove.

This left Mrs. Gaedel free, and I went over to her, introducing myself.

"Mrs. Gaedel, Bill Veeck sends his condolences," I told her, taking the seat next to her.

A pleasant-looking woman of sixty, salt-and-pepper hair in a bun, Mrs. Gaedel sat and listened as I told her how I'd been involved with Eddie in his famous stunt. I left out the part about the college girls in the lounge car.

"Mr. Veeck was wonderful to Eddie over the years," she said, her voice bravely strong. "Gave Eddie so much work. Eddie supported me, after his father died, you know."

"Eddie kept busy."

"Yes. TV, movies, stage . . . He lived with me, you know — had his little apartment with its little furnishings in the attic . . . ceiling so low I had trouble cleaning up there, but he loved it. That's where I found him . . . in bed . . . ."

I slipped an arm around her as she wept.

Then after a while I said, "You spoke to Mr. Veeck on the phone, I understand."

"Yes — this morning."

"I'm a private investigator, Mrs. Gaedel, and Bill asked me to talk to you about these . . . doubts you have, about the circumstances of your son's death."

"Oh! Are you willing to look into that for me?"

"Bill has hired me to do that very thing, as long as we have your blessing."

"Of course you have my blessing! And my eternal thanks . . . What do you want to know, Mr. Heller?"

"This is hardly the time, Mrs. Gaedel. I can come to your home, after the service sometime, in a day or two perhaps —"

"No, please, Mr. Heller. Let's talk now, if we could."

I was turning my hat in my hands like a wheel. "Actually, that would be wise, if you're up to it. The sooner I can get started —"

"I'm up to it. Start now."

We were interrupted several times, as Eddie's friends paid their respects. But her story was this: Eddie had been drinking heavily lately, and running with a rough crowd, who hung out at the Midgets' Club.

I knew this bar, which was over on Halstead, and dated back to the '40s; it had begun as a gimmick, a bar where the customers were served by midgets, mostly former members of the Singer Midgets who'd played Munchkins in *The Wizard of Oz*. An area was given over to small tables and short stools, for midget clientele, and eventually the midgets essentially took over. But for the occasional tourist who stopped by for the oddity of the joint — to pick up the trademark half-books of matches, see a few framed *Oz* photos, and get some Munchkin autographs — the Midgets' Club became the cultural center of midget activity in Chicago.

"I thought the Midgets Club was pretty respectable," I said.

"It is — Elmer St. Aubin and his wife still run the place. But a rough element — carny types — hang out there, you know."

"That blonde you were talking to. She doesn't seem part of that element."

"She isn't, not all. That's Betsy Jane Perkins . . . she worked with Eagle's Midget Troupe, does a lot of television, personal appearances, dressed and made up like a doll . . . the 'Living Doll,' they call her."

"Were your son and Miss Perkins good friends?"

"Oh yes. He'd been dating her. She was wonderful. Best thing in his life . . . I was so hopeful her good influence would wrest him away from that bad crowd."

"Do you suspect anyone in particular, Mrs. Gaedel?"

"No, I . . . I really didn't know many of my son's friends. Betsy Jane is an exception. Another possibility are these juvenile delinquents."

"Oh?"

"That's what I think may have happened — a gang of those terrible boys may have gotten ahold of Eddie and beaten him."

"Did he say so?"

"No, not really. He didn't say anything, just stumbled off to bed."

"Had he been robbed, mugged? Was money missing from his wallet?"

She shook her head, frowning. "No. But these juveniles pick on the little people all the time. If my son were inebriated, he would have been the perfect target for those monsters. You should strongly consider that possibility."

"I will. Mrs. Gaedel, I'll be in touch with you later. My deepest sympathies, ma'am."

She took my hand and squeezed it. "God bless you, Mr. Heller."

In the alcove, I signed the memorial book. The crowd of midgets was thinning, and the blonde was gone.

Nothing left for me to do but follow the Yellow Brick Road.

✗ ✗ ✗

The Midget Club might have been any Chicago saloon: a bar at the left, booths at the right, scattering of tables between, pool table in back, wall-hung celebrity photos here and there, neon beer signs burning through the fog of tobacco smoke, patrons chatting, laughing, over a jukebox's blare. But the bar was sawed-off with tiny stools, the tables and chairs and booths all scaled down to smaller proportions (with a few normal sized ones up front, for tourist traffic), the pool table half-scale, the celebrity photos of Munchkins, the chatter and laughter of patrons giddy and highpitched. As for the jukebox, Sinatra's "Tender Trap" was playing at the moment, to be followed by more selections running to slightly dated swing material, no rock or r & b — which suited me, and was a hell of a lot better than "Ding Dong the Witch Is Dead."

I had known the club's proprietor and chief bartender, Pernell "Little Elmer" St. Aubin, since he was, well, little — a child entertainer at the Midget Village at the Chicago World's Fair back in '33. He'd been tap dancing and I'd been busting pickpockets. Elmer had been in his teens when he appeared in *The Wizard of Oz,* so now — as he stood behind the bar, polishing a glass, a wizened Munchkin in an apron — he was probably only in his mid-thirties. But as was so often the case with his kind, he looked both older and younger than his years.

I selected one of the handful of somewhat taller stools at the bar and said to Elmer, "For a weekday, you're doing good business."

"It's kind of a wake," Elmer explained. "For Eddie Gaedel. People coming over after visitation at Keurtz's. You knew Eddie, didn't you?"

"Yeah. I was over there myself. Paying my respects, and Bill Veeck's."

Elmer frowned. "Couldn't Veeck make it himself?"

"He's pretty sick. So was Eddie ornery as ever, up to the end?"

"Christ yes! I hated serving that little bastard. Sweet enough guy sober, but what a lousy drunk. If I hadn't been secretly watering his drinks, over the years, he'd have busted up the joint long ago."

"I hear he may have been rolled by some juvies. Think that's what killed him?"

"I doubt it. Eddie carried a straight razor — people knew he did, too. I think these young punks woulda been scared to get cut. Funny thing, though."

"What is?"

"His mama said that straight razor didn't turn up in his things."

I thought about that, then asked, "So how *do* you think Eddie died?"

"I have my own opinion."

"Like to share that opinion, Elmer?"

"The cops weren't interested. Why are you?"

"Eddie was a friend. Maybe I'm just curious. Maybe there's a score to settle."

"Are you gonna drink something, Heller?"

I gave the Munchkin a ten, asked for a rum and Coke and told him he could keep the change, if he stayed chatty.

"Eddie was playing a puppet on a local kid's show," Elmer said, serving me up. "But he lost the gig 'cause of his boozing. So lately he was talking to some of my less classier clientele about going out on the carny circuit. Some kinda sideshow scam where they pretended to be Siamese triplets or something."

"Work is work."

"See that little dame over there?"

Every dame in here was little, but Elmer was talking about Betsy Jane, the Living Doll in her blue satin prom dress. I hadn't spotted her when I came in — she was sitting alone in a booth, staring down into a coffee cup cupped in her dainty hands.

Elmer leaned in conspiratorially. "That's Betsy Jane Perkins, the actress — Eddie was crazy about her, and she felt the same about him. She was trying to straighten him out, and I think she might've succeeded, if it hadn't been for that ex-husband of hers."

"Yeah?"

"Guy named Fred Peterson. He's a shrimp."

"A midget?"

"No, a *shrimp* — a 'normal'-size guy who stands just under five feet. He's a theatrical agent, still is Betsy Jane's agent; specializes in booking little people. Makes him feel like a big man, lording it over us."

"He is a regular?" I swivelled on the stool and glanced around. "Is he here?"

"Yes, he's a regular, no, he's not here. He wouldn't pay his respects to Eddie, that's for goddamn sure."

"Why?"

"Lately Fred's been trying to get back in Betsy Jane's good graces, among other things. Why don't you talk to her? She's a sweet kid. I think she'd do anything to help out where Eddie's concerned."

I took Elmer's advice, and my rum and Coke and I went over and stood next to the booth where the painfully pretty little woman gloomily sat. She looked up at me with beautiful if bloodshot blue eyes; her heavy, doll-like make-up was a little grief-smeared, but she was naturally pretty, with a fairly short, Marilyn-ish do.

"Miss Perkins, my name is Nate Heller — I was a friend of Eddie Gaedel's."

"I don't remember Eddie mentioning you, Mr. Heller," she said, almost primly, her voice a melodic soprano with a vibrato of sorrow.

"I'm an associate of Bill Veeck's. I escorted Eddie to that famous game in St. Louis back in '51."

She had brightened at the mention of Veeck's name, and was already gesturing for me to sit across from her.

"I saw you at the funeral parlor," she said, "talking to Helen."

"Helen?"

"Mrs. Gaedel."

"Yes. She feels the circumstances of her son's death are somewhat suspicious."

The blue eyes lowered. "I'd prefer to reminisce about Eddie and the fun times, the good times, than . . ."

"Face the truth?"

"Mr. Heller, I don't know what happened to Eddie. I just know I've lost him, right when I thought . . ." She began to cry, and got in her purse, rustling for a handkerchief.

I glanced over at Elmer, behind the bar, and he was squinting at me, making a vaguely frantic gesture that I didn't get. Shrugging at him, I returned my attention to the Living Doll.

"You'd been trying to help Eddie. Encourage him to stop drinking, I understand. Not run with such a rough crowd."

"That's right."

I'd hoped for elaboration.

I tried venturing down a different avenue. "I understand some j.d.s have been preying on little people in this neighborhood."

"That . . . that's true."

"Eddie might have been beaten and robbed."

"Yes . . . he might have."

"But you don't think that's the case, do you?"

Now she was getting a compact out of her purse, checking her make-up. "If you'll excuse me, Mr. Heller — I look a fright."

And she went off to the ladies' room.

I just sat there and sipped my rum and Coke, wondering if I would get anything out of Betsy Jane except tears, when an unMunchkin-like baritone growled at me.

"You got a fetish, pal?"

I turned and looked up at the source of the irritation, and the reason for Elmer's motioning to me: he was short, but no midget, possibly five foot, almost handsome, with a Steve Canyon jaw compromised by pugged nose and cow eyes; his hair was dark blond and slicked back and he wore a mustache that would have been stylish as hell if this were 1935. Deeply tanned, his build was brawny, his hairy, muscular chest shown off by the deep v-neck cut of his pale green herringbone golf shirt, his arms short but muscular.

I said, "What?"

"You got a scratch to itch, buddy?"

"What the hell are you talking about?"

He leaned in, eyes popping, teeth bared, cords in his neck taut; he reeked of Old Spice. "You some kind of pervert, pops? Some kinda letch for the midget ladies?"

Very quietly, I said, "Back off."

Something about how I'd said it gave him pause, and the clenched fist that was his face twitched a couple times, and he and his Old Spice aura backed away — but he kept standing there, muscular arms folded now, like a stubby, pissed-off genie.

"And you must be Fred Peterson," I said.

"Who wants to know?"

Not offering a hand to shake, I said, "My name's Heller — friend of Eddie Gaedel's, and Bill Veeck's."

He blinked. "What, you were over at the funeral home?"

"That's right."

"Paying your respects."

"Yes. And looking into Eddie's murder."

He frowned; then he scrambled across from me into the booth, where Betsy Jane had been sitting. "What do you mean, murder?"

"He was beaten to death, Fred. You don't mind if I call you 'Fred' . . . ?"

His hands were folded, but squeezing, as if he were doing isometrics. "The cops said it was natural causes. Why's it your business, the cops say it's natural causes?"

"I'm a private investigator, working for Veeck. When I get enough evidence, I'll turn it over to the cops and see if I can't change their minds about how 'natural' those causes were."

He leaned forward, hands still clasped, a vein in his forehead jumping. "Listen, that little prick had a big mouth and a lot of enemies. You're gonna get nowhere!"

I shrugged, sipped my rum and Coke. "Maybe I can get somewhere with Betsy Jane."

The cow eyes flashed. "Stay away from her."

"Why should I? She seems to like me, and I like her. She's a cute kid. She interests me . . . kind of a new frontier."

"I said stay away."

"Who died and appointed you head of the Lollipop Guild? I'm going to find out who killed Eddie Gaedel, and have myself some tight little fun along the way."

And I grinned at him, until he growled a few obscenities and bolted away, heading toward the rear of the bar, almost bumping into Betsy Jane, coming back from the restroom. She froze seeing him, and he clutched her by the shoulders and got right in her face and said something to her, apparently something unpleasant, even threatening. Then he stalked toward the rear exit.

Her expression alarmed, she took her seat across from me and said, "You should go now."

"That was your agent, right?"

". . . right."

"And your boyfriend?"

"No . . . husband. Ex-husband. Please go."

"Jealous of you and Eddie, by any chance? Did you go to him with the idea for a new act, you and Eddie as boy and girl livin' dolls?"

She shook her head, blonde bangs shimmering. "Mr. Heller, you don't know what kind of position you're putting me in . . ."

I knew that her ex-husband didn't want any man putting this doll in any position.

But I said, "I think for a little guy, your ex-husband and current agent has a tall temper. And I think he's goddamn lucky the cops didn't investigate this case, because he makes one hell of a suspect in Eddie's death."

She began to weep again, but this was different, this was more than grief — there was fear in it.

"What do you know, Betsy Jane?"

"Nuh . . . nothing . . . nothing . . ."

"Tell me. Just tell me — so that *I* know. I won't take anything to the police without your permission."

Damp eyelashes fluttered. "Well . . . I . . . I don't know anything, except that . . . on that last night, Fred was . . . nice to Eddie and me."

"Nice?"

"Yes. He'd been furious with me, at the suggestion that Eddie and I would work as a team, livid that I would suggest that he, of all people, should book such an act . . . We had two, no three, terrible arguments about it. Then . . . then he changed. He can do that, run hot and cold. He apologized, said he'd been a jerk, said he wanted to make it up, wanted to help. Sat and talked with us all evening, making plans about the act."

"Go on."

"That's all."

"No it isn't. I can see it in those pretty eyes, Betsy Jane. The rest . . . tell me the rest."

She swallowed, nodded, sighed. "They . . . they left together. Eddie lived close, you know, easy walk home to his mother's house — Fred was going to talk business with him. They went out the back way, around midnight. It was the last time I saw Eddie alive."

The alley behind the bar, bumped up against the backyards of residences, would be as good a place as any for an assault.

She was saying, "But I can't imagine Fred would do such a thing."

"Sure you can."

She shook her head. "Anyway, Eddie was no pushover. He carried a straight razor, you know."

"So I hear. But I also hear it wasn't among his effects."

"Oh, Eddie had it that night. I saw it."

"Yeah?"

"He emptied his pocket, looking for change for the jukebox . . . laid his things right on this counter, razor among them. We were sitting in this very booth . . . this was . . . *our* booth."

She began to cry again, and I got over on her side of the booth, slid an arm around her, and comforted her, thinking that she really was a cute kid, and midget sex was definitely on my short list of things yet undone in a long and varied life.

But more to the point, what had become of that razor? If Fred had attacked Eddie out back, maybe that razor had been dropped in the scuffle — and if it was back there, somewhere, I'd have the evidence I needed to get the cops to open an investigation.

"Betsy Jane," I said, "we'll talk again . . . when you're feeling up to it."

"All right . . . but Mr. Heller . . . Nate . . . I am afraid. Terribly afraid."

I squeezed her shoulder, kissed her cheek. "I'll make the bad man go away."

She put her hand on my thigh — her little bitty hand. Christ, it felt weird. Also, good.

Nodding to Elmer, I headed toward the rear exit, and stepped out into the alley. The night was moonless with a scattering of stars, and the lighting was negligible — no street lamps back here, just whatever scant illumination spilled from the frame houses whose back yards bordered the asphalt strip. A trio of garbage cans — full-scale, nothing midget about them — stood against the back of the brick building, and some empty liquor and beer cartons were stacked nearby.

Not much to see, and in the near-darkness, I would probably need my flashlight to probe for that missing straight razor. I had just decided to walk the several blocks to the side street where my car was parked, to get the flash, when a figure stepped out from the recession of an adjacent building's rear doorway.

"Looking for something?" Fred Peterson asked, those cow eyes wide and wild, teeth bared like an angry animal, veins throbbing in his neck, one hand behind his back. Though he stood only five foot, his brawny frame, musculature obvious in the skin-tight golf shirt, made him a threatening presence as he stepped into the alley like a gunfighter out onto the Main Street of Dodge.

I was thinking how I should have brought my gun along — only usually, attending midget funerals, it wasn't necessary.

"Get some ideas," he said, "talking to Betsy Jane?"

He was standing there, rocking on legs whose powerful thighs stood out, despite the bagginess of his chinos.

Shrugging, I said, "I thought Eddie mighta dropped something when you jumped him."

Peterson howled as he whipped something from behind him and charged, it was a bat, he was wielding a goddamn baseball bat, and he was whipping it at me, slicing the air, the bat whooshing over me as I ducked under the swing. Screw baseball, I tackled him, taking him down hard, and the bat fell from his grasp, clattering onto the asphalt. I rolled off him, rolling toward the sound, and then I had the bat in my hands, as I got up and took my stance.

That's when I found that straight razor I'd been looking for, or rather Fred Peterson showed me what had become of it, as he yanked it from his pocket and swung it around, the meager light of the alley managing to wink off the shining blade.

I didn't wait for him to come at me: I took my swing.

The bat caught him in the side of the head, a hard blow that caved his skull in, and by the time Peterson fell to his knees, his motor responses were dead, and so was he. He flopped forward, on his face, razor spilling from limp fingers, blood and brains leaching out onto the asphalt as I stood over him, the bat resting against my shoulder.

"Strike zone my ass," I said to nobody, breathing hard.

Finally I went back into the Midget Club, carrying the bloody bat, getting my share of my looks, though Betsy Jane had gone. I leaned on the bar and told Elmer to call the cops.

But the little bartender just looked at me in amazement. "What the hell did you do, Heller?"

"Somebody had to go to bat for Eddie. Call the goddamn cops, would you, please?"

✗ ✗ ✗

No charges were brought against me — my actions were clearly in self-defense — and Eddie Gaedel's death is listed to this day as "natural causes" on the books. Though I shared with them everything I knew about the matter, the police simply didn't want to go to the trouble of declaring Eddie a murder victim, merely to pursue a deceased suspect. Poor Eddie just couldn't get a fair shake in any of the record books.

A few days after the cops cleared me, Veeck spoke to me on the phone, from a room in the Mayo clinic.

"You know, ten years ago, when I sent Eddie Gaedel into that game," he said, reflectively, "I knew it would be that little clown's shining moment . . . what I didn't know was that it would be mine, too! Hell, I knew it was a good gag, that the fans would roar, and the stuffed shirts holler. But who coulda guessed it'd become the single act forever identified with me?"

"We're any of us lucky to be remembered for anything, Bill," I said.

"Yeah. Yeah. Suppose Eddie felt that way?"

"I know he did."

For years after, Helen Gaedel remembered me at Christmas with cookies or a fruitcake. Betsy Jane Perkins was grateful, too.

Veeck expressed his gratitude by paying me handsomely, and, typically, fooled himself and all of us by not dying just yet. The man who invented fan appreciation night, who provided a day care center for female employees before the term was coined, who was first to put the names of players on the backs of uniforms, who broke the color line in the American League, and who sent a midget up to bat — and who also bought back the Chicago White Sox in 1975 — lived another irascible fifteen years.

And wasn't that a hell of a stunt.

I Owe Them One

Despite its extensive basis in history, the novella "Kisses of Death" is a work of fiction; some liberties have been taken with facts, including compression of time. Most of the characters in this story are real people and appear under their true names. Thanks to my research associate George Hagenauer for suggesting this subject matter and helping gather material.

In addition to contemporary newspaper accounts of the Bodenheim murders, and "A Malady of the Soul," a fine 1981 *Chicago Reader* article by Michael Miner, the following volumes were of particular help: William MacAdams, *Ben Hecht: The Man Behind the Legend* (1990); Dale Kramer, *Chicago Renaissance* (1966); Ben Hecht, *A Child of the Century* (1954); Don Fetherling, *The Five Lives of Ben Hecht* (1977); Maxwell Bodenheim, *My Life and Loves in Greenwich Village* (1954); and *A Treasury of Ben Hecht* (1959), which includes Hecht's play "Winkelberg," based on Bodenheim's life. Thanks also to my wife, writer Barbara Collins, a Marilyn Monroe expert who contributed her insights; of dozens of Monroe volumes consulted, Randall Riese and Neal Hitchens, *The Unabridged Marilyn — Her Life from A to Z* (1987), was the most useful.

In "Kaddish for the Kid," names have not been changed, and the events are fundamentally true. Source material included an article by John J. McPhaul and information provided by George Hagenauer, whom I thank for his insights and suggestions.

The story "The Perfect Crime" originally appeared in the collection *Raymond Chandler's Philip Marlowe* (1988). That anthology included new stories about Chandler's famous detective by various mystery writers. A proviso of the story's inclusion in that volume was that any subsequent reprintings could not use the name "Philip Marlowe." I have re-written this tale into a Heller story (since I had used the techniques of my Heller stories in writing it in the first place), making shifts in background and voice; but my usual debt to Chandler hangs even heavier over this particular story.

"The Perfect Crime" is based on a real case, the probable murder of actress Thelma Todd. I have taken liberties, changing some names and fictionalizing extensively, and, while there is an underpinning of history here, this must be viewed as a fanciful work. A number of books dealing with the death of Thelma Todd were consulted, but I wish in particular to cite Marvin J. Wolf and Katherine Mader, the authors of *Fallen Angels* (1986).

In "Natural Death, Inc.," fact, speculation and fiction are freely mixed; the story is based on an actual case in the career of Eliot Ness. In "Screwball," certain liberties have been taken with the facts, and some names have been changed. Thanks again to George, who uncovered this little-known incident in the life of Frank Nitti.

Most of the characters in "Shoot-out on Sunset" appear under their real names; several — notably, Fred Rubinski, Didi Davis, Delbert Potts and Rudy Johnson — are fictional but have real-life counterparts. Research sources included numerous true-crime magazine articles and the following books: Tony Blanche and Brad Schreiber, *Death in Paradise* (1998); Florabel Muir, *Headline Happy* (1950); Ted Prager and Larry Craft, *Hoodlums — Los Angeles* (1959); Ovid DeMaris, *The Last Mafioso* (1981); *Mickey Cohen: In My Own Words* (1975), as told to John Peer Nugent; Ed Reid, *Mickey Cohen: Mobster* (1973); Jim Heimann, *Sins of the City* (1999); Charles Stoker, T*hicker'n Thieves* (1951), and Jim Vaus as told to D.C. Haskin, *Why I Quit Syndicated Crime* (1951). Thanks again to George, and to editors Bob Randisi and Joe Pittman for their permission to use this story — from their recent anthology, *Mystery Street* — here.

In "Strike Zone" (my preferred title — it was originally published as "Pinch Hitter"), fact, speculation and fiction are again freely mixed. George Hagenauer's usual good work was supplemented by personal knowledge: he knew Bill Veeck and kept me honest in my depiction. Newspapers of the day were consulted, and a number of books, including Gerald Eskenazi, *Bill Veeck: A Baseball Legend* (1988); Stephen Cox, *Munchkins of Oz* (1996); Hank Greenberg, *The Story of My Life* (1989); and Bill Veeck with Ed Linn, *Veeck — As in Wreck* (1962; revised 1976). Thanks to Otto Penzler for asking me to write this story.

And thanks to my wife and son; my agent Dominick Abel; and, again, especially to Doug and Sandi Greene at Crippen & Landru for publishing this second collection of Nate Heller's shorter cases.

A MAX ALLAN COLLINS CHECKLIST

This attempt at a full list of my fiction was the doing of two dedicated fans: Kevin Burton Smith and Norman Peeler. Kevin Smith discusses many writers of private eye fiction at his Thrilling Detective website (www.thrillingdetective.com/) with lots of coverage on yours truly. Norman has a website (www.angelfire.com/nc/macgallery/mac.html) devoted to my work, and I'm grateful to him for the attention. My thanks to both.

I have added a few items myself — some of this comes from my official website (www.maxallancollins.com, which my son Nathan oversees) — but may have missed a few things; any additions and corrections are welcome. I used to shake my head when Chester Gould and Mickey Spillane were unable to answer my questions about their work; now I understand — the professional storyteller is a shark, never sleeping, always looking for the next meal, sniffing after blood, never looking back.

Not included in this fiction-only checklist are non-fiction books, monographs and articles; film reviews and columns; introductions to books by other authors; trading card sets; and songwriting credits. Maybe another time.

NOVELS

Featuring Nolan:

Bait Money. Curtis, 1973; revised edition, Pinnacle, 1981
Blood Money. Curtis, 1973; revised edition, Pinnacle, 1981
Fly Paper. Pinnacle, 1981
Hush Money. Pinnacle, 1981
Hard Cash. Pinnacle, 1982
Scratch Fever. Pinnacle, 1982
Spree. Tor, 1987

Tough Tender. Carroll & Graf, 1991; combines *Hard Cash* and *Scratch Fever*

Mourn the Living. Five Star, 1999

Featuring Quarry:

The Broker. Berkley, 1976; reissued as *Quarry*, Foul Play Press, 1985

The Broker's Wife. Berkley, 1976; reissued as *Quarry's List*, Foul Play Press, 1985

The Dealer. Berkley, 1976; reissued as *Quarry's Deal*, Foul Play Press, 1986

The Slasher. Berkley, 1977; reissued as *Quarry's Cut*, Foul Play Press, 1986

Primary Target. Foul Play Press, 1987

Featuring Mallory:

The Baby Blue Rip-Off. Walker, 1983

No Cure for Death. Walker, 1983

Kill Your Darlings. Walker, 1984

A Shroud for Aquarius. Walker, 1985

Nice Weekend for a Murder. Walker, 1986

Featuring Nathan Heller:

True Detective. St. Martin's, 1983

True Crime. St. Martin's, 1984

The Million-Dollar Wound. St. Martin's, 1986

Neon Mirage. St. Martin's, 1988

Stolen Away. Bantam, 1991

Dying in the Post-War World. Foul Play Press, 1991; short story collection

Carnal Hours. Dutton, 1994

Blood and Thunder. Dutton, 1995

Damned in Paradise. Dutton, 1996

Flying Blind. Dutton, 1998

Majic Man. Dutton, 1999

Angel in Black. NAL, 2001
Kisses of Death. Crippen & Landru, 2001; short story collection

Featuring Eliot Ness:

The Dark City. Bantam, 1987
Butcher's Dozen. Bantam, 1988
Bullet Proof. Bantam, 1989
Murder by the Numbers. St. Martin's, 1993

Featuring Dick Tracy:

Dick Tracy. Bantam, 1990; movie novelization
Dick Tracy Goes to War. Bantam, 1991
Dick Tracy Meets His Match. Bantam, 1992

Featuring N.Y.P.D. Blue:

Blue Beginning. Signet, 1995
Blue Blood. Signet, 1997

Movie Tie-In Novels:

In the Line of Fire. Jove, 1993
I Love Trouble. Signet, 1994; written as by "Peter Brackett," the novel's
    protagonist
Maverick. Signet, 1994
Waterworld. Berkley, 1995
Waterworld. Berkley, 1995; young adult novel
Daylight. Berkley, 1996
Air Force One. Ballantine, 1997
U.S. Marshals. Berkley, 1998
Saving Private Ryan. Signet, 1998
The Mummy. Berkley, 1999
U-571. Avon , 2000
The Mummy Returns. Berkley, 2001

Other Novels:

Midnight Haul. Foul Play Press, 1986
Caribbean Blues. Paperjacks, 1988; a collaborative novel, benefitting Literacy Volunteers of America; author of chapters 4 and 12, co-author of chapter 18. Features Nathan Heller
Mommy. Leisure, 1997
Mommy's Day. Leisure, 1998
The Titanic Murders. Berkley, 1999
Regeneration. Leisure, 1999; co-written with Barbara Collins
The Hindenberg Murders. Berkley, 2000
The Pearl Harbor Murders. Berkley, 2001

SHORT STORIES

"Red Light," *The Files of Ms. Tree*, 1984 (Ms. Tree)
"The Strawberry Teardrop," *The Eyes Have It*, 1984 (Nate Heller)
"Public Servant," *Hardboiled*, 1985
"The Little Woman," *The Files of Ms. Tree, Vol. 2*, 1985 (Ms. Tree)
"The Love Rack," *Hardboiled*, Spring 1986
"House Call," *Mean Streets*, 1986 (Nate Heller)
"Scrap," *The Black Lizard Anthology of Crime Fiction*, 1987 (Nate Heller)
"Enter Nolan," written in 1968 but first published in *Hardboiled*, Spring 1987 (Nolan)
"The Perfect Crime," *Raymond Chandler's Philip Marlowe: A Centennial Celebration*, 1988; also published as a Mystery Scene Press Short Story Paperback and Limited Edition Hardcover with the name of the detective changed to Peter Mallory; in *Kisses of Death*, the character was changed to Nate Heller.
"Marble Mildred," *An Eye for Justice*, 1988 (Nate Heller)
"Mourn the Living" (Part 1), written in 1969; first Nolan novel, serialized in three installments, *Hardboiled*, Summer/Fall 1987 (Nolan)
"Mourn the Living" (Part 2), *Hardboiled*, Winter/Spring 1988 (Nolan)
"Mourn the Living" (Part 3), *Hardboiled*, Spring 1989 (Nolan)
"The Sound of One Hand Clapping," *The Further Adventures of Batman*,

1989 (Batman)

"A Matter of Principal," *Stalkers*, 1989 (Quarry)

"Private Consultation," *Justice for Hire*, 1990 (Nate Heller)

"Not a Creature Was Stirring," *Dick Tracy: The Secret Files*, 1990 (Dick Tracy)

"Dying in the Post-War World ," *Dying in the Post-War World*, 1991 Nate Heller)

"Louise," *Deadly Allies*, 1992 (Ms. Tree)

"Cat Got Your Tongue," *Cat Crimes III*, 1992; with Barbara Collins

"Robber's Roost," *The Further Adventures of Batman*, Volume 2, 1992 (Batman)

"A Good Head on His Shoulders," *Frankenstein: The Monster Wakes*, 1993

"Catgate," *Danger in D.C.*, 1993

"Inconvenience Store," *Deadly Allies 2*, 1994 (Ms. Tree)

"Reincarnal," *Hot Blood: Deadly After Dark*, 1994

"Quarry's Luck," *Blue Motel*, 1994 (Quarry)

"Guest Services," *Murder Is My Business*, 1994 (Quarry)

"His Father's Ghost," *Murder for Father*, 1994

"Rock 'n' Roll Will Never Die," *Shock Rock*, 1994

"Traces of Red," *Celebrity Vampires*, 1995

"Mommy," *Fear Itself*, 1995

"The Night of Their Lives," *Vampire Detectives*, 1995

"Wolf," *Werewolves*, 1995

"Firecracker Kill," *Shades of Noir: Book One*, 1996

"A Wreath For Marley," *Dante's Disciples*, 1996 (Richard Stone)

"Love Nest," *Lethal Ladies*, 1996, as solely by Barbara Collins; actually a collaboration

"A Bird for Becky," *Shades of Noir: Book Two*, 1996 (Richard Stone)

"The Chocolate-Chip Alarm," *Great Writers & Kids Write Mystery Stories*, 1996; with Nathan Collins

"Kisses of Death," originally available only as a 90-minute promotional audio tape from B & B, 1996 given away at ABA, read by Max and Barb Collins; first printed in *Kisses of Death*, 2001 (Nate Heller)

"The Cabinet of William Henry Harrison," *White House Horrors*, 1996; with Barbara Collins

"Interstate 666," *Hot Blood: Kiss and Kill*, 1997

"Regeneration," *Hot Blood X*, 1998

"Eddie Haskell in a Short Skirt," *Lethal Ladies II*, 1998, as solely by Barbara Collins; actually a collaboration

"Kaddish for the Kid," *Private Eyes*, 1998 (Nate Heller)

"Flyover Country," *Till Death Do Us Part*, 1999; with Barbara Collins

"Natural Death, Inc.," *Diagnosis Dead*, 1999 (Nate Heller)

"A Cruise to Forget," *Death Cruise*, 1999; with Barbara Collins

"I Had Bigfoot's Baby!" *Hellboy-Odd Jobs*, 1999; with Matthew V. Clemens

"Cat's-Eye Witness," *Crafty Cat Crimes*, 2000

"Screwball," *The Shamus Game*, 2000 (Nate Heller)

"A Woman's Touch," *Murder Most Confederate*, 2000; with Matthew V. Clemens)

"Flowers for Bill O'Reilly," *Flesh & Blood*, 2001.

"My Lolita Complex,"available online, 2000; with Matthew V. Clemens

"Shoot-out on Sunset," *Mystery Street*, 2001 (Nate Heller)

"Unreasonable Doubt," *And the Dying is Easy*, 2001 (Nate Heller)

EDITOR

Tomorrow I Die. Mysterious Press, 1985; collection of Mickey Spillane short fiction

Dick Tracy — The Secret Files. Tor, 1990; with Martin H. Greenberg; collection of short stories featuring Dick Tracy by various authors

The Dick Tracy Casebook. St. Martin's, 1990; with Dick Locher; includes both Chester Gould and Collins-scripted material

Dick Tracy's Fiendish Foes. St. Martin's, 1991; with Dick Locher; includes both Gould and Collins-scripted material

Murder is My Business. Signet, 1996; with Mickey Spillane

Vengeance is Hers. Signet, 1997; with Mickey Spillane

Private Eyes. Signet, 1998; with Mickey Spillane

Too Many Tomcats and Other Feline Tales of Suspense. Five Star, 2000; collection of Barbara Collins short stories

Flesh & Blood: Erotic Tales of Crime and Passion. Mysterious Press, 2001; with Jeff Gelb

COMICS (ALWAYS AS SCRIPT WRITER)

Dick Tracy comic strip, syndicated by Tribune Media Services, 1977-1993.

The Mike Mist Minute Mist-Eries. Eclipse Enterprises comic book, 1981 co-creator with artist Terry Beatty. Collection culled from self-syndicated feature *The Comics Page*, 1979-1980. Also, Mike Mist appears in *The Detectives #1*, Alpha Productions, 1993, and various issues of *Ms. Tree*. Later stories written with (and sometimes by) Barbara Collins.

Ms. Tree, co-creator with artist Terry Beatty. First appearance *Eclipse Magazine*, 1981. Began regular series as *Ms. Tree's Thrilling Detective Adventures*. Title changed to *Ms. Tree* with issue #4. Published in turn by Eclipse Enterprises, Aardvark-Vanaheim, Renegade Press, and D.C. Comics. Last issue to date published in 1993. Ms. Tree also appears in *The P.I. 's*, a mini-series published by First Comics, 1985.

Batman, regular monthly series, D.C. Comics, 1987-1988. Also author of first continuity of Batman comic strip, 1989-1990. Also, *Batman: Scar of the Bat* (graphic novel; artist: Eduardo Barreto; features Eliot Ness), D.C. Comics, 1996.

Wild Dog, co-creator with artist Terry Beatty. Subject of 1987 four-issue mini-series, a special, and several serialized stories in *Action Comics Weekly*, all by D.C. Comics.

Johnny Dynamite, four-issue mini-series ("Underworld"; artist: Terry Beatty). Dark Horse Comics, 1994.

Mike Danger, co-creator with Mickey Spillane of *Mickey Spillane's Mike Danger*. Tekno Comics, 1996-1997.

Wild Times: The Grifter #1. Wildstorm, 1999.

COMIC COLLECTIONS (WITH VARIOUS ARTISTS)

Dick Tracy Meets Angeltop. Tempo, 1979
Dick Tracy Meets the Punks. Tempo, 1980
Files of Ms. Tree, Vol. 1. Aardvark Vanaheim, 1984
Files of Ms. Tree, Vol. 2. Renegade Press , 1985

Files of Ms. Tree, Vol. 3. Renegade Press, 1986
Dick Tracy: Tracy's Wartime Memories. Ken Pierce Books, 1986
Ms. Tree. Paperjacks, 1988
Dick Tracy and the Nightmare Machine. Tor, 1991

Graphic Novels

Road to Perdition, with artist Richard Piers Raynor. Paradox Press, 1998
Scar of the Bat (see *Batman* above)

Produced Screenplays

The Expert. 1994
*Mommy. 1995
*Mommy's Day a.k.a. *Mommy 2: Mommy's Day.* 1997
*Mike Hammer's Mickey Spillane. 1999; documentary
*Real Time: Siege at Lucas Street Market. 2000

* Also producer/co-director

CRIPPEN & LANDRU, PUBLISHERS

P. O. Box 9315, Norfolk, VA 23505

E-mail: info@crippenlandru.com; toll-free & fax: 877 622-6656

Web: www.crippenlandru.com

Crippen & Landru publishes first edition short-story collections by important detective and mystery writers. The following books are currently (September 2006) in print in our regular series; see our website for full details:

The McCone Files by Marcia Muller. 1995. Trade softcover, $19.00.

Diagnosis: Impossible, The Problems of Dr. Sam Hawthorne by Edward D. Hoch. 1996. Trade softcover, $19.00.

Who Killed Father Christmas? by Patricia Moyes. 1996. Signed, unnumbered cloth overrun copies, $30.00.

My Mother, The Detective by James Yaffe. 1997. Trade softcover, $15.00.

In Kensington Gardens Once by H.R.F. Keating. 1997. Trade softcover, $12.00.

Shoveling Smoke by Margaret Maron. 1997. Trade softcover, $19.00.

The Ripper of Storyville and Other Tales of Ben Snow by Edward D. Hoch. 1997. Trade softcover. $19.00.

Renowned Be Thy Grave by P.M. Carlson. 1998. Trade softcover, $16.00.

Carpenter and Quincannon by Bill Pronzini. 1998. Trade softcover, $16.00.

Famous Blue Raincoat by Ed Gorman. 1999. Signed, unnumbered cloth overrun copies, $30.00. Trade softcover, $17.00.

The Tragedy of Errors and Others by Ellery Queen. 1999. Trade softcover, $19.00.

McCone and Friends by Marcia Muller. 2000. Trade softcover, $19.00.

Challenge the Widow Maker by Clark Howard. 2000. Trade softcover, $16.00.

Fortune's World by Michael Collins. 2000. Trade softcover, $16.00.

The Velvet Touch: Nick Velvet Stories by Edward D.. Hoch. 2000. Trade softcover, 19.00.

Long Live the Dead: Tales from Black Mask by Hugh B. Cave. 2000. Trade softcover, $16.00.

Tales Out of School by Carolyn Wheat. 2000. Trade softcover, $16.00.

Stakeout on Page Street and Other DKA Files by Joe Gores. 2000. Trade softcover, $16.00.

The Celestial Buffet by Susan Dunlap. 2001. Trade softcover, $16.00.

Kisses of Death: A Nathan Heller Casebook by Max Allan Collins. 2001. Trade softcover, $19.00.

The Old Spies Club and Other Intrigues of Rand by Edward D. Hoch. 2001. Signed, unnumbered cloth overrun copies, $32.00. Trade softcover, $17.00.

Adam and Eve on a Raft by Ron Goulart. 2001. Signed, unnumbered cloth overrun copies, $32.00. Trade softcover, $17.00.

The Sedgemoor Strangler by Peter Lovesey. 2001. Trade softcover, $17.00.

The Reluctant Detective by Michael Z. Lewin. 2001. Signed, numbered clothbound, $42.00. Trade softcover, $17.00.

Nine Sons by Wendy Hornsby. 2002. Trade softcover, $16.00.

The Curious Conspiracy by Michael Gilbert. 2002. Signed, numbered clothbound, $42.00. Trade softcover, $17.00.

The 13 Culprits by Georges Simenon, translated by Peter Schulman. 2002. Trade softcover, $16.00.

The Dark Snow by Brendan DuBois. 2002. Signed, unnumbered cloth overrun copies, $32.00. Trade softcover, $17.00.

Come Into My Parlor: Tales from Detective Fiction Weekly by Hugh B. Cave. 2002. Trade softcover, $17.00.

The Iron Angel and Other Tales of the Gypsy Sleuth by Edward D. Hoch. 2003. Signed, numbered clothbound, $42.00. Trade softcover, $17.00.

Cuddy – Plus One by Jeremiah Healy. 2003. Trade softcover, $18.00.

Problems Solved by Bill Pronzini and Barry N. Malzberg. 2003. Signed, numbered clothbound, $42.00. Trade softcover, $16.00.

A Killing Climate by Eric Wright. 2003. Signed, numbered clothbound, $42.00. Trade softcover, $17.00.

Lucky Dip by Liza Cody. 2003. Signed, numbered clothbound, $42.00. Trade softcover, $17.00.

Kill the Umpire: The Calls of Ed Gorgon by Jon L. Breen. 2003. Trade softcover, $17.00.

Suitable for Hanging by Margaret Maron. 2004. Trade softcover, $17.00.

Murders and Other Confusions by Kathy Lynn Emerson. 2004. Signed, numbered clothbound, $42.00. Trade softcover, $19.00.

Byline: Mickey Spillane by Mickey Spillane, edited by Lynn Myers and Max Allan Collins. 2004. Trade softcover, $20.00.

The Confessions of Owen Keane by Terence Faherty. 2005. Signed, numbered clothbound, $42.00. Trade softcover, $17.00.

The Adventure of the Murdered Moths and Other Radio Mysteries by Ellery Queen. 2005. Numbered clothbound, $45.00. Trade softcover, $20.00.

Murder, Ancient and Modern by Edward Marston. 2005. Signed, numbered clothbound, $43.00. Trade softcover, $18.00.

More Things Impossible: The Second Casebook of Dr. Sam Hawthorne by Edward D. Hoch. 2006. Signed, numbered clothbound, $43.00. Trade softcover, $18.00.

Murder, 'Orrible Murder! by Amy Myers. 2006. Signed, numbered clothbound, $43.00. Trade softcover, $18.00.

FORTHCOMING TITLES IN THE REGULAR SERIES

Thirteen to the Gallows by John Dickson Carr and Val Gielgud

The Mankiller of Poojeegai and Other Mysteries by Walter Satterthwait

A Pocketful of Noses: Stories of One Ganelon or Another by James Powell

The Archer Files: The Complete Short Stories of Lew Archer, Private Investigator, Including Newly-Discovered Case-Notes by Ross Macdonald, edited by Tom Nolan

Quintet: The Cases of Chase and Delacroix, by Richard A. Lupoff

A Little Intelligence by Robert Silverberg and Randall Garrett (writing as "Robert Randall")

Attitude and Other Stories of Suspense by Loren D. Estleman

Suspense – His and Hers by Barbara and Max Allan Collins

[Currently untitled collection] by S.J. Rozan

Hoch's Ladies by Edward D. Hoch

14 Slayers by Paul Cain, edited by Max Allan Collins and Lynn F. Myers, Jr. Published with Black Mask Press

Tough As Nails by Frederick Nebel, edited by Rob Preston. Published with Black Mask Press

You'll Die Laughing by Norbert Davis, edited by Bill Pronzini. Published with Black Mask Press

CRIPPEN & LANDRU LOST CLASSICS

Crippen & Landru is proud to publish a series of *new* short-story collections by great authors who specialized in traditional mysteries:

The Newtonian Egg and Other Cases of Rolf le Roux by Peter Godfrey, introduction by Ronald Godfrey. 2002. Trade softcover, $15.00

Murder, Mystery and Malone by Craig Rice, edited by Jeffrey A. Marks. 2002. Trade softcover, $19.00.

The Sleuth of Baghdad: The Inspector Chafik Stories, by Charles B. Child. 2002. Cloth, $27.00. Trade softcover, $17.00.

Hildegarde Withers: Uncollected Riddles by Stuart Palmer, introduction by Mrs. Stuart Palmer. 2002. Trade softcover, $19.00.

The Spotted Cat and Other Mysteries by Christianna Brand, edited by Tony Medawar. 2002. Cloth, $29.00. Trade softcover, $19.00.

Marksman by William Campbell Gault, edited by Bill Pronzini; afterword by Shelley Gault. 2003. Trade softcover, $19.00.

Karmesin: The World's Greatest Criminal — Or Most Outrageous Liar by Gerald Kersh, edited by Paul Duncan. 2003. Cloth, $27.00. Trade softcover, $17.00.

The Complete Curious Mr. Tarrant by C. Daly King, introduction by Edward D. Hoch. 2003. Cloth, $29.00. Trade softcover, $19.00.

The Pleasant Assassin and Other Cases of Dr. Basil Willing by Helen McCloy, introduction by B.A. Pike. 2003. Cloth, $27.00. Trade softcover, $18.00.

Murder – All Kinds by William L. DeAndrea, introduction by Jane Haddam. 2003. Cloth, $29.00. Trade softcover, $19.00.

The Avenging Chance and Other Mysteries from Roger Sheringham's Casebook by Anthony Berkeley, edited by Tony Medawar and Arthur Robinson. 2004. Cloth, $29.00. Trade softcover, $19.00.

Banner Deadlines: The Impossible Files of Senator Brooks U. Banner by Joseph Commings, edited by Robert Adey; memoir by Edward D. Hoch. 2004. Cloth, $29.00. Trade softcover, $19.00.

The Danger Zone and Other Stories by Erle Stanley Gardner, edited by Bill Pronzini. 2004. Cloth, $29.00. Trade softcover, $19.00.

Dr. Poggioli: Criminologist by T.S. Stribling, edited by Arthur Vidro. 2004. Cloth, $29.00. Trade softcover, $19.00.

The Couple Next Door: Collected Short Mysteries by Margaret Millar, edited by Tom Nolan. 2004. Trade softcover, $19.00.

Sleuth's Alchemy: Cases of Mrs. Bradley and Others by Gladys Mitchell, edited by Nicholas Fuller. 2005. Trade softcover, $19.00.

Who Was Guilty? Two Dime Novels by Philip S. Warne/Howard W. Macy, edited by Marlena E. Bremseth. 2005. Cloth, $29.00. Trade softcover, $19.00.

Slot-Machine Kelly by Dennis Lynds writing as Michael Collins, introduction by Robert J. Randisi. 2005. Cloth, $29.00. Trade softcover, $19.00.

The Detections of Francis Quarles by Julian Symons, edited by John Cooper; afterword by Kathleen Symons. 2006. Cloth, $29.00. Trade softcover, $19.00.

The Evidence of the Sword by Rafael Sabatini, edited by Jesse F. Knight. 2006. Cloth, $29.00. Trade softcover, $19.00.

The Casebook of Sidney Zoom by Erle Stanley Gardner, edited by Bill Pronzini. 2006. Cloth, $29.00. Trade softcover, $19.00.

The Trinity Cat by Ellis Peters (Edith Pargeter), edited by Martin Edwards and Sue Feder. 2006. Cloth, $29.00. Trade softcover, $19.00.

The Grandfather Rastin Mysteries Lloyd Biggle, Jr., introduction by Kenneth Biggle and Donna Biggle Emerson. 2006. Cloth, $29.00. Trade softcover, $19.00.

FORTHCOMING LOST CLASSICS

Masquerade: Nine Crime Stories by Max Brand, edited by William F. Nolan, Jr.

The Battles of Jericho by Hugh Pentecost, introduction by S.T. Karnick

Dead Yesterday and Other Mysteries by Mignon G. Eberhart, edited by Rick Cypert and Kirby McCauley

The Minerva Club, The Department of Patterns and Other Stories by Victor Canning, edited by John Higgins

The Casebook of Jonas P. Jonas and Others by Elizabeth Ferrars, edited by John Cooper

The Casebook of Gregory Hood by Anthony Boucher and Denis Green, edited by Joe R. Christopher

Ten Thousand Blunt Instruments by Philip Wylie, edited by Bill Pronzini

The Adventures of Señor Lobo by Erle Stanley Gardner, edited by Bill Pronzini

Lilies for the Crooked Cross and Other Stories by G.T. Fleming-Roberts, edited by Monte Herridge

SUBSCRIPTIONS

Crippen & Landru offers discounts to individuals and institutions who place Standing Order Subscriptions for its forthcoming publications, either all the Regular Series or all the Lost Classics or (preferably) both. Collectors can thereby guarantee receiving limited editions, and readers won't miss any favorite stories. Standing Order Subscribers receive a specially commissioned story in a deluxe edition as a gift at the end of the year. Please write or e-mail for more details.

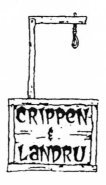

Printed in the United States
74267LV00007B/202-258

9 781885 941565